MW01226738

The

Venomsword

By Stephen Hagelin

Dedicated to my friend, Wesley,
who said I could make fairies cool.

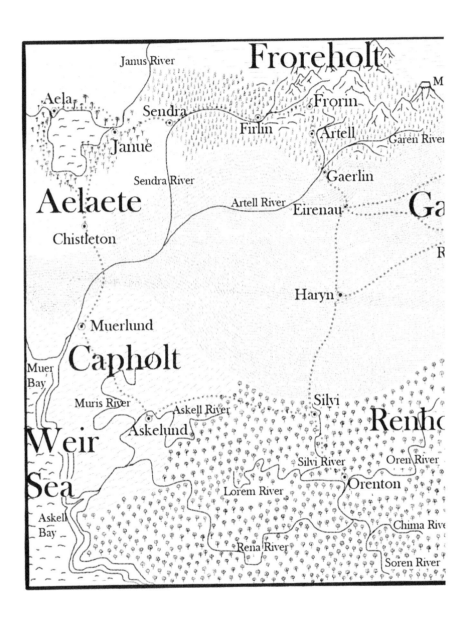

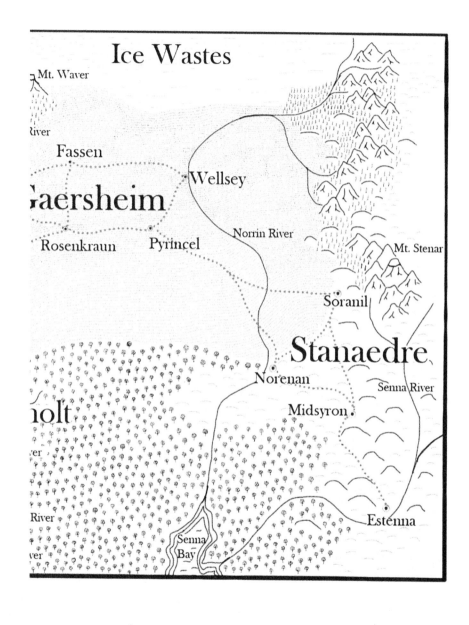

Party and Meeting

Frorin: Capitol City of Froreholt
Rain District
Faerie-Hunter Bounty Office

Leif tapped his fingers, wings twitching playfully, as he examined the features of the clerk through the glass. It was tough to decide, but he was determined to choose between her most appealing features, to be sure once and for all, which were her very best. She had three qualities that made an impression, first, her eyes, irises tinted white with a violet hint about the edges, second, her blue-tinged translucent white wings, and third, her mouth—red, shaped like a desert flower, perky and small, but not too thin either.

Her eyebrows narrowed as she leaned forward, sliding a small plaque through the opening in the window. "Here is your license, Sigleifr; you are now a full-fledged member of the Faerie Hunter Bounty Commission. Congratulations." She smiled sweetly, and Leif fell for her knowing that her best feature really was her tiny mouth.

"Thank you," he said, his heart twisting inside with pleasure, "do you have a break anytime soon?" He asked. "I would love to thank you more appropriately with a drink."

She chuckled, wings twitching cheerfully behind her back. "Oh, I work all day, even through lunch, which I take at my desk—most days," she demurred.

"Surely you've earned a lunch out then?" He insisted. "Today has to be at least a little special, right?"

"I really couldn't today, but if you stay in town, maybe tomorrow?" The clerk suggested, glancing at the calendar on the wall by the bounty board.

1

"What about after you get off for the day?" Leif pressed, searching her milky-white eyes.

"I'm afraid my hours keep me rather busy, and I have plans tonight." She sighed dramatically, and looked over her shoulder toward the back room where, Leif supposed, the other employees might be listening in.

"Well, then, as you say, I will return tomorrow." Leif picked up the plaque and examined its enameled, engraved surface. He turned it so it caught the light of her decorative starlamp, which drooped over her desk from its iron sconce like flowers with delicately glowing petals, and he considered the Commission's emblem and motto emblazoned onto the plaque.

"Justice is rewarding," he read aloud, tracing the emblem with his thumb. It had a set of scales balancing a dagger in one plate outweighed by a pile of coins in the other. His red-lined wings flicked unconsciously as he amused himself, shivering at the sensation of the cold of the silver on the plaque, and the place that had been warmed by the clerk's touch.

"It really is," she laughed, "we reward our partners on commission. Clever, isn't it, a commission in two respects?" She asked, playfully breathing on the glass.

"The more criminals we bring in or down, the more we are paid," he nodded, "it is rather obvious, but you're right, funny all the same." Leif forced an amused smile, but couldn't help thinking the only thing worth smiling about, was the smile she gave him.

"If you like, you can take a look at the bounty wall; the board should have a number of easy marks for your first job," she suggested, brushing the front of her green blazer jacket to smooth its negligible wrinkles, and tapping his papers on the counter to even them out, before sliding them into a drawer in her desk, and awkwardly coughing for good measure.

Leif turned left, keeping one eye on the slight color that showed on her cheeks, and scanned the east wall. Sure enough. There was a framed corkboard formed from the recycled stoppers of several hundred bottles of wine, arranged in a simple alternating pattern. On it, three wanted posters had been secured with silver sword-shaped pins, one of them through the nose of the exaggerated sketch of the face of a burglar with a scar on his chin. Apparently, whoever had submitted the bounty took his theft personally. "Wanted, Grendel Hamish, for robbery, burglary, and larceny, of the Frosthall Winery. Reward posted at 300-mint by the establishment above, approved by the Crown Prince Ieffin Martel," he read aloud.

"I am surprised that Lord Ieffin became involved in such a small matter, but if the rumors are to be believed, he is quite fond of their wine; so his pity might explain the quick approval," The clerk stated idly when he'd finished speaking, and her nameplate glinted as it caught the light, "Caelyn," spelled out in artistically printed typeface in black ink, and Leif wondered whether he should pronounce her name with a hard 'k' sound or a soft 's'.

"It seems rather simple, and recent you say, so I might as well take this one." He ripped it from the board with a firm hand, glancing at the scars that stood out on his left arm, and tugging at his sleeve to hide them.

"No, I sent another Hunter after him," the clerk stood, her stool sliding back with a rough sound, "another newcomer like you who, I admit, looked a bit familiar..." Caelyn, however it was pronounced, shook her head, and quickly adjusted her stool.

"I can't go chasing a mere pickpocket, or an unlawful solicitor," he complained, "is there anything else I can do?"

She paused, tapping her chin with her thin fingers, tilting her head just so as she thought. Finally, when Leif thought he couldn't bear watching such an attractive, charming, pensive sight any longer, she nodded with conviction and a cute tilt to her lips.

"Go look for trouble!" She exclaimed, beaming.

Leif laughed, louder than he'd intended, but the solution was brilliantly simple. "You know, I think you're right. I will go search the shabby streets; I will literally go 'looking for trouble' as they say." He gave her a wave and stepped out the thick double-doors onto the snow-covered street.

Thankfully it wasn't currently snowing, and though he didn't believe in the theory of Seasonal Disposition, he couldn't deny that he'd had a harder time summoning his elemental energies in a snowstorm than in his native desert. He stood on the edge of the South Cardinal in the Rain District, the road that went through the center of the city from the south with collinear sections in each district, not necessarily linked all the way to the center, but regular enough that he could find his way even being a stranger as long as he knew which way was north. He was about to move on when he walked straight into a pair of fae making for the Bounty Office, one practically dragging the other by his arm, and they all tumbled onto the street in a mess of dirty snow and the stench of old wine.

Leif stumbled to his feet, his face red as he offered his hand to the sharp-faced, beautiful fee he'd knocked over, and gave a suspicious glance

3

at her bound companion… who, at second glance, matched the thief from the board. He didn't help *him* to his feet of course; he reserved his attentions for the silver-haired beauty before him.

Though she accepted his hand, she did all the work as she stood, and dusted off her jacket in a perfunctory manner, especially her coattails and the back of her dark green skirt. "Sorry to surprise you, Hunter," she said politely, barely noticing his admiration, as she dragged her prisoner to his feet. "Are you off on a job?" She asked.

"Not exactly," he smiled awkwardly, "I figured I'd go tempt the undesirables into thinking I was an easy mark so they'd reveal themselves."

Her thin lips quirked, Leif hoped it was out of amusement. "We already have the Guard for that," she scoffed lightly, and her prisoner chuckled in agreement.

"Well, I can't live on my travel expenses forever," Leif said, waving his hands in resignation.

"Have you considered a life of crime?" the thief suggested, with a twinkle in his black eyes.

"I didn't say you could speak," the Hunter said coldly, turning on him with a clenched fist, shaking her head. "I literally told you not to say another word an hour and…" she glanced at the clock-tower peeking over the roof of the Bounty Office, "seven minutes ago."

He shrugged, looking relieved that his fate was being handled by her rather than someone else, with a face that said, Leif supposed, 'no offense'.

"I'm Sigleifr, by the way, though most just call me Leif," Leif said hurriedly as he tried to introduce himself, nodding excitedly as he accentuated the important syllables.

"Fryn," she replied.

"Grendel Ham…"

"We know," they said together, Leif giving him a dark look, hoping that he understood just how important this conversation was.

He looked away sheepishly, and scratched at the rope that bound his hands together at the wrists.

Just then, the flow of passersby increased, and fae flitted from office doors, and down the streets, and the clock rang the quarter till noon. Leif and Fryn stood on the curb as the people moved about, rushing to and fro in their business, watching them silently.

"Why'd you do it?" Leif asked the thief, adjusting his sleeves.

"I'm a thief," he said, forehead wrinkling in confusion.

"No, I know that, but I mean why rob a well-known winery that would only draw attention to yourself?" Leif gave up fixing his jacket and satisfied his nerves by playing with the sandalwood box in his pocket.

Grendel hiccupped. "Why do you think?"

"You drank it? How much?" Leif's hand paused, one finger tracing the hinge of his tiny box, and his eyes searching those of the thief.

Fryn coughed in her white-gloved hand, eyes flicking to the left to convey, Leif guessed, a pretty significant amount. "He made off with a full crate of wine, and there were only two bottles left when I found him." She smiled faintly. "They said I could keep them as a bonus."

"You must be a pretty accomplished Hunter," Leif said, admiring her pretty face, even if it looked a little cold and unused to receiving empty praise.

She shook her head. "I only just got my license three hours ago."

"What? I just got mine now!" He said, chuckling, "fancy that."

One of the passing faeries stopped as he said that and walked over carefully. He avoided any old patches of snow that might mar his fine suit and polished shoes, and as he approached, he fiddled with something in his pocket. "Did I hear you right?" He asked, his deep blue eyes searching, as he ran a hand over his combed blond hair.

"Yes," Fryn said with a start.

"And you, from Aelaete, you have the look of a Hunter as well, are you newly licensed, too?" The newcomer shuffled a small stack of postcards in his hand, watching their faces alternatively, openly, as if it was his pleasure, rather than his business.

Leif liked him immediately. He had that blonde hair that matched his own, and deep blue eyes that looked more mischievous than troublesome, and he had a comical smile that seemed self-aware of its own irony.

"I am." He and Fryn shared a look, and faced the stranger.

The stranger's smile broadened as held out two cards. "Congratulations! Our city is indebted to the valiant efforts of your organization, though really I should say it is indebted to the efforts of the Hunters themselves more-so than the Commission… but I am losing track of my thoughts… I would like to invite you both to a little celebration I am hosting as a token of my congratulations and thanks."

"Really?" Leif examined the cards, staring at the pale blue ink, printed in a fine script with lots of curls and loops, inviting them to the Final Needle, an establishment in the Snow District he'd heard of before, in the richest ring of the city just around the Palace, and just inside from the Merchant quarter they were currently standing in.

Fryn nodded politely, and the stranger bowed graciously, as he stepped back, and waved, before continuing on his errands, saying something about buying more food and drink that wouldn't be provided. They watched him walk back seamlessly into the noon crowd, until he vanished behind a hare-drawn cab.

"I wonder who he was," Leif said quietly, pocketing the card in his tan jacket.

"The card just says Mythrim," Fryn replied, taking a breath, "well, I'd best hand off my burden. I will see you again at the Final Needle, I should think."

"Yes you will, after all I only just got here, and what better way is there to enjoy the city, than being invited to a party I don't even have to bring a gift for?" Leif shrugged.

She looked him up and then down. "You should probably reconsider your clothes however: the Snow District can be very discriminating… and because of his invitation you'd better bring something small."

"I didn't exactly pack a large bag, crossing the desert," he hinted.

"Well then, at least iron your clothes." She dragged her prisoner into the Office, and left him alone, standing on the street.

Leif shuffled around his various pockets, finally locating the one that held the invitation. It provided an address, but he'd had very little luck trying to figure out the sprawling streets, and hadn't even bothered to study the map of the Snow District—since he'd figured he would never need to go there. He scratched his head, and adjusted his bangs carefully, before following Fryn inside.

Fryn was already talking to the clerk, shaking the thief by the shoulder of his jacket for emphasis, with his worn coat bunched up in her white-knuckled fist. "The reward was for 300-mint," she pressed, eyes glaring coldly through the glass.

"The amount was up to 300-mint. Part of that was reduced to account for the 50-mint of wine you are given as bonus," Caelyn said, strained sympathy plain on her face. "This is what dealing with the Snow District means. They are rich because they are miserly."

"Then they shouldn't have called it a bonus," Fryn said in an edged tone, looking down sourly.

"I am sorry to interrupt," Leif started to say, but Fryn cut back in.

"The Commission should award the promised amount, regardless of what they were paid by the client—the promise on the bulletin board should be concrete!" She muttered under her breath, something to the effect that that was what she'd been told before she obtained her license.

An older clerk wandered in from the back and pulled up a chair beside Caelyn. He watched the two, staring each other down, neither noticing nor acknowledging his presence. Leif felt there was a tug-of-war going on between their eyes, and that at some point the line had to break, and that when it did, it would erupt into an unpleasant explosion of sparks.

"I hate to interrupt here," Leif tried again, "but could someone help me with something really quick?"

As the staring contest continued, the thief escaped Fryn's grasp and stretched out on the bench beneath the bounty-board. The older clerk acknowledged Leif's resigned smile with a wave of his gaunt hand, and watched his face through the window, completely unfazed by the tangible tension between Fryn and Caelyn. Leif leaned against the counter beside Fryn—who still hadn't noticed him—and placed his hands on the marble countertop with a wry smile.

"I need directions to the Final Needle," he said, curling his fingers in and considering the roughness of his own skin as he tried not to look away from the impassive eyes of the old clerk.

The clerk nodded thoughtfully, and pulled a small silver watch from his pocket. "Caelyn, you are on break. You should go in the back room and eat your lunch undisturbed, while you have the opportunity," he said, not looking away from the hour-hand of his watch, pronouncing her name with a hard 'k' sound.

The two broke their contest and fixed him with their malevolent glares, but seemed to simmer off, and Caelyn departed through the arch into the back without a word. This new clerk had a refined, trimmed beard, and a more elaborately decorated nameplate pinned to the front of his black suit. It read 'Edgar' but no last name, just like Caelyn's had.

7

Edgar scooted his chair forward and smiled. "Now, as you said miss, the Commission will take on the difference, for that is our policy: but, what my colleague was trying to convey to you, Miss Martin, was the fact that the difference is not payable immediately, only what amount was set aside by whomever authorized the bounty. The difference will be placed in your account, accessible through the Hunter Bank in any of our locations. Transactions made in different locations must be made after the accounts are updated biweekly, but otherwise, our information travels faster than you can."

"Thank you," she said at last with a sigh of relief, and looked over at her bound prisoner where he had relaxed in a stupor, sprawled out on the nearest bench. "I'll leave him in your care."

"Of course," Edgar replied, "now, sir, you need directions." It was a statement, not a confirmation, and Leif disliked the way his steel-gray eyes bored through his sand-worn jacket.

"I do…" Leif glanced at Fryn curiously, "do you have a map I could borrow?"

"We provide local maps for all our members." He slid a folded document through the gap in the window, and dismissed him with his eyes.

Well, I guess that's done. Leif wondered, slightly miffed. He walked to the door and pushed it halfway open, when Fryn walked over with a small bag of coins clinking in her hand, and a satisfied smile on her face.

"I can lead you there," she offered with a victorious smirk.

"Really? That would be great." Leif grinned. "Where should we meet?"

She looked at the clock tower built into the Holly Inn on the west side and considered for a moment. "The party is in six hours, so I'd say meet up at the southern gate to the Snow District at 5:30. Where are you staying?" She asked.

"I only just arrived, came up to the Office as soon as I could..." He laughed. "Anywhere you recommend?"

She shoved her bag of coins into her pocket, and glanced around, and pointed up the eastward arc of the Ringroad. "About three blocks up from here there's an inn called The Hillock which is quite reliable, and known for housing Hunters and travelers alike."

He stood awkwardly for a few seconds, and then thanked her and walked off in the direction she'd indicated.

"Leif, don't you have a bag?" Fryn asked, her glacial blue eyes mocking him, even if she didn't laugh.

He did, but he'd left it sitting by the counter when he obtained his license, and he'd forgotten all about it when he thought he'd go searching for trouble. "I really do!" He slapped his forehead, and ran into the Office, returning seconds later with a drawstring travel bag, made of matching tan canvas to his red-trimmed jacket, and he waved to her as he ran toward the inn. She flitted away in the opposite direction, and Leif thought that she cut through the air rather than flew, like an arrow, or a wasp, or a viper when it sprang; he forgot about the clerk from before, with her white irises and flowering lips, he saw only Fryn's deadly, elegant speed, and watched in awe as one might at an ermine as it sunk its teeth into the neck of a winter hare.

The Hillock was a large building, set on a raised foundation from the street, with a wide covered porch, and little tables meant for enjoying tea or wine, while viewing the mountains. Leif left his bag there and pressed his clothes personally with their iron, even though they'd offered to do it for him. He didn't like other people handling his things, much less borrowing them. Usually nothing happened, but there'd been enough occasions where a new suit jacket or a favorite hat had been damaged or destroyed that he was not at all comfortable when other people handled his things... but it had been a while since he'd had a little sister try to be helpful, or a younger disciple try to earn points with unrequested favors.

He was grateful that his fighting style didn't require the use of a weapon because he saw himself panicking if anyone asked to hold his sword or whatever, if that had been the case. Still, he lounged in the inn's lobby by the fire with a hot cup of pine-needle tea, watching couples whispering, or sharing bites of cakes, or glasses of wine in the bar, waiting patiently till 5:00. When that time finally arrived, he wandered down the streets to the South Cardinal again and waited by the gate to the Snow District. Two guards in white uniforms, with glacier-blue piping, and silver decorative plates on their shoulders and chests, watched him nervously on either side of its unbarred opening. One kept checking the position of his short sword, and the other just gripped his halberd anxiously, eyes darting around, scanning fat merchants, and rail-thin messengers, as if they were really a threat... but if they were... Leif would've known.

Leif supposed they just weren't used to loiterers. "So," he addressed the one on the right, "what's the news in the city?"

9

The guard made a slight jump in surprise, hand dropping from, and then rising to the hilt of his sword, as he managed to assume a pleasant demeanor. "We… guard the city traveler; we don't collect stories for the journals."

"I see, I just arrived in town. Do you know of any places of interest I should see while I'm here?" He worried that his attempt at small talk wouldn't be successful in the least, and decided to scratch the back of his head purposefully to put them off guard.

"Well," the guard softened a bit, showing an awkward smile, "those of rank should visit the wineries along the Vineroad on the eastern and northern sides of the Snow District." He suggested.

The guard on the left frowned. "Those of less… nobility… should confine their visits to the Cloud or Pine Districts as there are plenty of common-houses and pubs to entertain country-folk."

Leif bristled, wings straightening, and tightening, as he tried to repress his reaction at what he *knew* was an insult, but before he could say anything he might later regret, Fryn appeared from the west end of the Ringroad, wearing a shining gray dress, with a silver scarf, and her hair pinned into an elegant braided bun. He softened immediately and stared in awe as she drew near, smiling wider and wider as she returned his smile without any of his awkwardness.

There was a slight wrinkle at the edge of her dress on the right side. Leif suspected she'd hidden something there, after all she *was* a Hunter. Sure, he couldn't be positive, but she was bound to have a hidden weapon, just like the Askasalè. And a Hunter should always be prepared.

The guard on the left tipped his white cap graciously, and smiled. "Greetings m'lady," he said, stepping aside to let her through with a proud wave of his hand.

"Leif," she turned, holding out her arm, "are you coming?" Her mischievous eyes laughed at the guards whose wings shot up in surprise.

Leif nodded stiffly, trying to look purposeful, as the guards watched him pass with a mixture of suspicion and understandable envy. Fryn was both wonderful and young, as well as pretty… and strong, and Leif couldn't come up with enough modifiers to describe her in any letter, if he ever decided to write back home. He took her arm for good measure, and they walked together until out of sight of the guards, when she withdrew her arm and coughed lightly into her gloved hand.

"Did you see their faces?" Leif chuckled. "I bet they didn't think I'd be in the company of such a fair lady."

She looked away for a moment, and when she faced him again, she looked much the same, except a little paler than before.

"I'm sorry; I didn't mean to... um... imply anything by it," Leif said, rubbing the back of his neck anxiously.

"It's nothing. We only just met, I don't know you well enough to be embarrassed," she smiled, "though I suspect you might give me plenty of reason to be." Fryn's cheeks revealed a bit of color, but it was quickly suppressed, and she looked ahead. "The Final Needle isn't very far."

They walked up the eastern wing of the Snow District's Ringroad. He supposed that was the Frorin equivalent of a main street, since all the others branched off from it into alleys and residential areas. "I have barely known you half a day, and already you tease me. What is it about me that invites it?" He asked, noticing how the well-dressed merchants made note of their passing, recalling how he'd always suffered under light jabs, and well-meaning disparaging remarks from friends, and family alike.

"Probably your naïve face, your sloppy hair, and that set smile. Do you make any other expression?" Her eyes were light, but a deep sort of light, blue, that matched the piping of the guards' uniforms, and the way they caught the light made them seem only more intent, and more interested in everything they looked at.

"Well, there's nothing I can do about that." He frowned, but it only made his mouth look flat, and it felt terrible, like it took too much effort to pull his face down.

"Now you actually look serious, it's unnatural, stop that!" She laughed, and pulled something from her clutch bag, it looked like a breath mint—a tablet of crushed mint and caramel. She popped it into her delicate mouth, not like the clerk's, hers was thin, not small, and she had dimples that appeared on her face with every sideways glance and self-conscious laugh.

"I think you look far more innocent than I do; for a Hunter that might not work in your favor." He shook his head. "Look, when you smile, with those dimples you look like a little girl."

"Thanks, that isn't exactly what I wanted to hear," Fryn chewed her mint with a sigh, and felt her cheeks subconsciously while smiling. She rolled her eyes, wings twitching in thought.

They walked in silence till they reached the East Cardinal. Fryn had grown quite serious in that time and Leif felt more uncomfortable than he could put into words, it was like there was a weight in the air, and it was

11

chillingly cold. Fryn's face had set into a blank look, as if she were reliving a grim memory.

"I'm sorry about what I said," he said, "I'm not very good at conversing naturally... especially with... foreigners."

She nodded, as if she only half heard him. "No matter. We feel the same about you. So, Leif, why did you become a Hunter?" She asked, looking painfully aware of the dimples that stood out with her smile.

Leif felt the sandalwood box in his coat pocket, carefully. It was something he always carried with him, engraved with the symbol of a silver serpent on the lid, which he traced with his thumb. "The school I come from has a very unorthodox way of graduating its students. Any Seventh-Rank student may compete for the honor of pursuing master status, but... it would appear that the test actually just required a term of service in the Commission. My master said that only when I become a recognized Hunter will I be called a Master of his School."

"What school is that?" She asked.

"Strafe-Curling-Viper school, it is a martial art native to my city, small but well-known among the Aelaete schools. My master was actually sent to prison for accidentally killing an opponent in a duel—only for three years," he added quickly.

"It sounds like a dangerous style, what kind of weapon do you use?" She brushed her leg, where Leif guessed she'd hidden her weapon.

"Just my fists and my sparks," he said, holding a hand up, sending a delicate tendril of electricity curling around his wrist and fingers, "What do you use?"

She nodded appreciatively. "I am a graduate of the Soft-Point-Fist, local to the city. We fight with a knife in one hand, and the other hand open for splitting strikes, or blocking, or grappling." She demonstrated a fist in her left hand, and her right arm swished through the air with a sharp cutting motion as if her hand were a blade.

Leif was about to ask another question when they turned down a side street and stopped before a large building, five stories tall, with a wide display of windows showing a view of the ballroom, and on the other side, a banquet hall.

A fae stood beside the door, greeting a trio of blondes in blue dresses with white crowns patterned on the fabric, and waved them inside. He wore a white suit with green lining, and the angled view suggested a matching bowtie. He cut a sharp figure as he turned to Leif and Fryn, and groaned magnanimously. It was Mythrim.

"Oh, how marvelous, I am so glad you were able to make it to my party. Please, come up." Mythrim said, coming down to meet them, with light steps, and an honest grin.

They ascended the steps and shook hands, looking inside curiously. Their host's wings shimmered and twitched excitedly, as he held the handshake for too long.

"Who is your tailor?" Leif asked without thinking.

"Now that would be telling," he laughed, and patted Leif's shoulder, "but I'm afraid I cannot reveal my secrets. You'll have to bribe me with wine. You! My lady, you look ravishing, positively stunning! Please, go and join the dancing and drinking. I have quite a few party games planned, and many toasts, so make sure to eat something."

They walked inside, and found eleven other guests, some twirling in pairs on the dance floor, others playing a game of cards, but most standing about talking with crystal glasses of wine and spirits in hand.

"I am going to get a drink," Leif said, "would you care for anything?"

Fryn looked at each guest carefully, but paused in her inspection to reply. "Yes, I'll have a glass of sparkling."

Leif walked over to the bar, and found once he had ordered her drink, he had no idea what to choose for himself. The shelves were lined with so many bottles of so many shapes and colors; that he couldn't even read the labels, their fonts so varied and unique that he entirely gave up hope of deciphering them. He rested his hands on the cedar-bark bar and stared intently along a single row, finally noticing a square glass bottle with a matching glass stopper, filled with an amber liquid, which caught the warm light of the stained starlamps and made him think of home.

"I'll have a glass of that sceppe there," he said, pointing with as much class and authority as he dared.

The bartender poured him two fingers of the liquid, but as he passed it over, he smiled. "This is ceren."

Leif's head slumped, and he gave a dramatic sigh. "Well, I won't drink that out of a tumbler, in fact, I think I'd like something else."

The bartender's eyes mocked him silently, as he picked up the glass, and raised it to his lips, and he downed its contents, eyes never releasing their hold on his. He set the empty glass down, and placed a fresh tumbler on the bar. "So then, have you decided?" He asked, smiling with his thin lips pressed together like the fingers of his hands.

Wine and Dine

Frorin:
Snow District
The Final Needle

In the end, Leif chose a glass of mead, dark, and cloying, made from caramelized honey that smelled like spices and, unsurprisingly honey. He found Fryn talking with a girl, maybe twenty or so, whose excited twirl as she talked, sent the edges of her dress spinning, a red and white dress that pulled in delicately at her waist and ended in a skirt a couple inches above her knees. It was both endearing and maddeningly attractive, and Leif had a hard time remembering Fryn's merits, until he saw her smile, and her dimples sprang rebelliously to life.

"And so that is how I was invited to the party!" The girl exclaimed, brimming with energy.

"I would never have expected that our host would be so well connected," Fryn said, taking the flute from Leif's hand, and sipping from it.

"Would you like a drink, miss?" Leif asked the fee in the red-swirled dress.

"Oh yes, please, that would be wonderful." She beamed, and looked longingly at the bar. "I'll have a glass of Yardall Sceppe," she added, casting a wink at Fryn, who nodded, apparently in on the joke.

"Coming right up." Leif wondered what he'd missed, but returned a few moments later with the drink she'd desired. "What's your name, miss?" he asked as she accepted the tumbler.

She took a healthy sip, and placed her hand over her chest as it went down. "That is much better, thank you."

Fryn placed a hand on his shoulder. "This is my colleague from the Commission, Leif."

She made an 'o' shape with her mouth, and blinked. "I am Clair Yardall." She punctuated this with a presentation of her glass, which nearly caused the contents to slosh over.

"Ah! Well, I am going to have to try your family's sceppe before the night is out," Leif said.

She nodded authoritatively, and stole a sniff of his mead. "You really shouldn't drink the Guldhand Company's wine—they are a crooked business."

"You seem to know an awful lot about alcohol," Leif grinned.

"I do, and I must, if I am going to inherit the business."

"How responsible," Fryn praised gently.

"I wouldn't object to learning a bit more," Leif said, taking a larger sip than he'd intended, spilling a small amount of it onto his jacket—luckily intended for travel, and already tan-colored to begin with. It didn't stain, but he turned away quickly to brush it off. The two snickered, but kept straight faces when he turned back, so he decided not to complain.

"Well then, perhaps I'll tell you." Clair winked. "Sceppe is made from malted grain. Here in the north we use wheat from the foothills, and occasionally we mix in rye." She leaned in confidentially. "I can't tell you the proportions, or our specific methodology."

He and Fryn leaned in close to hear, so that they all cracked heads, and rocked back, each expressing their own small amount of pain or discomfort. Leif rubbed his head with a smile. "I wouldn't dream of asking you to divulge your secrets."

Fryn's effervescent wine swirled as she shook away the ache in her head. "I think I could use something slightly stronger than this."

Just then, one of the waiters whisked by in a smart suit, cufflinks shaped like silver stars, wearing a blue cravat under his sharp chin. He interrupted Fryn cautiously and presented a tray of appetizers. "Would you care for a plate of cheese?" He pointed to the small dishes arrayed with several slices of different ages and consistencies arranged in a star-shape on the tray.

She nodded distractedly, and took one of the small plates, then, examining the cheese she sighed and passed it to Leif. "I can't stand the taste of blue cheese."

He gave the plate a sniff, and passed it to Clair. "Would you like some cheese?"

She laughed, and rejected the proffered plate with the palm of her hand, pushing it back. "No, I'm afraid that would be in conflict with my sceppe."

"Of course it would," Leif said, looking it over again, and decided that one of the types might go with his mead and hesitantly took a bite. It was a semisoft cheese with some kind of fruit, apricot perhaps, chopped and scattered throughout. He chewed it with a frown, and took a sip. The mead washed down smoothly, blending with the mild cheese. "That wasn't so bad. Fryn, are you sure you won't try one of the others?"

Her eyes rolled halfway before she thought better of the motion, and picked out a soft slice of brie. She popped it in her mouth and chewed it without reaction, and then finished with a gulp of her wine. "No, I think that'll do for me. I'm not fond of cheese to begin with," she said, "and I wonder if this was on the list of things Mythrim went out to buy... I thought he'd have better taste."

Leif raised his eyebrows at her, and took a bite of the blue. "Yeck, that's disgusting." He drank a large gulp and sputtered for a few seconds. "I think we should just set it aside until something nicer comes along."

"Agreed," Fryn chuckled.

Clair waved another waiter over and accepted a bowl of toasted nuts, and popped a couple in her mouth with a crunch. "So," she said, looking between them, "how were you invited?"

"Well, we met Mythrim outside the Bounty Office, and he congratulated us on obtaining our licenses." Leif stole a nut and tried it. "Mmm... that goes much better."

She returned a knowing look, and turned to Fryn. "So you are entirely new then? This must be a fine way to start a career."

"It is," she replied, smoothing her dress, still devoid of wrinkles. "In fact, I already caught my first prize."

"Really? Wow, you must be an incredible hunter." Clair's eyes widened considerably.

Fryn laughed. "No, I merely caught a drunk wine-thief."

She nodded. "I heard about that, Frosthall doesn't deserve such hassles."

"I've had several of their wines before," Fryn said, her eyes bright as if watching a happy memory, "I have a preference for their sparkling wine."

"I didn't ask what they were serving," Leif said, pointing to her nearly empty glass.

She finished it off and gave a slight calling gesture to a nearby waiter. "I'll have a glass of Frosthall."

He hurried away and returned soon after with a lighter-colored bubbly liquid in a crystal glass, and then rushed away to attend to one of the three pretty blondes they had seen when they entered.

"We don't see many Hunters at parties in the Snow District, or anywhere else for that matter," Clair said. "Most hunters, except some of the more renowned veterans, are a bit too rough to be invited. It takes a certain amount of class to fit in here."

As she finished her comment, Mythrim stepped in to ask how they were enjoying the party, an obvious pretense, as he had been listening and quickly joined the conversation. "Indeed Miss Yardall, but I saw something refined in our young friends here, and thought they'd do nicely."

She laughed prettily, and blushed. "I think you're correct, Mr. Mythrim."

"Just Mythrim, please." He pinched at an imagined piece of lint, on his sleeve self-consciously.

"Alright, Mythrim," she took a glass of white wine from a passing tray and sat at an empty round table, "anyone for a game?"

Mythrim nodded sadly. "Only one round, I have other guests to mind, you know."

They all sat down comfortably with a bowl of nuts, and various glasses, as Mythrim produced a deck of cards from his jacket. "The object of this game is to be the first to use all your cards," he explained, dealing a pair of face down cards before each of them, and then setting face-up cards on top.

"I think we all know the rules to 'Serendipity'," Clair interjected.

Leif's wings itched, and he straightened the fit of his jacket. "I haven't heard of this game…" he said, reaching for the cards on the table.

Fryn stopped his hand with a smile and a headshake. "Leif, these are the cards we use at the end, for the majority of the game we have a hand of five cards from which we play, and draw to refill that number."

Mythrim dealt five cards for their first hands, and placed the remaining cards in the center of the table beside the bowl of nuts. When they'd picked up their cards, everyone else proceeded to change out the face-up cards before them from their hands, favoring Kings and Dukes, and the occasional five, or nine. Leif had two threes, an eight, a nine, and a Queen, but had no idea how to play or whether he should replace the five and one, or whether in this game the five suits mattered.

"The loser has to get fresh drinks," Mythrim proclaimed, patting his shoulder, comfortingly, "I'll have a glass of Yardall."

"Oh will you?" Clair blushed again, and sitting to Mythrim's left, she played the first card, well cards plural actually: a pair of twos. "I think I'll make it easy for Leif since he's never played."

"I'll have as full a glass as they can give me," Mythrim added, "that I might enjoy it *all*, and all the more."

She blushed furiously, and then looked at Leif's cards. "You might not want to keep that five," Clair said, stifling a laugh.

Leif wondered if Mythrim had made some kind of euphemism, but focused on Clair's advice. "Why should I keep the one, and what do each of the cards do?" he asked.

Clair fanned her face with her newly stocked hand of cards, and nodded importantly. "I forgot to tell you, didn't I? Well, it's really quite simple, no really, don't give me that look. You can play multiples; five of a kind discards the pile, saving anyone from picking it up if they were unable to play, and there are a number of special rules. First, until the deck is exhausted, always redraw to five, and second… what was it?" She cast a desperate look toward Fryn, who smiled in return.

Fryn's smile, much more relaxed than Clair's, seemed to expand openly, and naturally on her face. "You can't forget that the most important rule in playing cards is that you must play a card greater than or equal to the one that came before, and, if it amounts to five of a kind, through however many people that have played in sequence, the pile is discarded as well."

"True. You are absolutely right, we should teach Leif the rules, if only so we can enjoy it all the more when he has to refill our glasses," Mythrim said, sharing a mischievous look with Clair. "But that reminds me, there is a special rule about primes."

"Primes?" Leif asked, feeling like he was the butt of some joke, but unable to grasp what it was.

"Prime numbered cards, five primes in a row also discards the pile, and if you play a non-prime number after a series of four, you have to pick up the pile. That is why this game is called serendipity, but it relies quite a bit on whether you have enough of the right cards, from the first, and in each play, so be wary of playing too many multiples of prime numbers." Mythrim took another sip of his wine, looking eager to move on to his promised glass of sceppe.

"So there're no wild cards then," Leif confirmed, draining the last of his mead, counting the cards in play. Out of 65 cards, 38 had already been taken from the deck, so he switched out the cards on the table, leaving his Queen and the five, to Clair's chagrin, and then playing his pair of threes. Fryn chuckled, but he drew a Duke and a seven, and leaned back in his chair, listening to the string quartet's strains of some chamber music, and watching the other partygoers alternate their conversational cliques, between the small society tables and the bar.

Fryn played a six, and Mythrim a pair of sevens, and Clair a matching pair, with a sly grin on her innocent face. Leif uncrossed his arms with an affected sigh, and placed the fifth seven on the pile, and as he cleared the pile, his eyes never left off their mocking at the ones who'd set him up. He led with his one, and drew another eight, and a ten, and from there it circled through four ones in a row, and Clair discarded the pile with a two, saying astutely that twos also counted as prime numbers.

After that, Mythrim got stuck with low numbers, picking up hand after hand, as Fryn tossed out her slightly higher cards with subdued glee. As Fryn ended up with just her face-down cards, Leif found himself picking up more and more cards he was unable to play. She won, only because Leif played four nines, and Fryn happened to choose the fifth nine from her unknown pair, and discarded the pile with one hand as she slapped the other, a five, alone on top of the table.

She cheered, blushing from the wine, and rested her chin on her hand. "I suppose the loser has to get the drinks." Fryn's eyes and dimples watched him impatiently, and Leif almost forgot what he was supposed to do if he lost.

"Oh!" He exclaimed, sitting up sharply, "What would you care for, sir, ladies?"

Mythrim shook his hand in disappointment. "*We* are going to have Yardall Reserve, and I believe your colleague was going to have Frosthall."

Leif ran off with their orders, frustrating the bartender in his haste, slurring over important syllables, and then considering what he should drink. The bartender just poured two glasses each of Yardall and wine. On his return, Mythrim took a sip and apologized, and sweeping out his hand led Clair to the dance floor, and they swayed carefully on the polished marble, her skirt swishing in the slight breeze they created. Leif set his glass of bubbly down, enjoying its refreshing variation of heat. Fryn placed her glass, noticeably lower than his, on the table beside his and looked at him expectantly, wings twitching, and a pulse of reddish color pulsed out to the tips.

Leif straightened his jacket seriously, and held out his hand. "Would you dance with me, Fryn?"

She smiled, and accepted it, and they moved to join Mythrim and Clair on the floor, easily matching the soft rhythm of the waltz and smiling.

"Who do you think would win in a contest?" Fryn asked him.

"We are the trained hunters. I imagine we are much more in tune with our own bodies, and each other, than they are," he said, holding her close, hand on her waist, thinking he felt a travel belt under the thin layer of her dress.

"What hunter goes without their means?" She whispered in his ear.

"Not a single one, I should think." He winked.

Mythrim gave Clair a spin, as if he had heard Fryn's challenge, and the music picked up a little. Fryn and Leif matched, he twirled her away, and spun her back, holding even closer, blood pulsing to the pace of the music, and the drink.

They danced, as the music quickened even more, and then, somehow as if they had expected it, Leif and Mythrim twirled their partners out, and switched.

Leif grinned as Clair laughed in his arms, and the music slowed to a more romantic waltz again.

"You're quite good at this, for a hunter, Leif," she said, looking up at him.

"And you seem to be quite a natural yourself," he replied, switching sides with another twirl.

"Shh…" she said, leaning her head against his shoulder. They slowed, swaying to the tempo of the new piece that the quartet seemed to choose simply because of the two pairs of dancers that the other partygoers had stopped to watch.

He glanced over at Fryn, slightly more reserved than Clair, suddenly looking unaffected by the wine she'd had, compared to the rosy cheeks that Clair tried to hide from him. Fryn met his eyes playfully, and gave Mythrim a twirl, making him laugh softly, and the other guests cheer, especially the trio of blondes in the crown-patterned dresses, who giggled and looked hopefully at the other men.

Clair stirred, and watched them, shaking softly with a quiet laugh. "My turn to lead," she said, moving his hands to her shoulders, and placing hers where his had been.

"This feels quite odd."

"Shh... It's not odd." She placed a finger on his mouth, and then gave him a spin.

He felt somewhat disoriented when she pulled him back, and found himself laughing. "Ha, ha, so this is how it feels?"

"Nice, isn't it?" She pulled him close, and they rocked to the music till the song ended, and bent him back dramatically.

The guests cheered the performance, and Mythrim called for a toast. The waiters brought out trays filled with glasses of Frosthall for all, and they raised them as Mythrim found a chair to stand on. Leif and Fryn returned to the card table and reclaimed their glasses.

"Hear me! Settle down," he said, waving them to stop their applause, "it is time to move to the dinner table, and enjoy the three-course meal our fine chef has prepared for us. I think we ought to honor him with our appreciation of his hard work, and, to thank these lovely partners with whom we have danced." He raised his glass clumsily, some of the liquid trailing down from the lip, and he looked as if all of Fryn's spinning had made him dizzy.

Leif and Clair clinked glasses, and cheered with the rest as they drank their own health, and that of their chef, and Leif wondered who the chef was, since he hadn't once come out into the party.

They drank roughly half the glass, and then moved to a long dinner table occupying the dining hall to the left of the dance floor, a room with windows lining each of its three walls, looking out onto the snow-covered roads and the cloud-covered sky.

Leif pulled out Clair's chair, and Fryn's, since Mythrim was now busy helping the blondes in the blue dresses sit by him. When everyone was settled, the chef came out in a black suit, with a blue cravat, a white apron, and midnight-black hair. He was young, and Leif supposed they were close in age, and the chef had deep blue eyes that looked cheerful and thoughtful at the same time.

He wondered whether 'calculating' would be a good word to describe him, but tossed the idea when the chef opened his mouth with a warm smile. "Greetings, everyone, I would like to thank you for coming tonight to my humble establishment."

There was a chorus of disagreement when he said 'humble' to which he grinned bashfully. "The first course I have prepared is a vinaigrette with gorgonzola and toasted pecans. It is nothing extravagant, but I hope it prepares you for the second course: a butternut-squash soup. Which in turn should ready you for the hare-roast at last."

Mythrim stood ceremoniously and held up a hand. "Is there some kind of desert or aperitif afterwards?"

The chef stared. "What dinner would be complete without one? I beg your patience, because that is a surprise."

There was a general "ooooh" among the guests, and they chuckled or laughed all around, and the chef gave a cough to call them back to attention. "I am Aldyr, by the way, and I hope this meal is to your great satisfaction. Thank you for your condescension." He waved the waiters forward, and they placed all the plates of salad down in front of each guest at the exact same time.

Leif looked between Clair and Fryn, but they didn't move to pick up their forks. Clair pointed surreptitiously under the table toward their host, who speared a bite of salad and took a bite. He chewed for a couple seconds, and swallowed. A few more seconds followed, and he looked relieved. "The food is fit for eating, or I have lost my mind."

Several people chuckled at his remark, and everyone took a bite, Leif slightly behind, trying to watch how they ate with a formal manner. He wished they'd taught him table-manners back home, but even if they had it wouldn't have suited this affair. He had no recourse but to copy everyone else… which was how he'd learned from his Master anyway.

Fryn smirked at his helplessness, and fixed his hold on his fork. "Two fingers and the thumb at the end, where it widens."

"I know how to hold a fork," he complained quietly.

Clair shook her head. "But you don't know how to use it correctly either." She turned the fork upside down with her forefinger along the shaft, and speared a bit of salad, and closed her mouth on it.

Fryn looked a little embarrassed.

"Salad is slightly different, Fryn, but I suppose you have as little practice as your partner," she continued.

Leif and Fryn shared a look.

"Oh, I just assumed you were a team," she said thoughtfully. "Many hunters work together when they first start, or didn't you know that?"

"We knew that," Leif said, turning to Fryn with one eyebrow arched up, "right?" He added to her in a whisper.

She shrugged, and ate her salad dutifully, ignoring the bits of gorgonzola. Leif agreed with her on that, the marbled cheeses did taste as bad as they smelled, though; Clair seemed to enjoy them. Perhaps it was an upper-class thing. They enjoyed the salad quickly, and sat waiting hungrily for the next course.

The soup didn't take long to arrive, but it was already cold by the time everyone took to eating it. It was so cold, that Leif wondered why no one complained, as if they didn't mind it at all.

"Is there anything wrong with your soup?" he asked Fryn.

She pondered for a moment, swishing a mouthful carefully. "No, it is perfect."

"Don't you think it is a little cold?"

Clair snickered. "It is supposed to be cold."

"Not to mention, whenever you receive something, you ought to assume that the state you find it in is the state it was intended to be in," Fryn intoned.

"Even if it's cold?" He thought the flavor was nice, but it was a little sweet and rich, almost like the next day's serving of gravy. He ate it too quickly, and hoped that the hare would be hot and spiced. He buttoned his jacket, feeling cold, and that was not something he liked when he was indoors.

The chef himself brought out the first plate for their host, setting the steaming porcelain, its contents drenched in thick gravy, before him with a dramatic flourish. One of the blondes clapped at his performance, and the others laughed.

Once more, Mythrim sliced a small bite of food, and smelled it on the fork, making the most engrossed sound of approval Leif could've imagined. "Mmmmmm… I have no doubt this is safe, but here, for the sake of propriety I will once more test its quality."

"Oh that's what he's been doing." Leif felt his box in his pocket. "I thought he was making sure it was safe for the guests."

"I'll have you know, Leif," Clair shook her head, her shoulder length hair swishing; "there hasn't been any need for that for a hundred years."

He'd thought her hair had been brown, when they'd met, but as it moved in the light, he saw that it was a subdued auburn. "That is nice to hear."

Mythrim chewed with the most foolishly delighted expression, and pronounced that it was fit for the King himself, and winked at the girl on the right, who laughed ridiculously.

"My cousin," he overheard her say, "has recommended me here many times, but I haven't had their roast hare before."

Their host grinned, but his eyes met Leif's and didn't seem quite as pleased as he made out. "Master Aldyr, this is the best you have made yet."

The waiters laid out the plates, heaped with meat, mashed potatoes, and gravy, before the guests with the same precision as before. Leif tried his best not to eat too much, but the light appetizers before had somehow only increased his hunger. The other guests seemed just as engrossed, and no one spoke for several minutes. Their glasses ran dry, and soon the guests drank a variety of beverages of their choice, red and white wines, sceppes, and clear cocktails, and Leif wondered what he should use to wash down the increasing warmth of his food, and whether just a plain glass of water or nectar might be better.

It seemed that the spice only grew more intense, and the hot food retained its heat even in his stomach, cleansing him of the discomfort from the soup. Fryn ate a little more than half her food, and leaned back in her chair tiredly, and Clair was only able to finish a third.

"Oh that is so filling," she said, using a handkerchief to fan her flushed face. "I'm not used to such spicy food, but my word, that is delicious."

Fryn nodded in agreement and brushed the front of her dress, as if worried about too much food ruining her figure for the evening. Leif had to admit that was his worry, since he'd eaten all of his food, and his jacket felt a little tight. He marveled that no one except he and Mythrim had been able to finish the meal, and they each sat back in their chairs with a mixture of satisfaction, and happy discomfort.

Mythrim stood stiffly, and waved the chef out to join them. "I remember a promise of desert, but I hope it is something soothing and light, that might make us feel as though we hadn't eaten so much.

Aldyr smiled, but Leif felt he was a little dismayed that so few had eaten as much as they were served. "It should please you to discover that my aperitif is one such item." He held out his hand, and one of the waiters placed a dark glass bottle with an obscure white label on his palm, and his fingers reflexively gripped it from the base.

"What is this, now?" Mythrim walked over and inspected it. "Stanaedre, hmm… I'm not too good at reading their script, but if I am not mistaken, this is an herbal liqueur."

"Precisely. In that land it is a common practice to lighten their stomachs so, and this has the perfect properties to alleviate such a… lethargy as the end of the dinner might bring. I wouldn't be surprised if you all felt like dancing again," he replied, taking a towel from his waist, and fixing it around the cork.

"It isn't bubbly, is it?" One of the girls asked.

"Not quite, but there is enough pressure that it requires similar treatment," Aldyr said, with a tilt of his head.

"Is this enough for everyone?" Mythrim asked, narrowing his eyes.

"It should be sufficient for the party, sir."

"No, I mean everyone." Mythrim patted his shoulder. "Here at the close, I would like to include, in appreciation for their service, *all* those who have attended here tonight."

"That is very generous, sir, but there is a policy against combining work and pleasure here." The chef seemed to hide a glowering look under an impatient huff.

"Nonsense. I'm paying, and the business is ended. If you would be so kind as to furnish everyone with glasses, I will give the meal's end toast." Mythrim puffed out his chest, and looked quite silly, but Aldyr consented, much to the waiters' delight.

In a minute, they had all gathered in the ballroom, holding tiny crystal tumblers filled with a nearly black, licorice-scented liquid. The guests beamed and loosened their coats, and the staff of the inn abandoned their aprons, and put on their matching jackets. *I fit in more with them now*, Leif thought, as they whispered and talked among themselves happily.

"Alright everyone, this evening is at an end." Mythrim began.

25

There was a spout of applause, which he waved away.

"And I would like to thank all of you for making this such a great occasion. It makes me sick at heart that it is the end." He held up his hand to forestall any more clapping. "Now, first, long live the King!" There was a general cheer. "And may his heir be his equal!" An even more enthusiastic cheer sounded through the crowd. "And, may you and your families, and this establishment be most successful in all your endeavors!"

The closest waiter, laughing with his coworker, remarked that he'd never had an opportunity to try anything like this liqueur before. There was general agreement amongst the group, and they looked at their host with a mixture of joy and respect. Leif hadn't either but decided not to comment.

Mythrim held his glass high, and with one final indistinct pronouncement, clinked glasses with the blonde standing before him. Everyone rushed to collide their glasses, and they all drank at once.

"This is amazing," Clair whispered, sipping like a lady.

Leif looked guiltily at his glass, it was nearly empty. "Aren't we supposed to down it all at once?"

Fryn rolled her eyes. "No, why would you do that?"

"This is not moonshine," Clair added.

They finished their glasses quickly all the same, and Mythrim himself turned his to his eye sadly. "I wonder if there is any more?"

Aldyr reappeared with two more bottles, his long coat trailing behind him. "A toast is not complete without a second," he said, shaking his head.

Mythrim waited as he filled all the glasses again, and passed them around. "I've already given a toast, who would like to give the next one?" He looked at Fryn mysteriously. "How about one of these two hunters? You know, they have only just obtained their licenses. Perhaps we should congratulate them?"

The murmurs in the crowd seemed to think so, and they were both pushed onto the musician's dais beside him. There were several calls for 'toast' and Leif shoved his hands into his pockets awkwardly.

Fryn decided to go first, swirling the contents of her glass in one hand, and fixing her scarf with the other. "Hear me," she said, somehow looking important, "I want to thank you all for your company and well-wishes. Further, I want to thank our host, who has entertained us so well."

Leif nodded cheerfully, and cut in with as much care as he could. "And to all who served us this evening!" There was a loud cheer of approval. "And to the fine ladies we've danced with!" An even larger cheer followed, and Leif thought he saw Clair blush. "And in closing, a very, very good night to all!"

Everyone applauded and clashed cups as they raced to finish their drinks. Leif settled against the wall beside Mythrim, touching glasses and drinking it pleasantly, though feeling a little nauseous. He really had eaten too much.

"You don't look too well," Mythrim said, examining his face, "don't let nerves get to you. It was a fine toast."

"I'm fine." His stomach didn't roil so much as ache, as if he were being stabbed by a pen collection. "I just…" Leif noticed that Fryn leaned against a music stand, gripping her stomach in pain. The other guests sputtered and coughed, and fell to their knees, or piled on the dance floor.

"I suppose it's time." Mythrim yawned. "I'm surprised it took this long."

Leif glanced around; Mythrim had his hands on his hips, and his jacket loosely thrown on. His eyes scanned all the guests, and met Leif's with surprise. "You're a lucky one, hunter, to have eaten so much." He walked over and kicked out his legs, and he slid to the ground against the window. It had begun to snow heavily. "You're lucky too, that you get to die such a nice death."

Leif dug his hands out of his pockets, and clawed his way to his feet with the drapes. "I'm also quite resistant to toxins."

Mythrim laughed. "Not this one." He held a wide cork in his white-gloved hand, and smirked. "The problem isn't the venom or a poison, per se, it is that it is naturally quite toxic… and only in Stanaedre are the people accustomed to it."

Leif coughed, and doubled over, spitting blood on Mythrim and the floor.

"Tch," Mythrim grimaced, "and I only just had this suit made."

"You killed them…" Leif struggled. "Even the staff… the chef?"

He did a quick spinning inspection. "I really did, Leif, and why do you suppose I did that?"

"So much for your generosity." It was getting more and more difficult to speak.

Mythrim smiled, and grabbed him by the collar of his jacket. "It's simple, they knew my face."

27

"I figured." His voice gurgled as blood dripped from his mouth.

Mythrim released him, staring at the blood that clung to his white silk glove, and Leif fell to the ground in a heap. "I should get going, I hope you enjoyed yourself before the end—it was a kindness." Mythrim laughed maniacally at his own joke, bent and checked the pulse of the blondes, and stalked off, waving as he strode out the door. The stained glove flew off, and covered the face of the chef.

Hills and Pine

Frorin:

Snow District

The Final Needle

Stars flashed before Leif's eyes, and he swung his head around trying to clear his vision and find someone else alive. He was fading fast, and drew a full charge of sparks into his hand, and arced the energy into his stomach with a sharp flash. His stomach burned, and the toxins broke up as he ionized them, and they bonded to his food. He vomited all over the floor, and wobbled on his knees to Clair, where her eyelids fluttered, and her delicate wings shivered, and foam gathered on her lips.

"I'm sorry," he whispered, placing his hand gently on her stomach as he shocked her as well.

All her muscles contracted, and she writhed in the forced convulsion, and he only just managed to turn her on her side as she spewed her meal onto the cloak of an already-dead waiter. She fainted, but the greatest danger was past, so he left her there as he rose to his feet and staggered to Fryn, where her head lolled against the window, seeking desperately for air. She mumbled, and her hand looked deathly cold against the glass.

Leif took her shoulders and focused her eyes on his. "Fryn, this is going to be painful." He used the last of his sparks on her, and they seemed to have an even greater effect, as a nearby spoon flung itself to rest against her leg.

Fryn relieved her stomach, and pulled the spoon from her magnetized hidden sheath. She struggled to her feet, pale as death, though she flushed with fresh color almost immediately.

"Fryn." Leif gripped her shoulder. "Are you alright?"

She grimaced, and looked at the singed portion of her dress sadly. "Better than my dress." She turned to Clair, who was coming back to consciousness, and moved over, wings drooping. "Clair! You're alive…"

"I couldn't get to anyone else." Leif sat on the edge of the dais, and sighed. "They'd never been included before." He trailed off, regarding the pained face of the nearest dead waiter. He felt the most pity for them. The other guests might've deserved a bad death for all he knew, but the staff, they were common, and had died with misplaced excitement.

Struggling to their feet and lifting Clair between them, Leif and Fryn stepped outside.

"We should report to the Office immediately," Fryn suggested.

"Can we make it there in our condition?" Leif watched the slowly falling snowflakes suspiciously. It was a wet snow, so he thought it wouldn't be dangerous, but he really couldn't say.

"I'll be fine," she replied, following his gaze. "They shouldn't be a problem unless it gets colder and sharper."

He didn't want to face a sharp snow.

Clair stirred, supported on either side. "The forecasters said it might shift that way, we should hurry."

Leif started, relieved to hear her speak, and rolled his neck. "Then, Fryn, I'll rely on your guidance back."

She led them back to the south gate and as they passed, they informed the guards and pointed them to the scene of the tragedy, who then ran off with an indistinct exclamation.

The snow fell thicker. Fryn batted flakes away as they went, but pretty soon they shrank and sharpened to delicate, vicious points.

As they neared the office, Leif tried and failed to dodge one, and it sliced his cheek. He pressed his free hand against the cut bitterly, and shivered at the cold water that went under his collar. They burst through the door right as the clerk, Caelyn, was putting on her coat, with the keys in her hands.

She froze, and stared as they collapsed on the bench where the drunken thief had slept. "What happened to you?" She asked, dropping the keys with a clatter to the ground.

Leif shook his head. "Trouble found me after all."

Fryn chuckled, but her throat was raw, so the sound was guttural and rough.

Caelyn checked their eyes and felt Clair's forehead. "You look like it was quite serious." Glancing toward Leif's cheek, she added. "Hold on a minute, I'll stitch that cut," and ran in the back before they could argue, returning with a small tin in hand, and her sleeves rolled up.

She knelt in front of him and surveyed the gash, and nodded. "It is a deep cut, but it's clean, and should heal nicely." Her white and violet eyes stared into his, and Leif was glad he was too tired to blush. Then, in one shocking movement, she leaned in close to his face, and licked the wound.

Leif shrank away, but couldn't get far because of the back of the bench, and found he wasn't too tired to blush after all. His cut tingled, and went numb, as a layer of ice closed the wound.

Caelyn looked away awkwardly, annoyed by his embarrassment, and her cheeks grew equally red. "I probably should've warned you. We all have some mandatory medical training here and that's the most effective way to clean a wound ..."

Her dubious explanation left much to be desired, in Leif's opinion, and Clair and Fryn laughed. "I guess that's another one of our 'foreign' customs you find so strange," Fryn observed.

Caelyn turned back, straight-faced and composed, and threaded a needle she'd produced from her sewing kit. "I always bring one of these in case I need to sew a button, but I'm glad it came in handy for this too." She held his chin with one hand, and pierced his cheek with the other, her eyes firmly on her work, avoiding his. Five stitches later, she tied it off, and leaned back, brushing her forehead with her sleeve. "Now, tell me what happened."

Fryn detailed their invitation to the party, rubbing Clair's back comfortingly, and related the end of the dinner, and their involvement in the toasts.

"Stanaedre liqueur, hmm?" Caelyn said at last. "I didn't know they had something like that." She rolled down her sleeves and buttoned the cuffs. "This Mythrim character, for such a serious massacre, I'm surprised I haven't heard his name before... but everyone was poisoned..."

"A fae so deceptively charming must have used an assumed name," Leif supposed.

Caelyn retrieved some forms, and asked them to write their account, and sign and date. She insisted that without documentation, the Crown wasn't very likely to issue a bounty.

"I don't care if there is a bounty at this point," Leif frowned. "I'm going to kill him."

"You should be wary of choosing your own marks. We are only authorized to go after approved targets, and only when there is a reward posted." Caelyn tapped her chin thoughtfully. "Still," she said, "I don't think there will be a problem."

"Mythrim thinks he killed us. It won't be safe to return to our homes, if he discovers we still live," Fryn said.

Clair shifted anxiously and Caelyn placed a hand soothingly on her knee.

"Employees of the Commission are welcome to use the Hunter's Lodge in the West side of the District. I'd recommend you stay there," Caelyn responded, patting Clair's knee as she added, "You should come too, I think."

They agreed, and followed Caelyn to the door. Clair didn't need as much help walking as before, so Fryn led her out with a steel umbrella, and Caelyn held one over Leif. The Rain District Ringroad was pretty empty, but even so, it took them a while to get to the Lodge because of the distance.

It looked like a five story apartment building, or a hotel, with windows glimmering with lights spread out across the corners of each floor. They passed into the lobby, and the desk secretary looked up at them in surprise. He rose from his seat and waved Caelyn over, who folded her metal-plate umbrella smoothly.

"What's this then, Caelyn?" He asked.

She explained that they were supposed dead, and needed to remain out of sight. Leif and Fryn presented their licenses, and were furnished with new clothes and room keys. Clair would have to stay with Caelyn, or Fryn, since they didn't give rooms to nonmembers.

"I am sorry about this, Miss Yardall, but I'm afraid I can't circumvent policy," he explained, subconsciously looking at the desk.

They parted at the stair-junction between the second and third floors. Caelyn led Clair away, arm in arm. "Come by in the morning. I'll see if there's a warrant by then," she said, with a wave.

Fryn and Leif had opposite rooms, and she paused with her door half-open. "Good work, Leif."

"You too Fryn." He folded his coat over his arm.

"It seems we're a team after all, huh?" She pulled her scarf from her neck and folded it carefully.

"Yes, I look forward to working with you."

She smiled, and was about to close the door, when he added, "Why didn't you point me to the Hunter's Lodge this morning?"

She shrugged. "I didn't know about it." She shut the door, so he went into his own room.

Leif wondered if he'd have any trouble sleeping, but when he'd changed into a thick set of nightclothes and crawled under the quilts, he felt his eyes closing, and relaxed.

These northern faeries really are something else, he thought, *So much more playful, yet reserved, than back home.* He slept soundly for most of the night, but close to morning, he saw Mythrim's face, and heard his mocking voice, as he choked him.

Leif shook himself awake, and noticed the small clock by his bed. It was slightly past three. He washed his face in the basin by the window, and meditated on the floor in the center of the room. His breathing calmed, and he went back to bed at four, and slept through the remainder of the night.

Frorin:

Rain District

Hunter's Lodge

Leif met Fryn in the Lobby. She sat in one of the cozy chairs in the lounge area on the opposite side of the reception desk, adjusting the lacing of her boots, glowing in the warm light of the hearth. Her wings twitched irritably as she undid her knots and unlaced her boot to start over.

Leif sat down in the chair beside her. "Good morning, Fryn, technical difficulties?"

She shot him a mean look, and returned to her business. "I didn't think I would have to wear a messenger's uniform."

Leif snapped his fingers. "I forgot all about that." He was wearing his usual travel set.

She shook her head. "I was going to ask what you were about."

33

"I wouldn't have been able to answer." Leif got up and stretched. "I'll be down in a minute," he said, and dashed back up the stairs.

The messenger's uniform was an unusual combination of the utilitarian and the fashionable. Leif suspected that it made messengers better regarded and received, since the gray vest, stenciled with green detailing, even on the inside, seemed of high quality. Apparently the entire uniform was tailored, the boots were cut with barely noticeable wingtips, and the slits in the shoulders of the coat were padded with silk. He buttoned up with purpose and rushed back down to the lobby, and stopped before Fryn with a flourish.

"So," he grinned, "how do I look?"

She shook her head with a smile. "Like a messenger?"

"Come on, stand up. Give us a twirl." Leif took her hand and pulled her up from her seat.

"I was perfectly comfortable, I'll have you know." She sighed, but tested the range of motion of her shoulders in the fitted jacket, which hugged her waist and shot out into long coattails, and continued around when she gave it a spin.

"Quite dashing I should say." Leif tapped his chin. "Just imagine how often you'll be harassed by the guards asking your business now."

She frowned. "I hadn't thought of that… but as it is I already have trouble getting through checkpoints without ten minutes of meaningless conversation."

Leif sat in the chair next to hers, where she stood. "Are there female guards in Frorin?"

"You're wondering if they'll stop you for conversation. That'd be a dream come true, wouldn't it?" She snickered. "I'm not sorry to tell you the truth, there are, but they are not at all as interested in flirting with the random passersby as are the low level officers."

"Such a pity," Leif smoothed his jacket, and flexed his upper and lower wings out to his fingertips, "I haven't looked so good in years."

She gave a snort and walked to the door. "Come on, we should meet Caelyn for breakfast."

He got up and hurried after her. Thankfully it was a clear day, and the morning sun bathed them in light from every angle thanks to the fresh layer of snow—which had yet to be cleared from the street. Their gray boots left crisp prints as they walked leisurely around the Ringroad. Few fae wandered about and they only passed one pair of guards on their rounds. *Rounds around the Ringroad*, Leif supposed, laughing to himself.

Fryn ignored him, and they arrived outside the Office at 8:05, where Caelyn and Clair were waiting for them. Caelyn was dressed for work, white blazer, black silk vest, and a jacket, with matching dress boots and slacks. Clair however, wore a messenger uniform, like Fryn's.

Fryn lifted one eyebrow at her. "I thought they said they couldn't do anything overt for nonmembers."

Caelyn nodded, and Clair looked away. "This morning I received a reply, in light of the circumstances Clair was inducted as a part-time member in the messenger division—which means she will have to do some running around looking busy—like the other messengers. Who knows when *they* do any real work."

Leif smiled. "If you are such a good dancer, I think you'll do fine with the extra effort," he said, turning to Clair.

She blushed, whether from the compliment or from disagreement, he couldn't tell. "I'll have you know I am not unathletic."

Leif bit his lip, but couldn't help but reply. "You mean you are athletic."

Her wings changed to a slightly redder shade, and she stuffed her hands in her pockets, mumbling.

Fryn placed a hand on his shoulder and coughed. "It is not acceptable to correct someone's grammar in Froreholt, Leif."

He nodded sagely. "I'm pretty sure that's true anywhere, but for the sake of humor – even politeness is at risk."

"Anyway," Caelyn interjected, "I only have a short amount of time to eat before my shift, so come on in and I will brief you before I have to start working."

They exchanged confused looks but followed her into the office. Apparently, in one of the back rooms the Bounty Office had a lounge with a hearth, a coffee table, and an assortment of chairs, benches, and bookshelves. There was a table by the array of windows on the west side with a stack of small plates, mini pastries, and a large pot of tea. The windows looked out on an alleyway parallel to the South Cardinal, but one block removed, and led into a small residential cul-de-sac.

They sat around the coffee table with their small plates and tea cups, and Caelyn allowed everyone to enjoy a minute or two before beginning

35

her brief. "Last night, the Justice Council decided to endorse the bounty of this killer known, in this case, as Mythrim. Therefore, the Commission is authorized to pursue him, for the reward of 5,000-mint."

Leif gulped. "That's more than I expected."

Caelyn nodded. "It turns out that three of the King's nieces were attending the party and were among those killed. He wants capital justice: Mythrim is wanted dead, not alive."

Fryn's eyes faded for a second and sharpened back to focus. "The three blondes."

"I see! That's why they had the crown-patterned dresses," Leif said almost in sync.

"Correct." Caelyn tapped the side of her cup idly and closed her eyes. "There have been other cases of guest poisonings in the realm, though none so large, and I wouldn't be surprised if they were all executed by him."

"Different names of course," Leif supposed, "it wouldn't make sense to use his name, or the same one each time."

They looked at him oddly. "What a cognitive leap." Fryn smirked.

Leif shifted, and mumbled. "Well, it makes sense."

"Exactly, it didn't need to be said." Fryn fixed her jacket.

"Do you still have the invitation he gave you?" Caelyn asked. "In each case, there was one common symbol, different shapes, sizes, fonts, but each one had a sword somewhere on the card the guests received."

Fryn pulled hers out promptly before Leif could even remember where his was. "Yes," she said, "there is a sword!"

Leif snapped his fingers as the image of the invitation flashed through his mind. "A threaded needle crossing a silver embossed sword!"

Caelyn nodded slowly. "That's why in certain circles, he is referred to as The Venomsword. You," she pointed generally at them, "are the first ever to have seen his face and survive."

They were silent for a moment.

Fryn changed the subject. "Since we are now uniformed as messengers, are we supposed to deliver letters around town?"

Caelyn shook her head. "No, I shouldn't think so. It is just a disguise, if anyone asks why you don't have a bag, you can always say you're on a break."

"That's a relief, but I don't see how we're going to find Mythrim," Leif said, reaching for the teapot.

Clair coughed lightly as she had reached for the pot as well, and had placed her hand on his.

"Oh, would you like some more?" He smiled, and filled everyone's cups. "But really, how will we find Mythrim in Frorin, of all places?"

"Is it that immense of a place?" Fryn asked. "I hadn't known."

Caelyn chuckled. "You could always go looking for trouble. It worked well for you last time."

"I wasn't actually looking for it then…" He sighed. "So what, we should just patrol each district, and ask questions?"

"I would advise against asking *too* many questions. Some information can only be gathered without looking for it," Caelyn said, tapping the tip of her nose with her finger.

"You mean asking questions would raise questions?" Clair laughed.

"I'm fairly sure that's what she meant," Leif said, taking another sip, and brushing crumbs from his jacket onto the marbled floor, regretting it as soon as he saw Caelyn's displeased glare.

They sat around the table quietly, each locked in their thoughts. Leif worried no one would speak again, but after about five minutes, Fryn made a 'hem' sound and drew their attention.

"Patrolling the districts is a good start. We could always eavesdrop or ask one or two questions periodically around various gathering places in the city." She lightly hammered her fist into the palm of her hand to accentuate her point.

Leif imagined a light 'ding' as if from a small bell, sounding from her gesture, and swallowed a laugh. "I recommend we check the restaurants and inns, maybe he frequents one."

"Just because you like your drink Leif, that doesn't mean he does," Clair said, swirling her tea. "But, it is a sound idea, better than most."

"You know, Fryn," Leif began.

"I don't…"

"There is a liqueur from Aelaete I think you should try." He held back a sly smile.

"If it's Agalia, don't even try." Her eyes narrowed.

"It's worth a try, you know."

"I don't…"

Caelyn coughed, and set her teacup on her saucer with a noticeable 'clank.' "That is probably for the best. Now, I should get started. You never know when a respectable hunter like Yarrow will appear—and they despise incompetence." She added the last part with a sharp, but playful, look. "Clair, I'll get you set with a few letters that need delivery, but I'll keep you moving around the Snow District. It's safer than the areas *they* will be frequenting."

"What if Mythrim is in the Snow District? He did manage to arrange such a high class party," she hesitated, her knees knocked together nervously.

"He won't notice you, but you can tell us if you see him." Caelyn waved Leif and Fryn over. "And when you are done for the day, go pick her up for dinner. Not safe to leave her out after dark."

Leif looked away, coloring slightly. "I had thought I'd do that, anyway."

"Well, both of you should go." She looked to Fryn, who nodded with a cryptic expression.

In the end, Clair ran off with a messenger bag strapped over her shoulder, and promised she'd meet them at the Tallow Inn restaurant at six.

Fryn guided Leif down to the farthest and most dangerous district of the city: the Pine District. Technically, there was a worse one but the Sky District barely counted; it was mostly populated by the poor, filled with slums, and did not have a restaurant to speak of. Fryn insisted that it wasn't the kind of place Mythrim would walk through, let alone, visit. Moreover, that it was actually less corrupt than the Pine District.

He wondered about that, but they rushed past the guards at the District checkpoints into the Hill District, and then followed the Ringroad around to the gate to the eastern end of the Pine District Crescent.

They walked down the main Crescent Road toward the north-east, looking down the long intersecting side streets where old houses and stale shops sat under tired awnings in the snow. The street was not as nicely cobbled as the upper districts. Here and there holes were filled with ice and snow, and Leif slipped across the first one he found.

He landed roughly on his back, limbs and wings spread-eagled, and shook his head. "Does anyone look after this place?"

Fryn bent over with a smirk, her braid nearly touching his face. "You could say that the Pine-Martin does."

"Who is the…"

She hushed him with a finger on his mouth. "It's best not to draw attention to that name."

"You just said it." He struggled to his feet and felt carefully on the ground to make sure he wouldn't slip again. An old fae watched them warily from the porch of a shabby bar, smoking a pipe, with an unwavering gaze. She took his arm and led him a little further. The wind bit his face: that was why he was a little red.

"The Martins have many eyes in this area. They control most of the district, and all the guards."

"What do they smuggle?"

"They deal in games, races, and everything where a bet is placed. I doubt Mythrim is involved with them, but they might know something of him," she said, adjusting her scarf.

They stopped before a lavish restaurant not unlike the ones in the Snow District. Leif coughed. "It's like they want everyone to know where they are."

"It's not like they're committing any open crimes…" Fryn smiled and pushed open the door. "But underneath that, they have power and connections."

Inside there was a giant staircase that swept from the back wall into two branches encircling a stage where a band of musicians played soft music as important-looking fae sat at various coffee tables with newspapers, pocket watches, and glasses of various drinks. In the center a sophisticated, but particularly rough-looking fae sat at a decorative table with a fur mantle over his suit and a cigar in his hand. He was the only one who looked, only with his eyes, in their direction.

"We wait here," Fryn whispered. Sure enough, an elegantly dressed waitress stepped forward, her slim-cut dress too thin to obscure the evidence of the knives beneath her apron, at least for his trained eyes. Leif swallowed.

The waitress was tall, with dark black hair, and maroon eyes. Leif forgot all about Caelyn. "Would you like to drink or dine?" She asked; her eyes narrow as they passed over their interlocked arms. Leif felt stiff.

"Dine, please, and if you have a paper?" Fryn asked placing her far hand over the one already interlaced with his arm, almost protectively.

The waitress blinked twice while surveying the tables, and spotted one behind the center figure. "Please, come this way."

They followed after smoothly but quickly, suddenly feeling as if everyone were staring daggers into their backs. Fryn mouthed "follow my lead" and they sat down at an oblique angle to what Leif guessed to be their host.

The waitress placed a single print-sheet menu on the table, and turned to the center figure. His hand tapped a newspaper on the table while he took a drag on his cigar. "Excuse me sir, if you are finished with your paper, may I let these other customers read it?"

He looked at her as if coming out of a daze. "What? Oh, yes, of course, could I have some tea?"

"As you wish, sir, thank you." She picked up the folded paper, and set it on top of the menu with an order slip and a pen. "Please look over the menu and write your order, when you are done, I will deliver it for you," she directed with a dangerously smooth voice. Leif forgot about Fryn on his arm.

Fryn unlaced her arm from his, and looked over the menu. She made a show of having mixed feelings, and wrote down "two specials with recommended pairing" on the slip. Then, picking up the newspaper, she found the daily puzzle: a crossword puzzle.

"Do you like this sort of thing?" Leif asked, leaning over it. "Oh, number twelve is frostbite."

She ignored him and wrote as she pleased: "Looking for information, Mythrim, connection to dinner-party incident" in various boxes.

She then worked to fill in the surrounding ones with correct answers and set it down on the table. The important fae with the cigar noticed, and grunted gently. "Excuse me miss, are you finished with that paper? I think I missed an article." He set his cigar in a notch on a porcelain ash tray, and leaned a white bone cane against the table.

She smiled and passed it over, and he nodded in thanks as he noticed the crossword and mumbled, "oh, frostbite" and smiled.

"Fryn, do they…?" *know you* he meant to ask, but she squeezed his arm slightly and glanced away. At that moment the waitress returned and took a look at the order slip. "It won't be a minute, two steaks, and reds."

It really wasn't even a minute before the wine arrived, a dark tannic wine that Leif had to smell three times before taking a sip. They leaned back and enjoyed the wine until their lunch arrived, and they finished eating. They didn't speak to the newspaper fae again. Fryn asked for the check, and left a generous tip, and led him back out.

They didn't talk until they passed through the gate to the Hill District when Fryn noticeably relaxed as she let go of his arm. "That was Eljaren Pine-Martin, the patriarch of the Pine-Martin clan. He governs the entire district, and deals with hunters in a very strict fashion. There has never been a price on his head, and I suspect there never will be."

"How will we hear from them?" Leif shivered.

"We will order a drink in the early evening tomorrow, or the day after. And yes, they know me. After all, I'm a distant relative—one of the ones who got rich and moved into the inner rings. I'm not popular, but I'm not unwelcome."

"Does that mean you're a Pine-Martin?"

"No, I'm distantly related. Anyway, let's go find Clair... I need a drink. I couldn't enjoy the wine." She led him north, growing more and more relaxed, the farther they got.

They found Clair in the Snow District at one of the police boxes chatting with a bashful guard, and went out for a late drink at one of the guard's recommended locations.

When they'd all ordered, Clair shifted her bag across the booth and sighed against the cushioned back. "I can't believe you went to Martin-hall, I suppose that's a good source of information, but it's going to be expensive."

"Well, even if they find nothing, I paid for food and drinks, so they won't complain, it's their entry fee," Fryn said, taking a breath as she relaxed in her seat opposite Clair.

Leif stood with a tray of snacks looking between them hesitantly, wondering where to sit.

Fryn shook her head and patted the place beside her. "Sit down and let me eat. The tension made the steak unenjoyable." She muttered something to the effect that they would make gourmet food turn to ash in a guest's mouth, and Leif guessed it was out of fear, or the kind of guilt one feels when they try to eat something extravagant in an impoverished area.

41

The bartender waved him over, and sent back three tumblers of honeyed Yardall. They all clinked glasses cheerfully. "You made it out Fryn," Leif said, "I'd say that means that you get to live to drink another day."

She gave him a cold glance, and smiled. "You were practically shaking. If I hadn't held your hand, well, you probably would have embarrassed all of us."

"What a thing to say, and so soon in our friendship." Leif took a sip of sceppe and looked at Clair. "Are you all like this?"

"Who?"

"Fee."

"No, I'm nice." She blinked. "But only to fae I like."

"I'm nice." Fryn chewed a piece of dried fruit. "At least, I didn't hurt you."

Leif was beginning to feel that she could just as easily hurt him by accident as on purpose. Still, he shifted in his seat and rested his elbows on the table. "Well, it won't be as tense tomorrow, right? And, Mythrim still doesn't know we're alive. I can't wait to see his face when we catch up to him." He laughed quietly, but still earned a raised eyebrow from the bartender.

"You shouldn't disturb the other guests in the Snow District," Fryn chided.

Clair agreed, pointing out that laughter carried, and it smacked of the lower classes.

"Well, I'm sure they make some allowances for foreigners," Leif said.

"Just don't push it." Clair chuckled, and took another sip.

Trials and Tails

Frorin:
Pine District
Martin Hall

Leif and Fryn walked up the steps to the covered porch of Martin Hall, arms hooked, trying to look nonchalant. Leif stepped on her foot and she shot him a pained look, but they caught the waitress's notice without any other mishaps. That morning, they had received a note while at breakfast in a tiny café in the Rain District; how they even knew to find them there, Leif didn't care to know, but he had the sense that they'd been tracked. He shivered and watched three older fae in slightly aged suits smoking and playing cards at a table beside the musician's stand. One of them threw down a trio of threes, smiling as the next player picked up the pile, apparently unable to play a prime.

"Ahem," the same hostess as the day before, only wearing a slightly thicker, longer, and more fur-covered dress, tapped a finger on the nearby desk. She wasn't attractive now, not with the pale light from the street-side windows, and the unlit chandeliers, she just looked impatient. "We have your reservation prepared. Follow me to your private booth."

He held back a swallow as they followed the waitress up the stairs and down a side hallway to a set of private box-seats overlooking the atrium. She swept back the black silk drapes and ushered them into their seats with her other hand, adding a cheeky wink at Leif, as he and Fryn finally unlinked their arms.

She left them with a flourish of the drapes and quietly disappeared. Fryn's mouth quirked slightly, but she picked up a breakfast menu from the observation side of the table and sighed.

"I don't like coming here. I feel like Harissa can't decide whether to hate me or idolize me…" she said, looking down at the faeries at their cards.

Leif pointed back toward the curtains. "Your… cousin?"

"Once removed. She's twenty. Don't consider it."

"I wouldn't." Leif groaned, and took the menu from her hands. "I'd feel uneasy." She smiled, but he felt she was merely humoring him. "What should we even get here?" he asked.

"We don't need to order anything, the menus are a formality," Fryn said, tapping her fingers on the table. "She'll probably deliver some drinks just for appearances but she won't ask what we want."

"Tough family," Leif said, "I only have two sisters, a younger brother, my parents, and grandparents on both sides. Normally I'd consider that a large family, but compared to this…" He didn't bother mentioning that his sisters were already married, with children of their own, or that his extended family comprised one of the larger clans in Sendra City.

"Funny." She looked back out over the balcony, following the three old fae with her eyes as they quit their game and wandered up the stairs. "I wonder what her whims will be this time."

"It is not a "whim" or a "fancy"," the waitress interjected, lifting the curtain and poking her head in from the hall, "I work to create a new favorite every time I mix drinks."

"Does that mean you can't make the same drink twice?" Leif smirked.

Harissa's mouth twitched, but she held back the frown, and presented a wooden tray with two tumblers of clear liquid garnished with flower petals and pine needles. "I see why she likes you… but no; it does not mean that at all." She set them down roughly, and some of Fryn's drink sloshed onto her sleeve.

She left without another word, walking away as if she had delivered a message, and they drank their mildly sweet beverages in peace. "All things considered," Leif said, plucking a pine needle from his mouth, "she makes a decent drink."

Fryn nodded. "It's passable." They heard a stifled sniff from behind the curtain. "But I wonder if she hasn't lost some of her original inspiration." Dull receding footsteps sounded outside, and they both relaxed.

"Does she always eavesdrop after delivering drinks?"

"Always? Well, I don't come down very often, once every few months or so."

"She does, doesn't she?"

"Yes, she does… I don't know where she picked up that trait though." Fryn took a sip and chewed on a pine needle. "I see, so that's why it's there." She smiled. "It tastes much better if you bite the needles."

Leif lifted his cup to his mouth, but before he could try it, the drapes parted and the Pine-Martin settled into a chair that appeared at the head of the table. Two waiters scurried back and left him with a glass of wine, and vanished around a corner.

"Fryn, Leif Aellin, I have investigated the matter you requested, and unfortunately the information we could gather was slight. We know that this Mythrim resides in the Snow District, but could not maintain a tail. Harissa wanted to follow more closely, but from what I can tell, he is a skilled fighter, of a class she could not attain."

"The Snow District… do you know his true identity?" Fryn scooted forward in her seat and set her glass on the table.

"No, we followed him from a sighting in the Stone Market, which led us to the edge of the Snow District, but unfortunately, we could not get through the checkpoint." The Pine-Martin took a sip of his wine and grimaced. "This is too bitter."

A waiter replaced it with a fresh glass and vanished again.

Leif coughed nervously and stole a draught of his drink. "What is the Stone Market?"

They both looked at him, Fryn with a slightly open mouth, and the Martin with a raised eyebrow. "You don't know?" they said in unison.

"Ha, ha, no, I'm afraid I don't," he replied, feeling cold.

"It is the unauthorized market, not entirely contraband goods, but one can go there to make connections with shady characters or purchase items without oversight." The Martin explained. "It seems that Mythrim purchased that Stanaedre wine there, and went back to persuade the vendor not to discuss it with anyone. He was handsomely paid, and what with the threat of that dinner party, I doubt the vendor would feel safe telling anyone."

"But does he know anything?" Leif asked. "Mythrim probably just bought the wine there; I doubt he even knows his name, or anything more."

"Perhaps not, but if he can be linked to anything there is a risk that someone, like us, might find him out. He does seem awfully confident in his secrecy, were I him I'd move less openly," Fryn suggested.

They sat back in their chairs thoughtfully, mulling over their drinks. Chatting voices trailed up from the floor below, and Leif wondered whether he should finish his drink now, or just take a small sip.

"...I see, this is a fine restaurant..." One of the voices mused. "I'm surprised there's such a place like this is the Pine District..."

Leif stiffened, Fryn's eyes widened, and the Martin placed a finger over his lips as he walked out. The voice was unmistakable. Footsteps receded down the stairs, and then returned a minute later and moved into the booth behind Leif's back.

Stifled voices whispered through the wall, and Fryn silently flitted over the table and pressed herself into the seat beside him with an ear against the stone. She levered herself higher from his shoulder and stood on the seat.

"...ood afternoon sir, is there something I can help you with?" The Martin asked softly.

The reply was inaudible, and they leaned closer to the rail.

"...see. That could be difficult..."

"...don't think so, not for one of your skill..."

"...ypically involve myself with Hunter business, what with the level of risk," the Martin replied.

"If this is a matter of payment, I can afford your fees, however if in fact you are sympathetic to said organization, I will take my leave."

"That is acceptable. I will initiate my investigations, and contact you when I have the desired information. Do you have a preferred form of communication?"

"...ere are relays for such things, drop the line at the Tipped Hat, and I will hear about it..."

Chairs scooted back, and there was a mix of shuffling, and the footsteps of the other guest left by the stairs. A minute later, Martin returned with his still full glass of wine and sat in his chair with a sigh.

"I am sorry to leave you in the middle of our conversation, but I imagined that such a person might call on our services. I cannot discuss other client's affairs, but I imagine that previously communicated information might be of use to you..." He trailed off with a smile.

Leif returned his smile and finally finished his drink. "Well then, thank you, I think we will take our leave as well," he said, placing a hand on Fryn's shoulder. "Now that we have a lead..."

She shrugged his hand off and made a face. "We should follow it."

They nodded to their host and ducked under the curtain, walking as quietly as they could. It didn't help; Leif wondered whether the floor had been designed to make noise.

They passed a trio of musicians setting up their instruments for an afternoon ensemble, and out the front door into the street. Fryn scanned the surroundings carefully, and relaxed when she didn't see Mythrim outright.

"At least he isn't on to us yet." She shoved her hands in her pockets.

Leif popped his collar and started back the way they had arrived. "I don't know how he'd feel if he saw two messengers leaving the Pine-Martin Hall."

She lost her relaxed posture and waved him in the opposite direction. "I think it'd be best if we went back a different way."

"I thought there wasn't one." Leif ran after her as she started down the northern curve, coattails swishing as she speed-walked.

She shook her head, and after a good five minute jaunt they turned into a dead end alley with the wall to the next district. "I didn't say we'd go through a watched pathway."

She climbed halfway up the stones and paused. "We need to be quick, if there is a patrol passing through we need to drop in behind them."

"I get the feeling you're used to this," Leif said, scratching his nose against the wall.

She didn't reply, but peeked over the top and looked down the neighboring curve. "It's clear for now, but we'd better drop now."

They dropped in without consequence, and stole their way up to the Snow District the same way. If Mythrim took the main roads, they might have a chance of spying him if they hid near the Snow District's checkpoint. Failing that, they'd change tack and head over to the Tipped Hat for dinner.

In the end, they didn't see Mythrim by the gate, so they stopped at the Lodge, and tried to dress in nondescript but clean-pressed clothes. Leif had to buy a new jacket at the market, since his travel clothes were not nearly fashionable enough, and Fryn insisted he'd have to remain behind if he didn't follow the dress-code. He settled for a tightly fitted gray suit jacket that matched his white linen shirt and pants, and they passed through the checkpoint on a date without trouble.

The guards, this time a fee and a fae, followed them with their eyes enviously, as if they wanted nothing more than to join them.

The Tipped Hat was in the western section of the district, and it took slightly longer to reach than the Final Needle had on the first day. It was a tall building, the lower section a restaurant, and the upper three floors a fancy hotel, with an apparently renowned bridal suite.

"I wonder how Clair is managing the deliveries," Leif wondered at the door.

Fryn shrugged, and locked arms. "We have our own concerns, first of which is you have to pretend you know how to entertain a date."

"That's cold, even for you." He sniffed, and opened the door. Inside the layout was almost identical to Martin Hall, except it didn't have an upper dining area, the far stairs led to the hotel lobby.

"Do you see him?" Fryn whispered, leaning close as if it were a pretty nothing she meant to say.

"I don't, do you?" He replied in kind, tempted to try and brush noses, and immediately blushed, even just pretending was harder than he thought.

She chuckled and waved a waiter over from the bar. "Well, you can manage that much at least."

They sat down in a dimly lit corner of the restaurant, where one of them could see the door from the side, but they wouldn't be seen immediately either. Fryn decided she wanted to be the lookout, so all Leif could see was the tip of her nose and chin in the slight light of the oil lamp in the center of the table. He thought it was a little odd for a restaurant in the Snow District to avoid using starlamps at the tables, since there was no doubt about their ability to afford them.

Fryn followed his gaze, and glanced down at the lamp. "Up here, the rich have a thing for romanticizing the commonplace and rustic as if it were special," she explained.

The waiter didn't ask their drink orders; he merely set down a tray with sliced bread and returned with a bottle of white wine. It was Guldhand, the wine that Clair complained came from a crooked business. "It's starting to make more sense," Leif said, placing his hands on the table.

Fryn's eyes glowed a little, and switched their gaze from the door to his hands. "What is?"

Leif poured their wine and pointed at the label. "Guldhand is quite popular isn't it?"

He slid her glass over, and she placed her hand on his. "It is starting to make sense. They have many connections, more than most would think."

The dinner was a delicious dish of pasta and mushrooms in a cream sauce, and the wine actually was really good. Leif figured since they were already mixed up in the underground it didn't matter if they drank it. Probably an hour passed before Fryn blinked and leaned in close to whisper that Mythrim had entered, their faces inches apart, and her expression entirely romantic. So good at acting, he thought. Leif couldn't act, but he could pretend. He smiled and placed a hand in hers.

"I suppose it's time for dessert," he said, eyes flicking to his right.

"The burnt cream is to die for, I've heard," she said, eyes locked to his, "perhaps we should stay and enjoy our time here."

He nodded and raised one hand to attract the waiter's attention. A desert menu appeared before them, and they promptly placed their orders. Their corner was dark, the burnt cream amazing, but they were tense, and Fryn constantly updated him with obscure remarks about what food sounded good, and how many lamps were needed per table to tell him what Mythrim was doing, eating the regular meal, talking with three guards in Captain's uniforms, and that he was also good at telling jokes... apparently.

"If he's got friends in the Guard, this is going to be much more difficult than I thought," Fryn sighed, biting her lip.

"We will have to tail him all the same." Leif nodded taking a sip of his fresh glass of wine. They were into their second bottle of wine, and Leif felt flushed, especially when he started to believe her acting.

"They don't have places this nice back home," he said, looking her in the eyes. "This is actually a lot of fun."

She smiled wanly, and nodded. "I'm not used to this either," she said, color showing on her cheeks, even in the dim light.

They ordered another bottle, mead this time, to finish, since Mythrim was really taking his time. The captains were laughing more loudly now, and they could even hear what kind of jokes Mythrim was telling.

"...so this kid comes into the post-box, and starts telling me that he'd been bullied by one of the guards. He's crying, and describes Heggil to the chin, I mean, we all know his chin, and the one hair that grows there, anyway, so I bring him in from the back and ask 'is this the fae who bullied you?' and he goes white as a sheet and starts spewing out apologies like nothing I've ever seen..."

"That's not that funny." Leif sighed.

"…so Heggil picks him up, gives him a hug, and says to tell mum he'd be back to discuss grades in an hour!" A loud roar of laughter sounded at the conclusion, and Mythrim walked over to the bar. "Give me another bottle."

The bartender, a young fae with a sharp face, went pale and passed over a bottle of red wine.

"You remember that right, Jared?" Mythrim asked, clapping the bartender on the shoulder. "That was when I was first promoted to Captain. What was that, ten years?"

"Eleven, sir," the bartender said, and wiped his forehead with his towel, glancing over his shoulder.

"You've certainly gotten better at remembering your history." Mythrim laughed, mussed his hair, and returned to the table.

"Captain?" Leif frowned, and opened his mouth to continue, but Fryn pulled him close and placed a finger over his lips with a sultry but commanding shake of her head.

"Save the commentary for after. We still have a long night ahead of us."

He blushed, and leaned back in his seat. "We should probably close out."

She nodded. "If we go up as if to book a room, I don't think he'd notice us, but right now he's watching everyone who leaves by the front door."

They spent a hundred and sixty-mint on that meal, Fryn covering most of it since Leif didn't carry much cash with him.

"I'm sorry," he said, tapping his fingers on the tablecloth, "I didn't realize how expensive it would be here. I don't carry much at one time, pickpockets, you know."

She laughed, and shook her head. "Don't worry about it. I got that wine thief the other day."

Mythrim glanced over at them, but whether he didn't recognize them, or because of the wine, he quickly ignored them and returned to telling jokes.

She took his hand and led him up the burgundy carpeted stairs to the black marbled lobby and they quickly followed the hall toward the kitchens and restrooms. They ducked into the kitchen, swept passed a confused chef, and stole out the back saying they needed some air. Leif leaned against the back stair rail and sighed.

"I thought he'd found us."

Fryn nodded seriously, pressing her temples with her fingers. "He may have just pretended not to notice."

They snuck around to the front, and waited from the top of the house across the street. Leif felt dizzy from the wine, but he didn't want Fryn to know, so he knelt and looked out thoughtfully. Mythrim took his time; nearly another hour passed before he and his friends staggered out the door and stood in a small circle in the street. They laughed over some joke of his, and broke off, waving to each other drunkenly.

Mythrim paused at the entrance to the main street, and looked over his shoulder warily, almost looking sober for a moment, before he turned right. They followed from the rooftops, hiding behind the shadowed slant of the roofs, watching as he meandered north.

He went straight north, following its curve for about ten minutes before they saw Clair approaching with her messenger bag slung over her shoulder with a wide accomplished smile. Leif stared as she neared Mythrim and her eyes widened as she looked away.

Mythrim stopped, following her with his head. Aside from them the street was empty, the windows shut, and not a sound to be heard. He scanned the roofs, and Leif barely dragged Fryn down just as he looked in their direction. They peeked over the lip, and watched, as all of a sudden, Mythrim stretched his neck and turned on his heel, and sped after her in one quick wing burst.

She let out a muffled cry as he covered her mouth, and pressed the sides of her neck, and she went limp. He slung her over his shoulder, and ducked into a nearby alley.

Leif and Fryn sped after him at a distance, on the wing, ducking around corners and waiting as he kept checking over his shoulder. "If he knows she's alive, he'll suspect we are too," Leif said.

"I think he knew all along," Fryn replied, watching their target skid to a halt at the end of a street. "How many people attended that party, and how many died? The report must have counted the bodies, not the number he meant there to be…" She added.

Mythrim jumped the low wall into the other section of street as he entered a gated community.

They went high, and scanned his path from the nearby clock-tower. He was watching every direction, but they were hidden behind the lamps lighting the clock's face. "So what, he lured us out?"

"I believe so." She dropped to the roof of the nearest gated-house and he followed quickly. "Shh!" She cautioned, glaring as he cast a pebble from the roof. Thankfully, Mythrim didn't hear it as it fell on the mossy turf below.

Mythrim took several turns, finally stopping before the back-entrance to a small estate with a white stone wall. He didn't bother with the door, but flit over the top and vanished from view.

They paused across the street, listening. "What do we do?"

Fryn scratched her neck. "I think he'll interrogate her before he kills her. That gives us some time to plan our approach."

"Still," Leif said, leaning sideways to get a view around the corner of Mythrim's house, "after we get her back, she's going to have to hide."

"So will we… unless we kill him now. I think Mythrim will try to get us even inside of the Commission if only to be rid of any liabilities."

They dropped to the ground and skirted the streets, staying out of the light. No light shone out of the windows, but Leif was sure he saw the curtains shift in the dim light of the street lamps. Scouting the surrounding area took about twenty minutes, during which time Leif saw repeated checks by Mythrim as he looked out from each window.

"There's no light from the house, she might be in the cellar," Fryn said at last. "Typically there's only one entrance…"

"I say that when we see him check a window in a higher room, one of us sneaks in and hides inside the cellar without letting Clair know. Then when he returns, the other one will kick open the door and surprise him while the first one knocks him out cold," Leif suggested.

"It's not a bad plan, but something doesn't seem right," Fryn said, grabbing his shoulder. "I just saw the curtain move at the top floor, now's our chance."

"Fine, let's both hide." They hopped the fence, and found the cellar door on the outside of the house facing the back gate. It was locked, but Fryn took her knife from her leg and slipped the point into the mechanism and froze the insides, then with a press of the blade, she broke it. In the dark, her knife looked almost pure black, like she'd stained it with oil, and he wondered if it were one of those metal-powder sintered weapons, lighter and thinner than what the blacksmith could usually forge.

They ducked in and shut the door. There was a long stair leading deep into the ground, lined with cold stone. At the foot of the stair, a soft light glimmered from an oil lamp that hung from a small sconce on the wall, and revealed several closed doors on either side of the hall. The far end had a heavy door with iron bands, but they checked each of the small ones first. The left side had an array of tools in a handy workshop, a room with shelves lined with boxes of unused utensils and dishware, and the right had a large safe and several strong boxes against the walls, and another room devoted to the storage of dried goods and food.

That only left the far room, which Leif supposed could hardly be anything but a wine cellar. They went up to the door and heard the muffled whimper of Clair through its wood. "She doesn't seem too well," Leif whispered.

Fryn smiled bitterly and lightly pushed it open.

Clair sat bound to a chair with a scarf wrapped around her face so she couldn't see or speak, and Mythrim stood before her with a tiny emptied glass bottle in one hand and a syringe filled with a vibrant green fluid in the other.

"I know how you lived, Clair, the only question that remains is, where are your friends?" He asked, pulling the scarf from her face with a flourish. It was a dark green that matched the fluid, and shimmered.

Her eyes locked on the syringe and she closed her eyes.

"You don't even know what this is, and you fear it. This could be tea for all you know." Mythrim chuckled, but it was hollow. Leif and Fryn stood frozen at the door. If Mythrim were down here, then who had been the lookout?

The cellar door opened, and footsteps rushed down the stairs.

Mythrim turned toward the sound and saw them. He blinked, and then laughed, and set the syringe on a side table. "It seems I had no need to investigate you after all. You're quite resourceful Fryn Martin."

She didn't bother explaining her mother's side once-removed connection. "You had an accomplice."

Mythrim's eyes ignored her and switched to Leif. "I'd say the same about you. I thought you were more independent—that would be much more convenient."

Leif and Fryn stood back to back as the door opened and a young fae in a black suit threw open the door with an exclamation. "They've broken in…!" He gaped at them, and they at him.

"The chef?" Leif asked.

"They're already here." Mythrim yawned. "You really expect me to manage an event on that scale by myself? You flatter me, but be more realistic." Mythrim reached out to a sword on the wall, one of the silver ceremonial weapons of the guard, and the chef from the party drew a black sword from under the tails of his long-coat. His eyes were cold, like Fryn's.

Leif settled into a stance with his legs at shoulder width, and felt Fryn stiffen behind him with her knife in hand. Her wings went cold against his, sharpening, laced with an edge of ice. He shivered.

"One brings a knife to a sword fight, the other brings none." The chef scoffed. "Dead or alive?"

"You can kill him, but I have questions for her." Mythrim leveled his sword toward Fryn's throat. "Where does your uncle spend the third day of every month?"

"I don't know," She smiled, "he doesn't tell anyone, in case situations like this occur."

"That's a pity, Havrshyk, it seems I'll have more work for you to do after all this. It's a pity they sided with you, Fryn, they would've been a useful resource." He stepped forward, lunging for her throat, she made to parry, but he disengaged, still moving forward as he plunged the tip of the sword toward her shoulder, it sunk in with a sickening crunch, as she held back a scream.

Leif ducked the slash of the black sword of the chef, Havrshyk, and stepped into his reach and threw a charged push through his center, blasting him through the closed door down the hall, with a loud crash of splintered wood. Havrshyk slid across the stones, smoke rising from his jacket.

Mythrim paused, and Leif reached around Fryn's waist and pulled her back as he kicked Mythrim in the gut, knocking him back against the wall.

"I don't take kindly to those who injure my assets." Mythrim growled, and slashed straight toward Clair's neck. Clair's eyes followed the arc of the blade, and she fainted as Fryn's knife, now in her left hand, parried the cut and slashed up Mythrim's arm, spraying frozen flecks of blood up into the air. Leif dragged Clair in the chair to the door and Mythrim and Fryn faced off, almost equally injured.

They slashed and stabbed and parried and reposted in a furious bout of moves, giving Leif the time to use one of the knives on the side table to cut Clair's bonds and sling her over his shoulder. She was incredibly light, and surprisingly thin. Fryn backed toward them and Mythrim trailed after, as they back-stepped over Havrshyk's unconscious form and out the door.

Mythrim followed them, a napkin tied around his arm, his sword in his left hand, all the way to the street, but he stopped, examined the tip of his blade, and touched the blood that Fryn had left on it, frozen onto the surface. He looked at it between his fingers and then glared at her. "I may not be a Bloodcrafter, but I will devour yours." He stared after them and withdrew back into the shadows.

With Clair over his left shoulder, supporting Fryn's frigid arm about his right, they walked the long way back to the Hunter Lodge. Each step drained him, the weight, and the cold, and the lack of sparks to keep him going, so that his legs trembled as they finally pushed through the double doors of the Lodge.

Fryn staggered to the front desk and leaned against it, and Leif laid Clair out on one of the couches in the lobby by the hearth and dropped into a chair, sweat running down his back.

"How did we get out?" He wondered softly.

"It was a surprise attack that caught him off guard, in close quarters, which made the use of his sword more difficult compared to our knife and fists. But I'd say we barely made it out," Fryn replied, as a slight bit of color crept up her neck, and the pain of the injury got the better of her control.

Her right arm hung limp and useless at her side, and she grimaced as she moved to sit on the low table before the hearth. "I need…" She bit her lip and groaned. "I need you to remove my jacket."

He moved behind her and slipped off the left side first, and noticed that even that hand had extensive bruising around the knuckles and wrist. "You should train more if you plan to parry the flat of a blade with your hands," he advised.

"I am aware of that fact," she said, closing her eyes and pressing her lips together as he started to pull the top of the jacket off her other shoulder. The wound had bled a lot during their walk, even though she'd obviously drained as much as she could into her blade, and her hand quivered. "I have not fought anyone that talented before in my life, not seriously anyway."

He pulled the jacket down her arm and just as he got it off her hand, she gave a cry. "Easy, that's it," he said, and removing the other sleeve, he folded the ruined jacket and set it on the ground.

"Not quite yet." Using her left arm seemed a little awkward as she reached the harness on her opposite leg and passed him her black damasked knife.

He shivered as he took it, at the way it clawed out the warmth from his palm, and tightened his grip.

"I need you to cut away the cloth around my shoulder."

Leif nodded, and started at the opening of her neck, cutting just under the collar across her shoulder, lightly pulling on her shirt to raise it from her skin. The white blouse was hopelessly stained with her blood and made a sickening sucking sound as he pulled it away from her wound.

"Ahh!" She clenched her left hand and closed her eyes. "How is it?"

"It went straight through, I think," Leif said, finishing his cut and peeling the folds of cloth aside to examine her shoulder. Her shoulder-blade had taken a direct crushing blow, and it looked misshapen under her skin, as for her collar-bone, it was broken in two, as shown by the sagging area of the wound. "This doesn't look good Fryn, I don't see how you can fight again in this year or the next. You may never regain full use of your arm either. I've seen soldiers ruined by the maiming of their forehand."

"Take the knife, place it in the wound."

"What?"

Her face contorted as she turned to look him in the face. "Just do it!"

He nodded, all the blood gone from his face as he lightly slipped the knife into her shoulder, somehow matching the path of Mythrim's sword until the hilt met the wound and the blade protruded far through it.

With his left hand bracing her shoulder, and the right on the blade, he felt it shiver, and her skin go cold. The blade darkened and grew heavy seeming to grow thicker and heavier by the second, as she grew colder and more pale.

She was completely white, her lips blue, and her eyes glazed, though they stared intelligently up at him, and her lips smiled, she looked dead. He recoiled, and fell back into a chair before the fire, but the fire went cold too. It seemed that the very air was crystallizing, and frost formed on her skin, and on the chair, and on Clair, and on him as well.

The edges of her wound still had color, and her pale face strained as a loud cracking and popping sound emanated from the back of the wound, and she slowly pulled the blade back out. Second by second she pulled, an inch taking twenty, and ice formed around the blade as it passed through, pulling back, firming up her bones where they should be, and fusing them together.

The knife gradually lightened, back to a charcoal-like color, where the lines could be seen again, and it looked pale as she finally let it fall to the ground with her weakening hand. Color faded back into her face, her lips turned pink once more, and ice covered the wound of her shoulder. Only then did she faint.

Clair woke with a start, and stared at Fryn in surprise, and shivered inside her coat. Leif sat beside her and wrapped one arm around her shoulders, and they watched Fryn till she awoke.

Back and Track

It took Fryn several hours to snap out of it, startling Leif and Clair from their unintentional naps. She woke, rocking forward with an almost comical lethargy, and then a painful cringe as she bumped her arm. Clair watched her expectantly, and Leif waited for her to speak.

"It's not that unusual," She said, cradling her arm. "Most Blood-crafts have some measure of the ability… though it is not easy to master a full Lichform.

"So it is true," Clair said at last, "but you're wrong about it not being unusual…"

"There's something in every tale," Fryn answered, "Leif, I'm sure you believe that there are giant serpents in the desert."

"I know it for a fact," he huffed.

"Well, most people in the east simply don't believe it."

Clair gasped. "Have you ever fought one?"

"A Lichform? No." Leif winked.

She shook her head, looking less shook-up. "I meant one of those lizards."

"They're snakes, and yes." He idly handled the sandalwood box in his pocket. "I still have my scars."

Fryn looked impressed, or at least she blinked at him and examined the fire, so what else could it be? "Does that mean you are more resistant to poisons?"

"Not exactly, I have some tolerance to snake venom, but I'm still just as vulnerable to other toxins." He examined a trailing white scar that ran across the underside of his arm, and quickly rolled down his sleeve.

"Then I think that our theory about the wine itself being toxic was misleading. You handled it the best, so it might have been venom." Fryn said, her eyes tracking his movement.

"But Mythrim himself told us it was the wine, why would he lie when he thought we were dying?" he asked, but then he had thought at first that he'd handled it better because of how much he'd eaten. Maybe there was a chance that there was some venomous element in the poison used.

Fryn shrugged and then bit her lip and went pale. "I should know better than to make gestures right now." She smiled wanly and took a deep breathe. "For all we know, the Stanaedre clans put snake fangs in the aging casks."

Clair coughed politely. "Shouldn't we plan what to do now?"

"Mythrim knows we are alive. Not only do we need to pursue him, but we also need to evade him at the same time." Fryn stood and paced, holding her limp arm.

"How long will it take for you to be back at your best?" Leif asked, following her path anxiously with his eyes.

"I cut him up pretty good, don't forget that." She replied with a vague smile. "Still, it should take over a week; even if I get a transfusion it should take about that long."

"Even with a transfusion?" Leif asked, wondering what she meant.

Fryn shot Clair a look, and Clair nodded sagely. "That sounds about right," Clair said.

Leif shook his head and sat back down. The wall clock discreetly chimed the hour, seven o'clock. He closed his eyes, and nearly fell asleep. But he rocked back forward and groaned. "We can't stay here any longer. We have to leave right now."

Footsteps announced the descent of one of the tenants. It was soft, as if trying not to wake the others, and snick-tapped its way to the lobby. The sound stopped behind them.

"Oh my!" Caelyn, the clerk with the tiny mouth, exclaimed. She was so pretty, even while, no, especially while worrying over them. "What happened? Clair, are you alright? Fryn, your arm!" She didn't fuss over him. "What happened, Leif? Did you get him?"

He waved his hand before her face, finding it difficult to get her attention. "Hey! Hey, listen! We did find him, but he had already caught Clair so we rescued her."

"Mythrim got away though," Clair added.

"He let us go more like it," Fryn interrupted, "I think that now that he knows for certain we are alive, we cannot hide from him, and that it will be a simple matter to silence us."

"I don't see why we don't just go to the guards and tell them who he is," Leif said.

"Because one, we don't even know his name, just 'that guy is Mythrim,' and two, because we have no proof." Fryn sat back down.

Clair sunk into her coat, and hugged her knees.

"Well, we just have to force him to act in public," Caelyn said, breaking the uneasy reverie that was descending on them.

"How?" They asked in unison.

"I don't know. You're the Hunters, aren't you? Next time you fight him, make it defensive."

"That won't work," Fryn replied. "It will make it seem like he is doing his duty as a guard, and that we are trying to run. We'd only make more enemies."

"I don't see why that matters," Leif yawned, "we just have to prove it after he's dead. Then, he won't have his friends, or be able to argue against us."

"There's still the chef," Fryn added. "We need to remove him. If we can do that, show that he was working that night, and link him to Mythrim, that could work."

"But what's to stop him from skipping town?" Leif asked.

"You have it backwards. We're the ones on the run now, Leif," Fryn snapped. "Sorry, it's just this." She pointed to her shoulder, leaned back in her chair, and closed her eyes.

They waited in silence till the clock read seven fifteen. Caelyn gasped. "I have to be in the office in fifteen minutes! Now I can't get my tea..."

They watched her go to the door, where she paused, and turned back. "Drop in as soon as the doors open. Write an account—just in case something happens to you."

Leif's eye twitched, and he looked over at Fryn with what he hoped was an ironic smile. She seemed to take it that way, and smiled back.

"She might know of a place we could stay," she said.

"Maybe the Commission will protect us," he wondered.

"I'm sorry to say that the only Hunters that spend time in Frorin are the weak and the inexperienced. That is mostly thanks to the low rate of violent crime," Fryn replied, shaking her head.

"Low?" Leif shook his head too, "you should spend time in my land."

"Well, what the law defines as crime or violent depends on the land I suppose," she allowed, and was about to open her mouth to continue, when her cousin, Harissa, burst through the door in a striking dark dress that clung to her figure but had slits down the sides of her legs to make movement more convenient.

Harissa's eyes found his first, and seemed to brighten, before she found Fryn, and went stiff and cold. "I heard about your exchange…" She said at last.

Leif walked over, took her by the arm, and led her to the couch. "Have a seat."

She blinked. Probably surprised to hear that phrase directed toward her. "Thanks…" She looked between them all and then shook her head with a smile. "I knew you'd do it."

"It was nothing," Leif said ambiguously.

"We didn't kill him," Fryn explained, "he nearly got us."

Clair watched her closely, but said nothing, so Leif interjected. "The chef from the event was an accomplice. We think if we can track him down we can get to Mythrim."

Harissa rolled her eyes. "Hold up a minute, I'm busy." She placed a concerned hand on Fryn's shoulder. "He will be chasing you now, but if anyone… well, you can do it."

Leif sighed and looked over at Clair. "I was going to ask if you wouldn't mind helping us uncover information regarding a fae named Havrshyk."

Harissa froze, and slowly turned her head toward him. "Oh I can tell you about him…" She looked furious. "That back-stabbing, silver-tongued devil! Yeah, I know him. He only left me waiting for three hours last night…" She trailed off. "Oh."

61

"I think Mythrim is going after… our… house," Fryn said, barely making it to the end of the sentence. "He said, 'they could've been useful.'"

"For what?" She asked. "He obviously has a network rivaling our own."

"You can always use more information, or informants," Clair said, catching Harissa's attention for the first time.

"You…" She narrowed her gaze. "Yes, you're that sceppe girl. How were you invited to the party?"

"That was…" She looked away, her eyes wet. "Miss Elena invited me."

"The Princess?" Fryn and her cousin asked together. "I guess you were important after all."

"It is not our friends who define our importance. It is our own actions that matter," Clair argued, "I went there not only to see my friend, but also because I thought I could make valuable connections for my family."

They fell silent, listening to the sound of the clock tick and the shoes of the doorman as he opened the door.

"…As you can see here, my lord, our agents are well in hand," the doorman explained.

"Yes they seem, for better or worse, alive," a young, confident voice replied.

Harissa's eyes widened and she turned away. "It's Ieffin."

Prince Ieffin, heir to the throne of Frorin, was a tall young fae, probably five or six years their senior, with blonde hair that was combed in a similar fashion as Mythrim's had been. Leif wondered if perhaps it had been the other way around, that Mythrim had been copying the style of the Prince. He had a lean, but not unkind face, and wore a simple suit of glacier blue with white piping to match his slightly blue, white-frosted wings.

"Master Aellin, Miss Martin, Miss Martin, and Miss Yardall, I am so glad to see you alive and well," he said gravely, standing obliquely to them, spreading his arms and wings magnanimously.

"I am sorry, my lord, but why should you concern yourself over my safety?" Harissa asked—the very picture of decorum, sitting with her back straight and her hands folded over her lap.

"Because, your family suffered a terrible attack last night. I have long understood the necessary work your family has done in managing the peace of the lower districts, and am very grateful. So I was much concerned when I heard the news about your father." The Prince's face adopted a sort of fatherly pity, as he bowed his head.

She bolted upright. "What… what news… my lord?"

"It seems our public enemy invaded the estate last night and cut a path to the penthouse, and stabbed your father in the heart." He pulled off his white silk gloves, and opened a leather-bound pocketbook that appeared in his hands. "I am sorry for your loss," he said, busily writing on one of the pages. "But I hope to expect your loyal service as I had from the Pine-Martin himself. My lady,"

He tore the page from his notebook and held it out. "Go on, take it."

She read the page and shrank back into her chair. "I am not…"

"Capable, worthy, or next in line…? You are all those things." The Prince said looking her in the eyes. "It was a bloody path to your father…"

She looked down and clenched her fists. "My brothers?"

"Heinric might live. He is being treated by your physicians now, I think. I am sorry that I cannot tell you more, but this is merely what was relayed to me."

Ieffin turned to Leif and Fryn. "I am so glad that you survived your encounter with that fae. There is no safer place for you than my estate. I ask that all of you, that is all four, stay with me in safety till this blows over. I might even request that you allow the Guard, or more experienced Hunters take over for this case."

"My place is with my brother," Harissa said.

"No, it is with me. I will not let a vacuum be created in the lower districts. While I am sympathetic to your situation, it would jeopardize mine if something should happen to you." He looked at Clair. "I'm sorry that you got mixed up in all this, Elena would be happy that you lived."

She cried softly.

"I am sorry sir, but what is to stop him from discovering that we are with you?" Leif asked.

Prince Ieffin laughed. "You don't know much about me, do you? I don't like your organization. I wouldn't take you in, which is why I must, if I am to avenge my cousins. But far be it from me to dislike someone simply because of their employer. I am sure if you knew the President of your organization personally, you'd hate him, too."

Fryn laughed. "President Hans has an odd reputation to be sure."

"And he's rude," Ieffin added, "Last summer he came to the Foreholt Fair, and insulted my crown. My crown! Well, not directly, but clearly enough."

Leif smiled and nodded. "I am grateful for your offer, Prince Ieffin, but if we are cloistered inside the Crown District how will we find Mythrim?"

Prince Ieffin swept his coattails to the side and sat beside Harissa and Fryn on the couch, and was about to place one arm around the shoulders of each when he thought better of it and crossed his legs and scratched his chin. "That is because I will not only give you access to undisclosed gates, but I think you might need the help of some of my informants."

"Just who are these informants?" Fryn asked, cocking an eyebrow.

"Merely loyal servants of the crown who will readily give an account of their knowledge when asked," he replied, "and seeing as how it is no longer safe for you to track him openly, I think you need all the eyes you can get."

"And what do you need?" Harissa asked.

"I need someone who can avenge my family on this criminal. We will find him, and you will bring me his head." Prince Ieffin folded his hands on his lap, and smiled as if he were asking for a cup of tea.

"I'd be happy enough to do that for myself," Leif stretched his neck, "but how should we go to your estate? Mythrim will likely be watching us. If he discovers we are there, why wouldn't he kill us?"

"I never said you'd be safe there." He shifted uncomfortably "I merely suggested you'd go unnoticed for a time. Isn't that better than walls and guards?

They agreed it was, and Ieffin took his leave, walking out with condolences and saying he expected them for dinner. But, he hadn't helped them plan any way of getting there. Leif supposed as a royal he had little understanding of the delicacy of the journey and expected them to simply walk through the front gate.

Harissa rose to leave, but Leif grabbed her wrist. "One last thing," he said.

She had lost her friendly, sultry posture and had long past gone pale. "What?"

"Where is the Stone Market?" He asked, searching her glassy eyes.

"Why would you want to go there?"

Fryn interrupted, meeting his eyes. "We need to find a way into the Crown District."

She withdrew her hand from Leif's grasp and smoothed the sides of her dress. "Yes well, I would suggest that you take me with you, but what of the sceppe girl?"

"Clair," Clair said, "And I am going with you. I will just need a change of clothes."

They all needed that, except for Harissa, though she insisted that her dress was inappropriate. Fryn changed into a simple skirt and blouse with a light jacket, since something too bulky would have been painful. Leif kept his new gray jacket on, but switched out of his linens to a borrowed set from the staff wardrobe—they wouldn't notice. When they'd all gotten ready, they waited for the noon rush and ducked into the crowds either walking on the street or hurriedly flitting above it.

Harissa followed the east-side Ringroad toward the north, leading them down side streets until they neared the east gate to the Sky District. "The market is not far now, and provides a connection between the three outer districts. People from each district can sell their goods or services at a steep discount or for an enormous profit, without worrying about city oversight. They sell their goods for what they sell for, and you can buy just about anything you might need."

They passed through the center of the gate surrounded by various traders and common folk going about their business so that the guards didn't get a good look. "We should be able to find someone to make us uniforms to sneak into the Crown District," she whispered.

Leif wondered if it could be done in time, but supposed they had little choice. It seemed he was right about that.

The entrance to the Stone Market was through the back door of a simple but well-to-do restaurant called the Pheasant. The proprietress saw Harissa and immediately waved them into a private room.

It was a small room with pressed-bark walls and a starlamp chandelier that cast a pale light over the sparse area around the round table. They took a seat and waited for Harissa, who watched them with a strange smile. Not long ago, Fryn had said the Sky District barely even counted as a district, but here, far from the center of the city, there was a restaurant with starlamps, that would have fit in well enough in the Rain District. Leif realized that each day it became more clear how little he knew about the city.

"What do we do now?" Clair asked, shifting the scarf she'd used to hide her face.

"Now we have lunch and hope that Camilla is pleased to send us below," she answered.

Camilla, the owner of the Pheasant, looked a bit like one, with a pudgy figure, and tiny feet, and a colorful comb in her hair. She insisted that they eat her mushroom soup and drink their proprietary pine-needle tea, neither of which suited Leif's tastes.

After what seemed like an hour, Harissa paid for the meal, hiding a smile as Leif complained about the 'mysterious mushroom mush,' and left a modest tip. Then, once Camilla returned, she swept up the cash in her hands, and slipped it into a tiny pocket on an oversized apron.

"Feel free to hold the room until you are pleased to leave," she said, waving as she walked out.

"That is what we've been waiting for," Harissa said at last, and gripped the edges of the tabletop with her hands as far apart as she could reach. Then, she rotated it ninety degrees, and heard a soft 'click' come from the wall behind her.

"How fascinating," Clair said quietly.

"I didn't know it'd be this cloak-and-dagger," Leif added.

Fryn sighed, and Harissa rotated the table counter-clockwise another hundred and eighty degrees, which pulled a section of wall back into a recess and cranked it to the side, revealing a tunnel roughly wide enough for two to walk side by side, and when they'd all entered the tunnel, Harissa pressed one of the stone bricks on the wall, and the door slid back into place.

It went down a slight incline with miniature lamps spaced out just enough that they could see their feet, then straight north for about fifty feet, and east for another hundred or so, before they reached a locked door. It was pretty cramped, but even though they were squeezed together by the door, Harissa didn't complain, she only knocked three times, and received four knocks in return, to which she gave two.

The door opened, but whoever had been watching it was gone, so they filed out and stared at the long street that stretched out before them. It was a wide tunnel that looked like a retired storm-drain, converted into a causeway lined with booths nearer to the center with an aisle between them. Then, on the outsides of the booths, lining each wall there were evenly spaced signboards hinting at shops built into the interior of the wall.

"This opens into a wider circular space at the end of the tunnel with a dome," Harissa explained. "From the dome you can exit to the Hill or Pine Districts."

"What if Mythrim comes for us here?" Leif asked.

Fryn tapped her cheek with her good hand. "He would have to come as himself, not in uniform, since they would never invite a guard down here, even if they were in someone's pocket, just so they don't scare anyone."

They walked down the far right side, examining the booths they passed. One sold 'second-hand' furniture, likely from repossessed houses or from places where the owner had died and then their property looted. Another had weapons, some impressive counterfeit guard weapons, or shields, or armor. One of the signs along the wall advertised the Guldhand Company.

"I knew they were crooked," Clair shoved her hands into her jacket pockets victoriously; "they must have a lot of connections to make it down here."

"There are honest businesses that make use of connections here," Harissa hinted. "My family employs one of the banks down here, simply because it is safer than using an above-ground one." She shot a glance in Leif's direction. "That goes for the Commission's Bank as well."

"Yes, I'm sure that's the reason." Fryn smiled.

They continued into the wide circle at the end, and found a series of booths rivaling that of the tunnel. They sold normal items, clothes, thread, pots and pans. As they walked half-way through, Clair gasped and pointed at one of the stalls.

"That's my company!"

Harissa laughed. "I didn't want to ruin the surprise," she explained. "I told you honest people sell their products here, but that's mostly because there's a lot of foot traffic. The Stone Market *is* a market after all."

"The Yardall company is set up in the Snow District, but only certain people are allowed in, so it isn't very surprising that they would want a larger market, or to sell their lesser quality batches at a discount to people from the common class," Fryn said, walking over and looking at one of the bottles. "Take this batch for instance, forty-two, is rated rather poorly, substandard for your company, so they decided to sell it to less discriminating people."

The person manning the booth turned to her with a smile. "And I will have you know, that it is still the very finest sceppe you can find in the lower districts." He had a trimmed mustache and thick arms, and dark hair that had a slight curl over his eyebrows. He froze when he saw Clair. "Miss Clair, what are you doing here? I assure you this is all above board, just getting rid of the sub-stock."

She waved away his concerns with a pale face. "I'm sure my father told you to do this... I just wish I'd been more informed."

"Something's not right, Clair, we haven't seen you around recently, and some were saying that you'd been killed or kidnapped by that madman a few days ago."

"I'm fine, as you can see, but I can't tell you more. Are there any skilled tailors in the market? I need a new set of clothes," She replied.

"It seems you are in some trouble, but I don't know any tailors, best check the store-fronts along the wall. They're more established businesses, helped set up this market," her friend answered. "I'll let your father know you're alright." He gave Leif and his companions an odd look. "What should I tell him about your friends?"

"That they are capable and in the same situation. Tell him not to talk to the guards, or look for me, I'll return when it's safe." Clair smiled prettily and walked off.

"I will do that." Her friend waved and turned to another customer and started praising the product and the outrageous price by which they could obtain it.

"Sceppe girl seems more important than I thought," Harissa said, sidling up beside Leif. "First she's friends with Elena, and then her family hides their works underground. I knew about the booth, but that fae seemed more than just a vendor. I think he gets information, or plays some other important role in the company, corporate espionage perhaps?"

"I wouldn't know," Leif said, scanning the nearest wall. "Ah, I think I found a tailor." He pointed sharply in the direction of one of the nearer signs, a circle of wood with a finch holding a thread in its beak trying to jam the end through the eye of a needle held by one of its feet.

They slipped into the dark space behind the door, and Leif immediately tripped over a ridge in the floor and fell flat on his face. Groaning, he got to his feet and dusted himself off. "You might want to keep your eyes open. This place isn't safe," he said, massaging his pride.

A mousy voice assaulted him from behind. "There's a sign on the wall beside the door. It clearly says 'mind your step.' So watch what you say about my shop being unsafe." It was a short pudgy fae with a bald patch on his head and plethora of different color threads on different color needles pierced into the sleeves of his shirt.

"I meant no offense, only a joke," Leif said, nodding to Harissa.

"Oh look here, a Pine-Martin. What do you want, a veil?" He smiled. "I'd happily offer a discount to the grieving."

Fryn stepped in and grabbed one of the needles with her free hand and looped it through the cloth of his two sleeves and cinched his hands together in an instant. "You should at least pretend to be sympathetic if a client has lost family," she said in a hushed voice.

Leif was about to pull her back by her shoulders, but stopped himself when he saw her flinch. "I am sorry about my acquaintances here," he took the scissors from the mousy tailor's apron pocket and cut the loops that Fryn had restrained him with. "They are a little shaken by recent events."

"You can leave my shop. I don't care about your events or your circumstances. I run a business, not an orphanage." He winked at Harissa, whose lip trembled, pressed thin.

"Oh? But I heard you were the fae to see about a special job," Leif said, "You come highly recommended."

"Who recommended you to me?"

"Why none other than Camilla herself."

"So she finally took notice of my talents, eh? Well, why should I think you are any friends of hers?"

Leif leaned over and placed his hands on his knees. "Because, if you don't believe us, you will find no friendship or help from my organization. We will disavow you."

Fryn stared, and Clair sucked in her breath.

The little fae eyed him warily. "And just what organization do you belong to?"

"I'm sure a knowledgeable fellow like yourself has heard of the Strafe-Viper school in Aelaete, and their practice of sending their masters-students out into the lands to help keep the peace, and save people from harm? What would happen if there was someone they decided not to help?"

Leif's eyes bored into the man's forehead, causing a gradual drooping of his wings.

"Bah, you don't have that kind of influence. They stick to their compass like wax," the tailor said, looking away.

"If you don't believe me about that then what do you think of their other tradition, the one where they must distinguish themselves in the Commission?"

"You expect me to believe that you're a Hunter? They don't let Hunters in here."

"They don't let them attack people, or track their targets," Fryn clarified, "but say someone else attacked you, there are no guards, and hunters might be persuaded that you don't deserve to be saved."

He saw the bandage on her shoulder and his eyes narrowed. "You two, you're the ones he wants. You'll get no help from me; you couldn't protect me from him anyway."

"What if we forced you, he might forgive you then," Leif said, turning to the others. Clair and Harissa watched him mysteriously, "how much for counterfeit uniforms?"

"Eighty a set," He answered, watching them with his bulging eyes.

Leif patted his shoulder. "So we can purchase them after all." His hand shifted to the man's back, and he zapped him with just enough of a shock that he passed out.

"Leif! What are you doing?" Harissa asked in alarm. "If it's discovered that we attacked someone we'll never be let back in."

"We can fix that once we're safe." He threw her a glance. "Now, we need… three hundred and twenty mint. Feel like being our benefactor? Our current one is not very reliable." Ieffin probably hadn't even thought about their need for expenses… but then, even if he had, he probably wouldn't provide any.

She fished out the correct amount from her small clutch bag and sewed them into a fold on the inside of the tailor's pant-leg. Then they rushed over to the lines of shelves and cupboards. There were all manners of shirts and jackets with colors ranging from orange to blue, and even one matching Ieffin's own clothes.

Harissa looked over the wardrobe and sighed. "I don't know, I just don't know, do we go in as servants? Guards? What?"

Leif found a trim glacier blue suit with white lining and stitching. He stepped into the dressing room and came back with his old clothes rolled up into a bundle under his arm.

"An Attorney's uniform?" Clair asked.

"Is that what this is?" Leif smiled. "I will deal out justice," he said, striking what he hoped was a dramatic pose.

"That's hardly what that's like." Fryn shook her head. "I will go as an assistant."

"Can you handle the job?" Leif asked.

She shook her head. "This isn't about showing what I'm capable of, it's about going unnoticed." She took a similar uniform with a blue blouse, matching blazer, and skirt and found a pair of flats that went perfectly. "Harissa, I'll need your help."

They came out of the dressing room in a few minutes, Harissa in a gray servant's uniform, and Fryn decked out in the cheery blue one. It made her eyes seem like an even deeper icy blue than he'd noticed before.

"What a happy set of colors," Leif said with a grin, "it's hard to think about who's after us just being around them."

Clair stepped into the dressing room and returned in moments in a matching uniform to Harissa. "That's half the reason they chose that color and fashion, too many attorneys had problems with depression and crises, so they decided to brighten the job."

"I see." Leif walked to the back of the store and found a tight alley that ran around the circuit behind all the shops. "We should exit this way, someone may have seen us. Best if we make our move now."

They crammed into the space and carefully made their way back to the exit. Camilla took note of their leave, and they hurried out to the street and back to the Rain District. Just as they were about to make a turn onto the Ringroad, Harissa pulled back and pressed herself against the wall.

"I just saw Havrshyk walking by the Hunter Bounty Office. They'll be watching the gates to the inner districts, well, probably all the gates."

"Sh." Leif turned around. "Maybe we should take a cab." He threw his hand in the air as one of the street-cabs was pulled onto their street by a driver holding the reins of his hare, a light brown creature with an anxiously twitching nose.

It pulled to a stop as the hare gave them a sniff and relaxed. The driver took off his tall hat and flitted down to hold the door open. "Come aboard, where would you like to go?"

Fryn, posing as his assistant, waved the two 'servants' aboard and stood beside the driver as Leif settled onto the bench opposite them. "We need to get to the Grand Assembly. These witnesses need to appear for a trial my associate is advocating."

The driver nodded seriously. "Because of the recent killings, I'm afraid we will have to pass through inspections at the gate but I am sure that you can arrive in time." He hopped up and they took off at a gentle but quick pace.

The gate to the Snow District had a very informal screening. Fryn stepped out, her arm no longer bound, looking undamaged in every respect, as she explained their purpose with her damaged hand stuffed in her jacket pocket. The guards nodded and waved them through, and they made it to the gate at the Crown District without trouble.

There they were all required to step outside. One of the guards wore a thick scarf and had dark eyes and the other yawned tiredly. "I'm going to need to inspect what you're carrying there," He said.

Leif didn't like his voice. "I am a very busy man," he said, pointing a finger at him. "My case starts in fifteen minutes and I need to prepare my witnesses."

The dark-eyed man's eyebrows lifted mysteriously. "There are no cases being judged in the Assembly today. I need you to show me your papers."

Fryn stepped forward and presented her Hunter License, and whispered. "We are tracking a criminal who has breached the Crown District. We are on important business, please let us through."

Leif placed his rolled up clothes in Clair hands and moved Fryn aside. "If you would allow me to handle this," he said, giving her a sharp look. "I think he knows why we've come…" He whispered.

The guard warily placed his hand on the hilt of his sword and clapped his companion on the shoulder. "You won't be passing through this gate, foreigner, as if you'd pass for an Attorney."

The other guard drew his black sword and felt the tips of his mustache. He gave it a quick tug and tossed it away like molted skin, clubbing his companion with the pommel and aiming a slash at Leif in one quick movement.

He had dark hair and a young, but cruel face. "You think I'd let you get away again?" He said, stabbing toward his heart with a thrust. "You won't beat me now that we're outside, Hunter."

"So the chef comes at me with his knife." Leif smirked, dodging the thrust, and stepping back into a low stance, sliding back over the iced cobblestones. "What do you know of me, little chef?"

"More than you know me." Havrshyk grinned, and swung his blade at his face.

Leif parried with a jab under the flat of the blade and stepped into his arc, making as if to go for another push, which Havrshyk expected, and tried to counter with a downward hacking blow.

Leif grabbed his wrists and wrested the blade from his grasp, sending it flying, where it sunk into the stone wall. "What is that thing made of?"

Havrshyk's hands went pale, like they had been drained of all blood and frozen, like Fryn's Lichform. He stepped forward and shifted to a tight stance, boxing for position.

"Whoa!" Leif skidded back over the ice and sighed. The punch had grazed his shoulder and torn the uniform and given him a gash across his upper arm. Blood congealed instantly, covered with a small amount of frost.

Havrshyk bounced and tossed a couple punches in the air. "You think if you disarm me you might win?" He glared at Fryn, who had neared the wall, reaching out with her good hand. "Don't make me take you." He loosened his fists and held out braced fingers, and skidded in a short step to her position, and plunged a hand into her injured shoulder.

But she'd hardened her skin, and his hand bounced back like an arrow hitting steel.

Leif rushed, and with a quick wing-burst, he twisted and kicked him in the back, sending him face first into the wall, where he fell with a crack in his frozen nose.

"Well, what is all of this then?" A new voice asked, walking down the steps from the Assembly.

They all stared as a young blonde-haired fae approached in a white suit with blue lining. "I expected your counsel an hour ago Attorney. It shouldn't take this long to vet a secretary." He shot Havrshyk a look, who seeing him, skipped to the wall and grabbed his sword and flitted down the streets.

"Prince Ieffin?" Leif asked.

Fryn returned to her normal color and sighed.

"Well now he knows we're here. How are we supposed to catch him?" Harissa asked, closing her eyes, and then opening them, and looking at her now useless expense on the uniforms.

"I might have a couple of ideas," their host replied, "but my goodness, Fryn, I should've hired you a long time ago." He winked.

She looked away and adjusted her coat. "I am quite happy with my current job."

He laughed. "That's all fine then. You must be hungry. Please come with me." He turned on his heel and started toward the Assembly. "Actually, Leif, seeing as how you are already wearing that uniform, I could use an Attorney's services at the moment. This Mythrim might know you're here, but I'd rather that no one else finds out. Think of the damage to my reputation."

Leif looked at the sorry state of his jacket and shrugged. "As long they accept excuses about getting into a fistfight with the opposition."

"I'm sure they won't complain." Ieffin walked up the twenty or so steps to the great doors of the Assembly and held one open as they filed in. Just then however, one of the Prince's staff ran gracefully over and drew Clair and Harissa aside, muttering something about needing them. Fryn and Leif shared a look, and Clair waved awkwardly as she was herded off toward the main building. Ieffin showed them into the building.

He sat them down in a large office room where an equally large attorney sat in an immense chair behind an extremely wide desk. The old fae leaned over his desk with his head on his hands, looking sickly and pale.

"There is a small matter here that I could use your services for in the meantime." Ieffin lifted the man's head by his white hair and they saw the blood on the desk and the slit in his throat.

"He was garroted," Fryn said, stepping closer. "How will this help us find Mythrim?"

"Oh it won't, but I need your help, and will tell you if my people hear anything." He let go of his head and it fell unceremoniously back to the desk. "See, he was investigating a conspiracy involving, well, that's probably best if you don't know. All I want is the person hired to kill him."

"Alive?" Leif asked.

"I don't care about that. I know who hired the assassin; I just want to remove one of their tools. It's much easier to fight an opponent without letting it come to the surface. Sometimes it's best to let things remain as they are." He took a seat in one of the chairs at the long meeting table.

"There's a strange mark on his hand," Fryn said, lifting it in her left hand. "It looks like a knife piercing a coin."

"That is something you'd best avoid." Ieffin advised. "Now, let's eat."

Dun and Done

Frorin:
Crown District
Grand Assembly

Leif lifted the late attorney's head and examined the precise slit in his throat. "Well it's not good, I'm afraid," he said, smiling morbidly.

Prince Ieffin laughed. "I know he's dead."

Fryn knelt by the door examining something on the floor, turning and bending down to see whatever it was more clearly.

"That is not quite what I meant, your Majesty," Leif said, "I think you have a turncoat in your guard. I have good reason to believe that Mythrim is one of the city guards, but I'd wager that he has an accomplice on the inside of this very Assembly."

Ieffin paced in front of the desk, giving his former attorney an odd look, smirking, then grimacing, as if he were disturbed and then amused in alternating moods. "I know who wanted him dead, but what I don't see is how you know the assassin worked here." He looked at Fryn with a distracted smile, and then turned to Leif. "But I really must eat." He produced a silver bell from his jacket pocket and gave it a sharp ring, and stood facing the door expectantly.

Within moments, a sharp-nosed servant burst ceremoniously into the chamber and froze with a look of horror on his face. Thankfully, he recovered quickly under Ieffin's withering, uncaring gaze. "What is it you require, my lord?" He asked, hands tightly clasped behind his back.

Ieffin nodded. "First, where is William?"

"He... he's dead my lord," the kid replied, stammering as he looked down over his shoes. "The guards found him in an alley on his regular route here this morning."

Leif let out a sharp cry. "Aha! I knew it was an inside job. Our killer impersonated your servant and obtained access directly to his target."

Fryn's eyes narrowed, but she didn't interrupt.

Ieffin did though, "I already figured that out myself. What I find more vexing is the fact that I lost the only reliable butler I ever had." The whites of his eyes accented his vexation with veins popping out across the whites.

The youth stood there in front of the door watching the exchange with a blanched face, looking for all the world like he hoped he'd been forgotten.

Fryn hadn't forgotten about him apparently, "We'd like lunch," she said, eyes sparkling for some reason. Leif had the impression that she was probably enjoying the kid's discomfort, and hoped to exacerbate it for some reason.

He jumped and stuffed his hands in his apron, and searched his pockets for several moments, until he found his memo pad. "What kind of wine would you like?"

Ieffin turned his head slightly so he barely looked at him out of the corner of his eye. "I want ceren."

"C'ceren? Yes, of course, right away." He turned on his heel and ran straight into the door, and rebounded onto his rear rubbing his sore face with one hand, and his backside with the other. Without another sound, he dashed out.

When the door had swung shut, Ieffin burst into a fit of laughter, leading Leif to join in, and then Fryn at the strange scene they had just witnessed. "I don't know whose kid that is, but I assure you, he's the youngest," the prince predicted, settling in one of the embroidered chairs, wings stuck out the back through the thoughtfully placed holes.

They waited about ten minutes for the new butler to bring in the lunch at the long table. He pushed open the double-doors discretely, and brought in a rolling cart laden with trays of bread, cheese, meat and roasted nuts, that filled the room with a spicy aroma. There was a crock of creamy soup, and a carafe with ceren set over a bowl of steaming-hot water. When all had been placed in a line on the table, the kid leaned back proudly and avoided looking at their absent guest. "Is there anything else, my lord?"

"Yes, have a seat. I need you to taste everything." He glanced over at Leif. "You can use his plate."

Leif almost complained, but at Fryn's slight headshake, he sighed. "I don't mind."

The servant pulled up a seat and served a modest portion of each item, including the ceren—which he seemed only too pleased to taste. He methodically took bites from each, alternating with small sips from the ceren, until he leaned back and waited for their response.

"Well you're alive, let's eat," the prince said at last. "You may go. When I ring, you can come back and clean up." He looked at the desk. "Except for that, you don't need to deal with that."

"Thank you sire," he replied, and walked backwards out the door.

"I'm still just a prince," Ieffin shook his head, "and with the way my father ages, it will take twenty years before I become king."

Fryn filled a cup of soup from the crock and set it down carefully. "Didn't your mother, the queen, die ten years ago?"

"Just about, may she rest in peace, but my father, he has taken great pains and expense to prolong his life," he said it almost with a tinge of disgust. To Leif he looked like the sort that felt sick at the thought of the desperate way people clung to life only to die in a sickbed, that he might prefer a 'glorious' death such as what the attorney had attained.

Leif watched him finish his glass of ceren in his third swig, and refill it from the carafe. "I am not well versed in the intricacies of this country, but I imagine you are much too busy to spend so much of your time with us," he said, searching for something in Ieffin's moody face, the way he leaned his elbow on the arm of his chair, and rested his cheek on his half-curled hand.

Fryn sucked in her breath.

"Why do you think I have servants and errand-boys? I can't bear to run all the affairs. I must keep in mind the greater scheme of things." He took a small sip from his glass. "That is why I have time to investigate the murder of one of my loyal subjects, and to protect Hunters who might be of use to me," he frowned as he said it. "It's not that I like your kind; mercenaries are without honor, or direction."

Fryn blinked, but Leif laughed. "Well, thankfully we are not just any hunters, I come from a tradition of honor and nobility, and Fryn is a citizen of the highest quality."

Ieffin leaned back with a smile. "That is gratifying to hear. Tell me, which tradition do you hail from?"

"The Strafe-Curling-Viper school, in Sendra City," Leif said, hoping it would at least be recognized.

"You don't say. I once met a member of that order in my youth, a Master Yarl. Sadly he didn't accept my offer of employment. I see it as my first failure as a member of the Crown."

"That was my Master!" Leif exclaimed. "How old were you?"

"I was five," he shrugged, "but it doesn't matter."

Fryn took a small sampling of the meats and nuts, but none of the cheese. "Do you know Master Hrensil?"

Ieffin nodded. "I do, he is a personal friend. I had heard your name before we met. He even recommended that I hire you… but you pursued a different line of work."

"I didn't know," she said, looking at her plate awkwardly. "Perhaps when this is over… I don't know what I will do."

Prince Ieffin watched her closely, shifting from his relaxed position to sit forward with an earnest interest. "I recommend that you pursue this track a little longer, so that you might well see what this organization is before you stay or leave. I can imagine that tracking down criminals is exciting, but you must always mind your employer."

Sound logic, Leif thought. "You said you want us to track down the assassin, but you also said that you wanted us to remain inside the district. Which is it? If I may ask…"

The prince took some of the nuts and crunched lightly for several moments. "I did say both of those things. Therefore you should investigate here, and hope the perpetrator is still inside the estate. Otherwise, I will send someone out with any information you uncover."

They finished their lunch over smaller gossip, and Ieffin rang his bell and left the kid to clean up while they examined the room. Soon it was only them, finding every scuff mark on the floor, each scratch on the desk, and finding the areas that the servants were too lazy to dust. Fryn copied the tattoo that the attorney had, of the knife piercing a coin, into a journal, and moved on to checking his pockets, lips pressed, her discomfort evident as she found a thick wad of pocket lint.

"You know," she said, tossing the article on the ground in disgust, "this isn't quite what I envisioned when I wanted to become a Hunter."

Leif checked the drawers, and shoved the top one back with excess force in frustration.

Fryn looked at him, startled, and sat on the edge of the desk. "Guess you thought the same, huh?"

"I don't mind the intrigue. I always thought a murder mystery would be more exciting. It's just I feel like he just wanted to keep us occupied, and out of the way." Leif's eye caught the tense muscles of the corpse's left hand, and he pulled the fingers open, finding a crumpled piece of paper.

"What is that?" Fryn leaned over to read it. "9:00, Excise Representative, Case number 213…"

Leif opened the third drawer from the top on the left side, and pulled out the late attorney's day-planner. "There is a section for today that has been torn out."

Fryn bent over from her side of the desk, boots thudding softly as she unconsciously swung her heels, and flattened the piece of paper and set its torn edges against those of the planner. "It fits," she said, and hopped down, and walked around the body to see it better.

"He left a dying message, of a sort, probably felt the meeting was suspicious and hid this in his pocket or something," Leif said.

Fryn sighed and walked back to the table, and took a seat, folding her wings back, and crossing her legs. "I still don't see why he has us investigating this. Why not the guard?"

Leif chuckled. "Probably because he has his trusted guards investigating the murder of his butler. That, or, he doesn't want us running off."

"More likely the latter," Fryn said, absently reaching for a ceren glass that wasn't there. She pulled her hand back with a disappointed grin. "I forgot it was gone."

"I could use a drink myself," Leif said, "I held back around Ieffin. It's not wise to drink much around your betters, you know."

"I know," Fryn said, raising an eyebrow, "which is why I also held back, but now, I really need to do something."

She was being honest: Fryn sat there, eyes avoiding the corpse, because she was tough, but even toughness required a little numbness—especially the kind that comes from a bottle. Leif sat in the chair across from her with a sigh. "This is an ugly business. I keep thinking of the day we met, of the fun we had, and I wish that we could have just gone on from there. But no, Mythrim had to be crazy."

She laughed. "It was fun. You aren't a bad dancer, you know."

"That's because we're hunters. It's our job to understand how to move in any situation," he explained, "and there may yet be a chance to practice again when this is all over."

She gave a slight headshake and traced a small circle on the table with her fingertip. It made a perfectly circular line of frost, which faded quickly, but looked nice nonetheless. "But what do we do in a situation where we can't move?"

"You know what they say, actions are not the only actions we can 'do' since speaking accomplishes some 'object' intentional or not," Leif replied, crossing his legs to mirror her.

"You read philosophy, huh?" She asked, looking at him closely. "So who do you think our killer is?"

"I think it is that chef, Havrshyk. He seems like the guy who might garrote somebody." Leif resisted the urge to reach out for a nonexistent glass.

"No, he was dressed as a guard to try to stop us from getting in. I doubt he had time to switch disguises. I believe our killer is unrelated to Mythrim, which is why Ieffin put us on the task. Not only that, but I think Havrshyk would use his sword, or just stab someone with hardened hands."

They sat there quietly, no sound but their breathing, only silence outside the windows, which showed fresh snowflakes winding down. "I guess I'm not going anywhere," he shivered.

Fryn followed his gaze and smiled. "Representative of the great multi-national Hunter's Commission, master of the Strafe-Curling-Viper school, but you still can't handle the snow."

"I can... sort of," he frowned, feeling the mostly healed cut on his face, "I don't see you running out to play."

"I don't really have time to play, now, do I?" She took a deep breath and then looked hard at the door. "Where are Clair and Harissa?"

"I was just wondering that." He hadn't. He'd been too absorbed in their little adventure, and subsequent banter, to notice they hadn't returned.

She ignored the topic. "Our attorney died around nine to nine-thirty, because that was the timeframe of the appointment. We arrived at eleven. How did our killer escape?"

Leif had spent some time examining the body, but he hadn't thought to check the doors. Was that what she'd been doing when they first entered?

81

"I found several marks at the door, and some at the windows. It looks as though someone tried to pick the locks on the windows, for which I doubt the attorney carried a key, but upon failing that, they locked the doors and stepped out."

"Why?" Leif asked.

"I wouldn't know," Fryn replied, "probably to delay the discovery of the body. Anyway, anything after that is a mystery."

"It is all a mystery to me," Leif said. "Why do you think the door was locked? Ieffin didn't mention it."

She held up a small pin with thread. "Because he used this to lock the knob and pulled on the string to get away. Sadly, for him, it snapped and left this behind."

"You could have been a decent investigator." Leif gave a low whistle.

Fryn smiled sheepishly and set the item on the table. "Well, what is it that we're doing now?"

He nodded and tapped the table with his hand. "Exactly that. Now, how about we tell the prince that we have exhausted our leads?"

She went to the door and turned the handle, only, it didn't turn. It just rattled a little, and stuck. "I don't believe this. He's locked us in." Fryn returned to her seat and scratched her chin. "Now I suppose we wait."

"I'm sure there are plenty of things to talk about to keep ourselves entertained," Leif said, "like you could tell me why you and Harissa weren't so close until the whole Mythrim thing happened."

She shook her head, "No, not unless you feel like talking about your exes or how you can't decide between infatuations."

"I'd be happy to." He gave a false smile, and let the conversation drop.

***

It was a long time before the door opened again. When it did, it was courteous enough, but Clair and Harissa were let in and then closed in within the span of a few seconds. They were still wearing the server's uniforms they'd obtained from the Stone-Market that morning, and it was now afternoon. They looked well-questioned and tired, too.

"Oh Leif," said Clair, sitting in the chair beside him, "they asked us about a murder, of an attorney no less. Which of course made me think of you," She glanced back at Fryn, "and Fryn, because what if it had been you?"

"We are fine, as you can see," he said.

Harissa covered a sound like a bitter laugh.

"What?" He watched her, whispering in her cousin's ear, their previous distance now forgotten.

Harissa stared back at him cynically, silently pointing toward the desk with the well-aged corpse, and waited with her hand over her mouth for Clair to notice.

Clair rolled her eyes at her. "I can't tell you how troublesome she is, bribing guards, making deals, and whispering secrets to officials... why I thought she might even be Mythrim himself."

"She is the heir of the Pine-Martin..." Leif said, though he had only recently learned what that was.

"Heiress, thank you," she sniffed. Suddenly Leif remembered she had reached that position only that morning and wondered how she was able to stay focused on the job at hand.

"Quite." Leif placed a hand on Clair's shoulder. "I'm afraid there *has* been some nasty business with an attorney." He pointed her to the desk, resisting the urge to jump as she gasped.

"Who is that? What happened?"

"That is the attorney in question. He was murdered," Leif said gently, "Prince Ieffin asked us to look into it."

Clair stood and walked about the table purposefully. "Then why are you still here?"

"Because he also doesn't want us to leave," Fryn added.

"What? Why?"

"Because he doesn't want Mythrim to catch us," she replied.

This could last till winter. Leif thought, glancing ironically at the snowflakes falling outside of the window. "Alright, Harissa, what did you learn?"

Her knowing eyes blinked innocently. "Oh? Did I learn anything? Well, of course I did. That new servant has impressed the Prince with his antics, the old one died miserably, and the attorney was killed by a renegade hunter."

They all stared. "How?" Leif asked.

"He was garroted." She grinned. "But you already knew that."

"How do you know the killer was a renegade hunter?" Fryn clarified.

"Well Fryn, I am sure the name Fildar the Red is familiar to you, since he was once a top-tiered hunter of the commission till five years ago, when he killed his partners and started doing assassinations for contract." She tapped her cheek with her mouth shaped like an 'o' to make a hollow sound. "His fame as a hunter meant that he was quickly hired by all the reputable, and disreputable, and made a name for himself in the trade."

"Who would hire him to kill an executive of the Grand Assembly?" Clair asked.

The door opened, and Ieffin stepped in with a pitcher of iced tea in hand. "Well, I thought that would be obvious. I predict it was none other than your commission."

Clair stared, open-mouthed, but the others just looked at him, Leif with narrowed eyes, Fryn with her head cocked to the side, and Harissa with a light smile. "Why would the commission hire a traitor, much less assassinate a high-ranking official?" Leif asked.

Fryn opened her notepad and examined the symbol that had been on the attorney's hand. "Perhaps he was close to pushing through legislation that would diminish or eliminate Commission influence in Frorin."

Ieffin snapped his fingers and sat beside Clair, looking lost in her eyes for a second before returning. "That is right Fryn, he was. My father has had long-standing relations with the Commission, but there are two factions in the Crown District, one in favor of their influence, and one that is wary of losing its own. It is only natural that there should be some who work to mitigate that, but for the Commission to potentially kill one of my attorneys, that is something that might have the opposite effect in the long term."

"Then, perhaps someone wanted to make it look that way. I doubt the Commission would work against itself," Fryn said, "for all we know Mythrim hired the assassin to act as a distraction."

"Fildar doesn't go through intermediaries. The benefactor would have to be Mythrim himself; and he'd have to have a big enough name to hire someone like him," Harissa pointed out. "He'd have to be an equal figure in the trade, no less than The Venomsword… which is possible given his habits."

They sat around the table, Ieffin drinking iced tea, lost in thought. "My guards found the first clues from my butler's death. He was also garroted, and dumped in an alley: just the sort of work that Fildar is known for," the Prince sighed.

"Just let us track him down, 'send a hunter to catch a criminal', right?" Leif interjected.

"He's a far better hunter than you, Leif, no offense intended. Besides, you're out of your element in the city. Fildar knows both streets and forests, and how to erase his tracks," he replied, watching Leif's eager face. "Fine, but you can only check this district. If you find him, I want him alive."

They all rose in a flash and raced to the door; but it was still locked.

"Not all of you, I don't want to sit by myself at the moment, Misses Yardall and Martin, would you join me for a stroll in the garden?" Ieffin walked to the door.

Clair looked like all she wanted was to be anywhere other than that room. "Sure!"

"Don't just volunteer me." Harissa scratched her head. "Alright, it isn't very often I can talk with royalty." She looked embarrassed by her informality and looked away.

Ieffin nodded and slipped a key into the door, but it wouldn't turn. His head slumped. "I must've grabbed the wrong key." He knocked on the door. "Hey, could you open the door?"

The reply sounded like that kid from earlier. "Right away sire!"

The door handle rattled for a second, and then the door slid open, and they all stepped out, and breathed in the 'fresh' air of the foyer.

"Alright, you guys, have fun!" Clair waved as she trailed after the prince and Harissa, who were already making for the exit. The new kid closed the door and looked expectantly to Leif and Fryn.

"We're just going to explore the building for a bit," Leif said, not sure why he bothered to explain.

"I'll be right here if you need anything," he answered, and returned to a spot beside the door.

Fryn shook her head and they walked down the far end of the foyer, which had roughly four office rooms connected through the walls on either side, with a central corridor running into the heart of the building. They entered the Assembly Hall through a wide set of double-doors and stared at the dusty benches descending from above the entrance to an open space before a dais with a long booth. Five chairs sat behind the booth facing the benches in their arc around the room, and one small booth with an iron ring set before a single wooden chair marked the seat of inquiry. There were windows from the domed roof that shone their expansive circles in a clear and slightly blue color that reflected coolly off the dark wood and the white marble.

Fryn walked up the side ramp and around the first ring, looking for marks and clues, so Leif did the same, looking at the doors and the floor for prints or signs left in haste.

"Why do you think he did this?" He asked. "Do you think Mythrim is *the* Venomsword?"

"I don't know," Fryn said, picking up a used handkerchief from one of the spaces behind the Attorneys' Seat. "Gross." She dropped it on the long desk in disgust.

"I don't want to imagine what Fildar's trial would look like, especially with one seat empty." Leif hopped on top of the chair by the Attorneys' Seat and paused. "Huh, what do you make of this?"

Fryn followed his pointed hand and flit up in the air beside him. He traced a black scuff on the wall just above the molding of the white marble stones that comprised the dome, and floor. "Hmm… It looks like a boot-mark," she said, "do you think he… but why? He'd be seen if he flew out during the day."

Leif sat on the back of the chair and dangled his legs over the seat. "What if he did?"

"He'd be seen." She leaned over him, shaking her head. "Unless he couldn't."

Their heads shot up and she scanned the ceiling, there was a small ledge that led to a tiny circular panel around the side over the double-doors. "Is that a vent?" Leif asked.

"I think it is for the staff to access and secure themselves when they clean and repair this area." She sped over and slid the edge of her knife under the panel, and pried it open carefully. Leif joined her in a second, and they peered into the hole. "Hang on; let me get a better look." She pushed him sideways and stuck her head inside.

She gave a soundless jerk, and thrashed a bit, and grabbed her knife with her good hand and stabbed it in blindly.

"Whoa!" Leif rushed to catch her as she was sent flying from the hole with a cut around her ice-encrusted neck, and slid across the floor coughing. Two hands reached out and braced themselves on either side of the hole, and a slender fae darted out, metal wire gripped between his hands as he closed in on Leif, with a dispassionate smile as he advanced with the loop of wire.

Leif ducked and the wire closed over thin air, but Fildar spun overhead and kicked him in the back of the head. He fell on top of Fryn, and the assassin made a dash for the door.

"Follow him," Fryn hissed, her neck sore and red even with the ice-shield. They ran after, disoriented but excited to be on the scent. They flitted down the corridor to a turn where they barely saw their target's form blur around a corner into a stairwell. He landed in a crouch at the base of the stairs, and threw up the wire across the space from wall to wall as they hurtled toward it.

Fryn smiled as she flew at it, her left hand reaching out, pale and cold and drained of all blood. Frost formed up her fingers to her shoulder, and then her neck, as she grabbed it and wrenched the wire from his grasp. The metal cut blue lines across her frozen skin, but the wire snapped as it grew brittle in the cold.

Leif launched forward with a wing-burst and landed beside the assassin, whose eyes were wide with surprise, and he socked him in the jaw. Fildar rolled with the punch and grabbed him by the wrist, twisting his hand back, and pressing the nerves of his elbow, with a laugh.

Leif groaned, but sent a surge of sparks through his arm to the palm that Fildar had confiscated, and blasted the shock into his stomach. Fryn landed and kicked him down the hall.

Metal coated boots clanked on the floor above in a mad dash to search out their fight, and Prince Ieffin's excited voice rang out indistinctly, as if on a royal hunt. Leif could almost hear the horn, and the leaves in the wind.

Fildar spat and pulled out a set of spiked knuckles from one of the pockets of his butler's suit, and folded his wings. The air twisted around his hands, and a gust blew down the hall, tossing Fryn's bangs out of her eyes. "You think you've won? You can't claim me, not even the Commission can touch me."

He bounced on his feet, and gave a couple test jabs, and crushed one of the marble stones of the wall. Leif frowned, but Fryn and Fildar just looked more excited.

"Fryn, we'll need to work together on this one," he warned.

"No thanks, take a break." She gripped her knife in her left hand, still coiled in discarded wire, her right hand secured to her chest in a tight sling.

She brushed past him and settled into her forward stance, knife held before her like a foil.

"Oh this isn't a good idea Fryn." Leif edged to the wall and watched her balestra into a lunge, pulling in her back foot, and then bursting forward with her blade out in a fleche, sailing across the distance, aiming to pierce his heart.

At the last second, he twisted his body, and punched with his knuckle blades under her armpit, and her advance failed, her arm hung limp, and cold, and she crumpled under her own momentum.

Fildar backed away, and dashed into the kitchen, but Fryn jumped up and tripped him, her arm undamaged in the feint. He slid across the marble and crashed into the worktable of the kitchen, scattering flour and sliced vegetables over himself and the floor.

"Give it up Fildar, there's no other exit here, and you've forgotten how to fight," Fryn said, twirling her blade in her good hand.

The guards had apparently heard the clatter and sounded closer than before. Leif moved in beside her and looked down at the slender fae covered in flour. "You will live if you come quietly," he said.

The wind picked up, and spun into a cyclone around his form, and he stood with his eyes bloodshot and open wide. "You think you led me here? I let you! It is so much easier to kill in close quarters." The wind burst outwards, and threw them back into the hall. Fryn hit her head and fell, out cold, and Leif's shoulder popped and he cradled his arm in pain.

The air was growing thin, all being sucked into the high-pressure zone, and Leif felt his lungs burning as he gasped for air. He summoned all this strength, and charged all his sparks in the palm of his good hand, pointed at Fildar, and let it fly.

Fildar twisted the air, and the lightning curved and arced behind him into a statue of one of the Frorin monarchs in an alcove of the room.

"See?" He gloated, but fell silent, and the wind died down. Pots, pans, ladles, and spoons, all the metallic items in the kitchen converged on him on their way to the statue, and a tea-kettle knocked him out.

"You see that, Fryn?" Leif stood and braced himself in the doorway, and slammed his arm back into joint. "Ahh!" He screamed, and fell to the ground beside her. "I just got the renegade with a tea-pot.

She mumbled incoherently as he checked her head. It wasn't too serious, but the ice had been slightly cracked at the base of her skull. He hoped that wasn't bad… it was just ice.

Ieffin and his personal guard gathered around them, and stared in awe at the mess displayed on the statue and at the large bump that had formed on Fildar's head.

"When all else fails, just throw something," Leif said, "they can't dodge forever."

Ieffin waved the guards forward, uncharacteristically serious. "I didn't want to think he was still here… he could've been waiting to kill someone else."

The guards secured the assassin, and the captain, Leif judged by the silver bands on his robes, coughed gently. "What do you want us to do with him, sire?"

The prince looked at him in a daze. "What? Oh, right, secure him in the prison for sentencing tomorrow. Sedate him."

The guards filed out with their package carried between them, and Ieffin sat on the floor beside them. "I'm glad I kept you here," he said.

"Well, I don't know how happy I am, but I could use a bath." The wind had strewn all the flour and small items on them and around the hall, and Leif absently brushed what he could out of Fryn's face.

"That kid is going to complain about this," Ieffin observed. "Come on up, I'll help you with her."

"No need to ruin your clothes, I can carry her." Leif's arm ached, but he swung her into his arms and carried her toward the stairs. They walked back into the study, where the corpse had been removed, and Leif moved toward one of the chairs when Fryn's eyes flickered and she groaned.

"Just a little longer, I promise." She closed her eyes and slumped against his chest.

He set her down in one of the cushioned chairs and exhaled. "I didn't know that he was that dangerous. For a minute I thought his reputation was just an illusion."

"People like that will always keep you guessing," the Prince replied, ringing his silver bell. The door opened quickly and the kid stepped in, already looking more confident; which only made him look more comical—straight-backed, chin up, and scrawny like a finch. "I want a bottle of Yardall, and three glasses."

"Ice, sir?"

Ieffin smiled. "No need. Oh, and when you're done, I need you to reorganize the kitchen."

"Yes my lord." He almost skipped out the door and returned minutes later, one thick crystal bottle of sceppe, fifty-years old, with matching crystal tumblers with the Yardall label cut into the base.

Ieffin held one glass in his hand and a layer of frost formed across the cuts. He did this with all three glasses and then filled them with three fingers of sceppe. He leaned over Fryn gently and wafted the contents of the glass before her nose.

Her eyes burst open, and she looked around in a daze. "What happened?"

Ieffin proffered the drink, and sat when she'd taken it. "You did it, that's what. We solved the crime."

We? Leif took a sip and set the glass down, enjoying the smoky burn that went down his throat. "This is the best thing I have ever tasted."

The prince rolled his eyes. "We allow merchants with useful products to pay their taxes in such tribute. We have a stockpile of fine wines and such going back two hundred years. Of what we take, roughly ten percent is locked for fifty years, another ten for seventy five, and the rest can be used whenever."

Fryn drank her sceppe carefully, but looked much better, probably because the alcohol numbed the pain. Perhaps that was Ieffin's reason, or maybe he just wanted a drink. They finished their glasses, Leif, with a warm glow suffusing his stomach.

Fryn sat up straight and professional. "Prince Ieffin, I wonder if we shouldn't question the perpetrator, find out who hired him."

"We are going to sentence him tomorrow, there will be a public questioning, but I doubt he'll tell us anything about his previous employers… or his purpose," he said yawning as he poured a small amount in their glasses. "Don't try anything. I do not want to contaminate the proceedings."

"Of course," Leif and Fryn agreed.

As they sipped their sceppe, Fryn felt her leg, and looked around the chair distractedly. "Has anyone seen my knife?" She asked.

Leif remembered the pots and pans and silverware that had knocked out the assassin. "It might still be in the kitchen."

Ieffin nodded slowly and rang his bell. In a few seconds, the kid returned, with flour on his suit, and a cloth tied around his head.

"You called, sire?"

"Fryn is missing her knife. Have you found any weapons in the kitchen?" He asked, matter-of-factly.

The servant's head bobbed with each bit of information, and he finally nodded. "I found something a bit odd, sire," he said, pulling out a cloth-wrapped bundle from his apron, "it was stuck to the statue of King Davis." He uncovered it, and showed the black-damasked Bloodknife that Fryn had made somehow.

"That would be it. Pass it over then," Ieffin said, holding out his hand. He took it and dismissed the kid with a wave and stared deep into the surface of the blade. "It's funny," he said, "I almost feel like the folds are shifting." He shrugged and passed it off to Fryn, who took it with a sigh of relief.

"Thank you sire," she said, and raised her glass in his honor, and took a healthy sip.

"I still wonder why it did that," Leif said, joining them.

"It's the iron." Ieffin finished his glass, and poured another round.

When they'd finished the bottle, Ieffin slept with his face on the table, and Leif and Fryn having had about fifty percent less were only quite intoxicated. They snuck out the door whispering and missing stairs they as found their way out into the night and across the courtyard. The sky was clear, and they supported each other as they walked over the shoveled stones.

"Mythrim had to have hired him. We need to find out where he is," Fryn said with slurred certainty.

"He'll tell us everything or else," Leif assured her.

They stumbled down the stairs of the palace detainment prison, where prisoners awaited their trials, and crept around the area of lamplight where the warden slept with his head on his desk.

They heard footsteps coming from the hall around the corner, and ducked inside the coat closet and peered out of the crack between the doors. A guard walked out with his helmet on and a scarf around his face, and he patted the warden on the back. "There, there, bad fish is best avoided, don't you know?" The voice was thick and accented, and the guard walked out into the night.

They crept out, avoiding the warden, hoping he would stay out because of the bad fish, and found their way to the cell of Fildar the Red. Fildar lay with his back to them, wrapped in a thick blanket since he was from Gaersheim.

"Hey, wake up, we have questions," Fryn whispered. She gripped the bars with her left hand and watched him closely. "It gets pretty cold here. You don't look very well, if you tell us where Mythrim is, I can get you more blankets."

"I think he's had more cold than he can take," Leif said looking at the small amount of skin that wasn't covered by the blanket pulled over his head. "I'd say he looks quite blue."

Fryn stared at him and shook her head, all of a sudden becoming much more lucid than before. She reached in and turned him over, and went pale as the rest of her blood drained into her blade. "Leif, you need to focus, alcohol can't affect me when I have no blood, but I think Fildar has been killed."

She directed his view to the pale patch of skin. It was covered in ice.

"Oh no, then that means…" Leif shook his head, trying to gather his bearings.

"It means that warden is dead, and Mythrim found his way here."

They rushed back into the study where Ieffin still slept, only now with a blanket thrown over his shoulders, and they shook him awake. He looked at Fryn. "What? You got tired of the sceppe?" He poked her face. "So cold yet so fair. I knew a Lich once. He stored his wine in a bottle, and felt it whenever he wanted." He said with a yawn.

She patted his shoulder. "I'll need you to listen. Someone got to Fildar and killed the warden as well.

The prince went cold and sighed. "Well, there goes my sleepiness. They may come for you. Do not leave this room." He rose, and slightly wobbly, made his way to the door. "Don't go poking around for trouble next time I advise otherwise. Whoever killed Fildar might just have easily have killed you in your drunken state." He stepped out and caught his balance with the door. "Well, our drunken state," he added, and then left them staring after.

Free and Clear

Frorin:

Crown District

Botanical Gardens

Leif and Fryn occupied one of the benches in the domed greenhouse opposite Clair and Harissa who sat tossing crumbs in the pool between them. Fish with sparkling colors or dull matte skin poked their heads up and ate what they were given with a sort of placid docility, and Clair enjoyed herself with giggling whenever two fish collided. Harissa looked less than interested, but Leif felt that she was hiding a smile, as she couldn't look away.

Fryn picked a bright red berry from a shrub behind their bench and popped it in her mouth with a grimace. "It's been almost week," she said, working to rid her mouth of the bitter taste. "We've heard nothing and Ieffin still won't let us leave."

Fildar's death had caught them both off guard, and Leif felt, more than surprise, disappointment that his efforts had gone unrewarded. Sure, Ieffin had promised them a bonus, but they had no idea when he was going to pay them. Leif leaned against the back of the bench and closed his eyes.

Suddenly, he realized that someone was talking, so he opened his eyes and found he had been leaning against Fryn's shoulder which was now fully healed. She was also a bit dazed. *Guess I fell asleep,* he thought, stretching his arms over his head. Across the pond Prince Ieffin was chatting with the other two girls, with a young fee on his arm. His companion had styled shoulder length blonde hair and pale gray eyes and a face that looked like a more feminine version of the Prince. She wore a thin white dress with a light green scarf, and light brown leather boots.

93

"Princess Savis," Fryn said, adjusting her coat. "I didn't realize she'd returned."

"Who?" Leif stood, trying to get a better look.

"Ieffin's elder sister, she's the Ambassador to Gaersheim," Fryn replied, and walked over, with Leif trailing behind. "She must be here for a special occasion," she added over her shoulder.

"I see." But what, he wasn't sure. Royal House politics had always been inscrutable. It wasn't as clear-cut as clan hierarchies that generated a government by the excellent, or of the clan-based councils of Aelaete.

"Ah, you're awake," Ieffin turned to address them, holding his sister's hand and pulling her close to his side. "This is my beautiful sister, Savis, beloved by all, and… betrothed. So you will have to relinquish any dreams you might have had."

She laughed, in a soft, but bright voice and took her hand away. "He isn't spoken for." She winked to the girls. "But then, unfortunately there are other barriers."

"If only you would dissolve your association with mercenary groups, then perhaps you could be treated like a noble; if my petition for the uplifting of House Martin is granted. It would do good to enfranchise the lower districts, you know." Ieffin smiled.

Harissa's cheek twitched. "You put out a petition?"

"I didn't tell you?"

Savis shook her head. "He likes surprises. In fact, he called me over for something, but won't tell me what it is."

Clair furtively tossed the last crumb from her pouch out over the pond and a pure white fish caught it before it even touched the water, and fell with an obvious splash. She hid her hands behind her back and smiled.

"I thought you weren't going to fatten the fish anymore," Savis said, turning to her brother with a frown, "you and your promises."

"I swear I haven't, but I cannot speak for other people; guests, servants, or father." He sat beside Harissa and rested his chin on his hands. "I know I had something important I wanted to tell you."

Everyone waited, as he bounced his heel on the ground in thought. "Of course! I remember, I am pleased to tell you that there has been no sign of Mythrim in a week, so my investigators predict that he has fled, or gone on to another job."

"You should have let us out sooner," Fryn said, crossing her arms. "How are we going to track him down now?"

"I can't tell you that. Maybe wait for him to strike again, and then follow the trail," he answered, "Still, you are free to leave. I hope your time here has been as enjoyable for you as it was for me. I had a wonderful time! It isn't very often I find people entertaining for this long."

"Thank you, Prince," Harissa said, "then we will take our leave so that I may begin rebuilding my House."

"I will call on you when I know the results of my petition, Pine-Martin, but for now I leave the lower districts in your hands. All I ask is that you remember the light hand of your father and his deference to the Crown." Prince Ieffin looked deep in her eyes, and then nodded to himself.

"Of course, I would do nothing else." She bowed her head and went to the walkway. "It was a pleasure to meet you, Princess."

"And you." Savis nodded.

Leif and the others said their goodbyes and followed Harissa to the front gate. They were let out with polite waves from the royal guards, and stood on the Crown Ringroad intersecting the South Cardinal wondering what to do next.

Clair spoke first. "I must get back home. I have been away for far too long. My parents are probably worried sick."

"Of course, we'll walk you there," Leif said.

"You just want to try some sceppe," Fryn narrowed her eyes.

"What at this time of day?" He shrugged, giving a quick spin, presenting the morning view of the city.

"If it's a drink you want, after we drop off Clair we can go to my house and I'll mix us something," Harissa said, "now, let's be off."

They followed her down the South Cardinal to the Snow Ringroad and up the western arc till they arrived before Clair's estate, a large manor with warehouses off to the southern side of its walled-off courtyard, and they left her at the gate.

Going all the way to the Pine District took longer than Leif expected. They stopped before the doors of Pine-Martin Hall around three, all wearing clothes provided by the Prince, white with blue decorations, everyone feeling somewhat out of place. Leif looked at the brown canvas and leather that the people passed by in, wondering if they didn't stand out too much.

There was no sign of damage to the front doors, or even the foyer, the marble floor had been polished recently, and the chairs where the old card-players had sat were empty by the musicians' stand. Newspapers were stacked on one of the tables by the door, and Harissa grabbed one and took a seat where the eldest fae used to sit in the center. She glanced up and gave a soft smile. "This is where my father used to sit, and there," she pointed to the nearest chair, "my uncle. He's the one who taught me how to read, how to make the perfect cocktail, and also how to use a cane."

Just then, a waiter in a smartly-pressed black-and-white uniform popped out of the kitchen and froze when he saw them, and then ran back inside. They could hear him yelling "She's back!" and then suddenly the foyer was filled with Pine-Martins back in their chairs, playing music, and reading books in loud but orderly celebration.

The waiter stopped by Harissa's chair, and she muttered something, and he sped off upstairs.

"What was all that?" Leif asked, peering at the headlines of the newspaper.

"They want to welcome me back. I'm the heir so they're going to throw a party." She spread her hands wide as if to say, "like this."

The waiter returned in moments with a bottle of sparkling in one hand, and the polished bone cane that *the* Pine-Martin once held, its smooth surface lined with crisscrossing red metallic lines that curled like veins in and throughout the material. He stood in the center of the musician's stand and waved them to stop playing, and began his speech.

"Ladies and Gentlemen, I cannot express my joy at the return of our Heir; the last survivor of the line of the Old Martin, of his pure descendants: my cousin Harissa." The applause was deafening, as the room filled up with people coming in from the door dressed as if they had been waiting for this party. "We have suffered a grievous loss at the hands of the infamous Venomsword, who not only killed our family, but also the family of the King; but even so we are not defeated. We have our finest here with us today, with the ascension of Harissa as The Pine-Martin, and the return of our estranged cousin Fryn."

The crowd was solemn as they nodded and trays loaded with half-full glasses were distributed by passing them around. No servants in fancy dress delivered treats or wine, they served themselves and each other regardless of age or rank. Leif supposed he'd ask Fryn or Harissa about their customs later.

The young fae holding the cane raised the bottle high to gain their attention once more. "As is our tradition, we will give the symbol of our house to its heir, and she will cut the cork and drink straight from the bottle. Harissa, this is yours now." He tossed the cane towards where she sat in the chair, rotated to partially face him and the people, which she caught in one hand without looking.

She stood and walked languidly onto the podium beside him, and accepted the bottle. "This bottle is from the vintage of our founder, which he stored and set aside so that his successors would always mind his legacy and walk according to his standards. We are in a sense our own nobility, our own royalty. Our clan is sovereign in itself, something established by our ancestors. We make no claim to the throne of Frorin, we have ourselves, self-sufficient, independent, and answerable only to the laws that we have set for ourselves."

Leif watched in awe as she proclaimed such an impossible statement. Why did the King tolerate such insubordination? What 'deference' had Ieffin been referring to?

"How have we continued to exist in a greater world where others can exercise their will upon us? Because we have been benevolent, we have been honorable, and reliable; these are things that bring us notice and acclaim. If we had been contemptible, we would have lost through our folly what our ancestors established by their virtue, and we would deserve our fall. So now, on my ascension as your head, I confirm the values and traditions established by the foundation of this house, and I promise that I will lead us to greatness with honor, and benevolence."

There was a loud roar of applause, even the city folk in their rough brown clothes, who had been ushered into the room by the noise, were excited. They watched her like she was their folk hero, someone who made them matter, who enriched their lives.

She examined the cane, and the red lines shifted color as her eyes took on a faint glow. She twisted the handle, and drew from its length a beautiful steel foil folded with wavering red lines in some of the layers. It was double-edged, and ran straight to a fine point, but it was flexible and the light took on a surreal tone under its reflection. She passed the sheath of the cane-sword to her cousin, and held the blade against the neck of the bottle beneath the cork, and with one invisible stroke, the top of the bottle sailed across the room with a loud pop, and she drank from the sharp lip of the bottle.

Everyone cheered and clinked their glasses, provided for all who had stopped by, and they drank her health and her leadership. Leif and Fryn touched their glasses and he met her gaze. "This is much more wholesome than the extravagance of the Crown District, isn't it?" he asked, sipping from his glass carefully.

He wasn't sure, but he thought he saw a flash of color on her face. She smiled. "She is like the pauper's princess. The people have always been in awe of her. She played with the regular children when she was young, she fought bullies to protect her friends, and she even published a small book of poetry about the beauty of the lower districts and their way of life. It made her very popular."

Harissa stepped down, the bottle half empty and sat back in her seat. "Pauper's Princess, I like that," she said, giving Fryn a playful look. "I know you didn't have time to buy me gifts, so I will make it simple."

"Gifts?" Leif swallowed, and leaned over to Fryn. "I didn't know she expected gifts."

Harissa accepted the sheath of her foil from her cousin, and sheathing her sword; she rested the cane across her lap, and waved to the musicians. "I want a lively waltz, and then more traditional folk dance."

They responded by setting their bows to the strings and their lips to their mouthpieces and played the first notes of a familiar waltz. Leif stood and straightened his coat and reached out his hand to Fryn. She chuckled and reached out her hand in response, but before she could grasp it, Harissa leapt out of her chair and grabbed it, and dragged Leif out to the center of the floor. "This is my gift from you, Fryn," she said, looking over her shoulder.

Leif laughed and they settled into a quick pace, stepping and twisting into the first movement of the dance. "Then what is my gift?" He asked.

She tilted her head, stepping away from him and side to side with her hands on her hips. "Your gift is to dance well." They stepped forward and locked again, and twisted to face the people behind them, and switched momentarily into two lines, rotating partners and then circling back into their original pairs. "See," she said as he placed his hand on her waist, and the other in her hand, "you're already doing well."

Leif felt Fryn watching them, and grew a little nervous, but Harissa was a good dancer and drew his attention back with a squeeze of her hand.

They rocked side to side, wings twitching in time to the music, Harissa's with a bluish tint, and Leif's with coursing red.

"Don't stop now, Leif, this piece has another movement," she said as they stepped back, and switched partners with the person on their right, then switched positions forward and switched right again, and swung into a series of steps that brought them in a spiraling course toward the edge of the floor, where everyone was brought into a wide circle facing each other. The waltz slowed to a stop, and Leif wondered if it were about to end, when the flute broke in with a quick melody and the fiddle joined in next in harmony, and Harissa gripped his hands and they simply spun in circles in their own space. At a rest, they stopped spinning and released one hand so they opened outwards with a flash, and then spun back in and did the same spin in the air on the wing, this time breaking vertically, so that Leif landed on the floor looking up at an upside-down Harissa with her black hair streaming toward his face, and her feet pointing toward the ceiling.

They spiraled back to the center, now in the air, horizontal to the floor, spun, and released parallel to the floor at a loud crescendo breathless, and everyone else watching them as they glided to the floor to a cheer from everyone. Dizzy, they found their seats as the folk music started and the people rejoined the dance.

Fryn held a fresh glass, and Harissa worked on finishing the ancient bottle that sat on the side table with her newspaper, and Leif felt parched. "I need something to drink. Harissa, didn't you promise to mix us the perfect cocktail?" He hinted.

"I did at that," she said, running her hand along the smooth cane. "Do you know what this is?" She tilted it so he could get a better look.

"A cane-sword?"

"Yes, but it is also so much more. This was forged, according to the instructions left in the original Pine-Martin's will, out of the finest steel and the bones of my ancestor." She caressed the handle and admired the polish it had gained with centuries of use.

"Why did he do that?" Leif asked, her actions reminding him of Fryn and her connection to her Bloodknife, what little he understood.

"We cannot be entirely certain. Maybe he knew something we don't about magic, but whatever the case may be, this blade cannot be scratched by normal materials, and is able to cut through ice and Bloodcraft like nothing else." She twirled it in her hand and drank from the bottle, cutting her lip on the sharp glass.

"Ah! Are you alright?" Leif leaned forward in his seat.

"I'm fine." She pressed the cut until it stopped bleeding, and gripped the cane so that the blood ran down the handle and sheath. Fryn lifted an eyebrow, and Leif watched in awe as the blood was absorbed into the cane and the cut fused on her lip. "See, I knew there was a reason we had to drink from the bottle. This blade had to attach itself to its new owner now that my father is passed. This blade will only recognize those descended directly from the Old Martin, and if we fail, then our clan will, too."

"So you can transfer an item like that?" Leif asked, looking at Fryn.

"I had never heard of it happening before. Typically, Bloodcraft items belong only to their creator. They cannot be far from their item, or else they will die, or go comatose in a near-death state until their item is returned," she replied.

Harissa set the cane aside and waved to her cousin. "Jason, could you bring me my bar-kit? I think we need some new drinks."

"Of course," he said, running his hand through his slicked-back hair.

He ran off, and Harissa returned her attention to them. "How did you make your blade, Fryn? It isn't part of the Soft-Point-Fist curriculum."

Fryn smiled with her mouth, but her eyes narrowed, as if the subject were dangerous or private. "No it is not." She glanced around the party at the merry people, members of the clan, of the city, and smoothed the wrinkles in her jacket. "I discovered it on my own, and it is not something that I would like to discuss."

"I thought so." Harissa nodded.

"What am I missing here?" Leif sighed.

"Most Bloodcraft is created in times of dire, traumatic experiences, and is itself extremely traumatic," Harissa explained, "I can only imagine the situation she must have been in, disarmed, severely injured, on the point of death, before crafting a weapon to turn back the destruction that had been pointed at her."

Leif nodded seriously, examining Fryn's composed look of discomfort. Somehow now, she seemed even more incredible than their experiences had shown her to be.

"You once said that you had defeated one of the sand vipers back in Aelaete. How did you survive?" Fryn asked, eyes glazed over with a thin layer of frost.

He realized that his hands were in his pockets, one of them tracing the silver serpent on the lid of his sandalwood box. Periodically the scars on his arm burned. Traces of the venom had worked their way to his heart. They burned at that moment. "I crushed its head and fried its mind with my sparks, from the inside of its mouth. It took a long time to claw my way out."

"How many warriors have defeated one?" Harissa asked with extreme interest on her face. She'd probably never even left the city.

Leif smiled proudly and finished the last of his sparkling wine. "There are probably only fifty such people alive at present. Most are masters who teach their own schools, but I am the first to use sparks. Previous attempts were dismissed on the viper's hide, and the successful warriors had all been other elemental types," he said glowing with pride.

"And how have you changed?" Fryn asked.

"Well that... that's not something I can say." He scratched his head and fixed his hair. "It's not something I can really explain."

"That's how it is for anyone." Harissa smirked. "Like this, I'm not the same girl you danced with, but I can't explain why, there's something more to what I see now that I can touch the heart of my ancestors."

"That's a pretty eloquent explanation, and one that serves well enough for anyone," her cousin in the waiter's uniform said, appearing by her side with a tray of bottles, glasses, and mixing utensils. "Your accoutrements as requested."

She stood seriously and took the mixing cup. "I think we need something sceppe-based, little bit of citrus... it's expensive to import, some mint, and cured berries." She stirred the sceppe in the ice, muddled it with citrus-rind, and poured it into tumblers over large square blocks. Then with a flourish, she dropped in several ceren-cured frost-berries and placed a single leaf of mint over each block of ice. She passed the glasses over, and returned to her seat, twirling the contents of her glass around its block of ice.

Leif took a sip. It was chilling, but refreshing, and had the heat he'd expect from the sceppe, but it was subdued by the added sweetness. "Fryn, why did your family split from the clan?"

Harissa and her younger cousin watched them quietly, and Fryn's lips turned up slightly at the corners. "While I did spend a good deal of my childhood visiting with my extended family, going to special occasions and the like, my parents decided to move away from the clan in order to pursue a life in the Rain District."

"I don't see why you can't be part of a clan if you are spread out between districts. That's what reunions are for," Leif said. His family was well connected, and equally dispersed.

"We had reunions, and were invited, but as my family gained influence in the upper districts they had to disassociate themselves from the clan in order to be seen as truly 'high class," Fryn said, watching his face.

"So they offended the clan, by being ashamed of them?"

"That is how my father reacted," Harissa added, "I don't know why I'm telling you this, but when they cut ties it hurt us very deeply. We were family, and suddenly they pretended we weren't a part of their lives." She folded her arms and looked away. "And I lost the only girl close to my age."

Leif nodded and watched the dancers. There was one couple doing a spectacular job at the Acorn, stepping in quick, careful succession around some imaginary point. The girl had white eyes with a violet tint, and wore a tan vest over a white blouse to match her boots and pants.

Fryn followed his gaze. "Is that the clerk? What is she doing here?"

The clerk danced with a dark-haired fae in a party mask decorated to look like water with fish swimming toward his eyes, who wore his pale gray sleeves rolled up, and his pinstriped black vest close to his athletic waist.

"Quite a dashing figure." Harissa leaned over her chair and whispered to Fryn.

Leif agreed that he was an impressive dancer with impeccable taste, so far as he could tell when it came to that, but he had the nagging suspicion that he'd seen that fae before. He took a contemplative sip from his glass and watched the clerk, Caelyn, grin as they moved to the next phase of the dance, which if memory served, was called 'the chase' and involved partners switching through the lines at right diagonal, then left, and the male partner trying to find his original dancer. It was based off the life of squirrels, and was one of the few Froreholtian dances that had caught on in Aelaete.

Caelyn had a great smile, seemingly brightening the other dancers as they tried to match her enthusiasm.

"Leif, are you going to watch all day, or do you want to learn this dance?" Fryn stood, setting her glass down on the newspaper table, with its ice block swirling air.

He drained the contents of his and placed his glass beside hers in similar fashion. "I'm going to learn how to dance." He took her hand and twirled her into the chaos of the dance floor, and scanned where she flitted between pairs and loners searching in the mass of people. She appeared for an instant in a space that opened up between them, doing the loner version of the acorn, hopping to one side of the circle, landing on her toes and spinning to step in the opposite direction.

Leif slid between the people, keeping out of her varying line of sight and had to duck more than once as he got close, but within thirty seconds, he hopped out of the group and landed opposite her on the acorn and they matched their steps with opposite hands held over the space.

They jumped, spun, and landed facing the opposite way, switching hands, and pulled together for close stepping around an even smaller invisible space. Leif held her right hand in his left, and his right on her waist as they stepped side to side, slowly rotating to the softening music, and they caught their breath as all the couples rocked to the dying beats with heads against shoulders, bodies in close embrace, and one even finished the dance with a delicate kiss.

They watched that one, not being distracted by their own ending, and Leif suddenly felt an awkward impulse to step back, or forward—but he didn't, he met Fryn's eyes with a smile. "I guess we missed the timing on that ending."

She laughed, and they left the dance floor, returning to their seats. They found a richly-dressed fae waiting by Harissa with one of her custom cocktails in his hand. He seemed satisfied with it, but set it down as they approached, and gave them a polite bow with his round head.

"I was hoping I might find you here," he said enigmatically.

"Is that so? I was thinking just the same," Leif said with an ornery, but polite smile.

He smiled in return and waved them to their seats, as one was pulled up for him. "I understand that you are the Hunters who encountered Mythrim, and are responsible for the resolution of the attorney assassination. My employer has a job that might interest you, as it involves a party not unlike this, only difference being the potential danger of similar madmen and their unpredictable machinations."

"I'm not entirely sure I understand," Fryn said, crossing her legs.

"The annual Guardhouse Ball is in a few days, and someone dear to my employer is invited to attend. With the recent tragedies occurring in the city, my employer does not feel that it is safe, and would like you to watch for any threats to the party-goers and eliminate them without alerting the person whom you are protecting that you are Hunters; as this could cause undue panic," he explained.

Harissa twirled the cane in her hand idly as she listened, and her younger cousin, whose name Leif really wished he knew by this point, stood behind her with his hands behind his back.

Fryn bit her lip, and Leif considered the proposal while he watched the dancers. "So we are to attend the party, but not as guests, otherwise it might be known we are Hunters?" he confirmed.

The nobleman, as well as Leif could peg him, nodded. "I do not know many things about your trade, but I have heard that you are adept at using costumes; even gaining entrance to the Crown District in the capacity of an attorney. I am sure you could attend as guard recruits, servants, someone making a delivery… there are many ways to belong at a party, but we only ask that you remain anonymous. As for payment, if you stop something terrible from happening there will be a bonus of fifty percent to the base of 300-mint; if you manage to do so without alerting anyone, the bonus will be increased a hundred percent, for a total of 600-mint."

Leif and Fryn leaned in close together. "Well, what do you think?" he asked.

"I think that since Mythrim skipped town, we need to do as many jobs as we can to save up enough mint to follow him. We should do this, quietly." She said seriously.

"I agree." He nodded, and they turned to face their potential employer.

"We'll do it," Fryn said.

Their employer smiled. "That is most excellent. My benefactor will be pleased to hear that you will be there. I leave the logistics of the operation to you, but ensure that no one dies, because my employer will not divulge the identity of the person you are to protect: therefore anyone attending the party could be the person you need to protect."

"Understood, anonymity on both sides," Leif summarized. "Will you be attending the Ball?"

"I will not be required, since you will be there. We will send payment to the Bounty Office upon your success." He bowed his head once more and stood, nodded to Harissa, and adjusted his jacket. "Lady Pine-Martin, I hope that you will be recognized as the first of the peripheral Nobility, that Lord Ieffin's petition goes according to your wishes. You can expect greater notice by the Snow District. We will be watching how you manage this ring."

"I am sure you will. If there is anything else you need, you are welcome in the Pine-Martin Hall anytime." She bowed her head in turn and watched him slip through the crowd and out the door. "How do you plan on getting into the Guardhouse anonymously?" She asked without turning her head.

"I liked the idea about posing as guards," Leif said.

Fryn coughed on a glass of water and sputtered for a second. "It was hard enough for you to 'pass' as an attorney. You are far too tan to be from here. No. As an immigrant you'd need something much more common."

"I don't want to be common." He frowned.

"I'm afraid she's right," Harissa interjected. "Perhaps delivering RSVP's or crates of wine, but you cannot use a high profile identity to remain anonymous." She shared a look with Fryn. "Did you have much experience in impersonation before coming here, or was everything based on impulse?"

"Everyone has had experience 'playing pretend' from their childhood. I happen to think I'm pretty good at it," he replied.

"So, that means you're a novice. Well, the first rule of infiltration is to not draw attention to yourself. You must be mediocre, and you cannot be funny," Harissa explained. "We have what, three days before the Ball?"

"Two days, if we are talking about preparation time," Fryn added.

"Then we need to choose your roles tonight, send orders for disguises, and start practicing tomorrow," Harissa continued.

"Shouldn't we get there the night before?" Leif asked.

"What? No, that'd be a terrible idea. The Ball starts at six, so it'd be better for you to get there early in the morning, and help with the preparations on the pretense that you are the morning shift and then take a break, to go search for anything suspicious," she replied. "Oh! That's perfect, help set up the party, going as 'the help' would be the best way to get accepted, make an impression as mediocre and not worth bothering with, and then come back to help serve when the party starts."

"You are just about the cleverest girl I've ever known," Leif said, leaning back in his chair.

"And what, you've known a lot? Don't be so easily impressed. Some people have minds so sharp they'd cut you with it if they could figure out how. Take Princess Savis for example, she is the Froreholt Ambassador to Gaersheim. She deals with plots, machinations, and the influence of the heart of the Commission on a daily basis. That is the kind of person you should keep an eye on," Harissa countered, her cheeks slightly reddened.

"Ahem," Fryn rejoined, "I think he's right cousin, you deserve notice, even if you would prefer to remain anonymous." She folded her hands on her lap and looked at her empty tumbler. "Jason, if you wouldn't mind." She glanced up at the Martin in the waiter's uniform.

"So that's his name." Leif muttered softly. "If it isn't too much to ask, Jason, I would appreciate a little more myself."

Harissa caught him by the arm.

"You too? That's fine," he smiled.

"No, have a seat, I'll get it." She pulled him into the chair previously occupied by their new employer. "We have enjoyed bubbles, and sceppe, but times like this call for wine." Harissa produced a bottle of Gaersheim Rosenkraun from the tray Jason had brought out, and placed four crystal glasses, cut with the design of a pine marten on the limb of a tree, and divided the bottle equally.

When they had all sniffed the wine, swirled it in its glass, and tasted it, Fryn continued where they'd left off. "Since we don't have the cooperation of the guard, we will need to learn to act the part. It would be wise to start practicing now."

They sat in their semi-circle in thought till Jason gave a polite cough. "I happen to know a few things about the trade, and if you are willing to endure criticism, I would be willing to teach you how to serve."

"You would?" Leif asked.

"I think I should," he replied, looking at Fryn. "We have suffered enough losses to the clan, and now that we have you back, Fryn, I want to ensure we do not lose you again."

"I'm not exactly involved in the clan's affairs," she answered softly.

Harissa smirked. "It's safe to say that you are now. We lay no claim on your activities since you are a Hunter: independent and free by nature—but your success or failure reflects on us, as ours does on you. That is the definition of family."

"Fine," Fryn chuckled, "but I cannot always attend events as my occupation will keep me busy."

"Shouldn't we focus on the occupation we just obtained?" Leif asked.

"Yes, of course," Jason replied. "I agree that going as servants is your best option. We can get you there as hired staff using our connections with the Butlers' Guild, and I am sure they'd willing to help prevent a tragedy as long as you can look the part."

"Why would they help us?" Leif took a long sip of his wine, and saw Caelyn sitting with her partner at one of the tables, face red, from dancing, wine, or blushing, he couldn't tell.

Fryn tapped her glass with her fingers, in a ¾ pattern. "I think I know why. Recall that Mythrim killed all the staff as well as the guests? Well, if the Butlers' Guild knew we were there to prevent a potential tragedy, we would be helping them avoid losing any more of their members."

"Quite so," Jason clapped his hand softly against his wineglass, "I will go over to their department tonight, and obtain uniforms and cooperation, thereby eliminating the need to scrounge the Stone Market, and tomorrow we will have you practice wearing them as well as learning to serve and set up what will be required of you."

They watched the people as they all found tables and benches to relax. The music stopped, and the fae with the fiddle desperately drank from a glass of water set beside his chair. Caelyn parted with her dance partner, and sat looking dreamily off into space.

"So, Harissa, how does it feel to be the Pine-Martin?" Fryn asked, looking at Harissa's cane as her hand brushed the sheath strapped to her thigh.

"That isn't something I can easily answer. For now, we will have to affirm our contracts with the people, arrange a proper memorial service for my father, and brothers, and continue with daily life... but after that, I am not sure what state our clan will be in, only that regardless of the affairs beyond us, we will remain the same."

Leif leaned back in the upholstered chair and sighed. "I think you ought to write poetry."

"I do. Don't you remember? It was brought up earlier." Harissa looked at him closely. "I think you'd do well to drink a bit more water, keep your head clear."

He alternated sips of water and wine, watching the people as they came one by one at their own time to congratulate Harissa before leaving the

Hall. Eventually it was just them, family members reading books, a fire in the hearth, and Caelyn, the clerk, asleep on the bench beside it.

"I think she danced herself out," Jason said, shaking his head with a smile, "I wonder who her partner was."

"What should we do about her?" Fryn asked, taking off her boots, dropping them to the ground with a few light thuds.

"She'll be fine there till morning, it's a comfortable bench," he said, going to a cupboard built into the wall by the kitchen. He pulled out a red and green quilt and draped it over her, and tossed another piece of wood on the fire. Then, returning to his seat, he said, "It is a lot safer in this house than many of the streets of the Snow District, whatever they may say about crime in the lower districts. The people like us, and we look out for them, so criminals make sure not to bother us."

"I'll take your word on that," Leif said. "I haven't been here long enough to know the city very well. Isn't that right, Fryn?" He glanced over, but she had pulled up her feet, jacket discarded on top of her boots, curled up on the chair with her eyes closed and her head against the wing of the back, and her white socks, with blue snowflakes contrasted with the leather.

"I guess I'll get another blanket," Jason said. "Leif, I'll show you to a room with a real bed. Harissa, do you have them?" He turned to his elder cousin and sighed. "She's out like a candle."

Her legs splayed out from the chair, toes pointed in, with her head resting against the cane which she hugged to her chest.

"I guess you'll need two more blankets." Leif chuckled. "This is something that a servant needs to do, right?"

"It certainly is, but they won't test you on it." Jason retrieved two more quilts and covered his cousins to the chin. Then, he locked the doors and led Leif down a hall by the kitchen and showed him into a guest room with a window looking out on the empty street, a porcelain washbasin by the dresser, and a wide feather bed with red and green quilts. "It looks like it'll snow tonight, so if you need another blanket, there are more quilts, and a fur spread in the closet," he said.

"Thanks." Leif opened the closet and pulled out the fur and tossed it on the bed. "It is most appreciated."

Jason nodded and closed the door as he left, and Leif wondered if all the Pine-Martins needed to learn how to serve or act in different positions. It wasn't that long ago that Harissa had been showing them to a private table to speak with her father, making them drinks, and flirting with the guests.

He was feeling more at home and pampered than he had during any of the days spent at the Palace. Ieffin was odd, and generous, but also a little dangerous, and so he hadn't truly relaxed the whole week. He slept better than he had for ages.

Serve and Guard

Frorin:

Snow District

Snow Ringroad & South Cardinal

Leif adjusted his bowtie against the north wind. Harissa and Jason had educated them for roughly two days, in an equally rough manner. His knuckles had taken more than a few raps from the ruler that Jason used to check his sleeves to make sure they were never long enough to hover over the top of a drink, and made good use of it whenever he spilled a drop or poured from the wrong side.

"They will think you're dosing their drink, sleeves back!" He'd said, snapping the ruler with glee.

Fryn had it slightly easier, but that was mostly because she picked up the trade like a natural, and was forced to leave the room when her laughter became an unwelcome distraction. Still, they'd been approved by the Guild hired by the guards, so it had been worth a few bruises to his pride; he suspected that he'd value the skill set later anyway.

"I wonder who is going to attend this party," Leif said, admiring the sleek profile of his suit.

Fryn chuckled. "Stop that, you look like Clair."

"You look better. It's like you were meant to wear it," he said, pointing at her cropped jacket and black vest.

"Stop it, I'll blush," she said without expression, watching his discomfort, with her wings alone betraying her amusement.

They stood before the doors looking at the Guardhouse, an asymmetrical building with angled roofs and a ballroom lined with windows granting a view of the western slope of the city. It was built with eaves covering a veranda around the ballroom so that people could escape the party but still feel like a part of it, or so Jason had explained.

"We could probably find a way in under the veranda. I bet there's a service entrance," Leif suggested.

"Weren't you listening? Harissa said the servants go in through the back. Now come on. If we're late, it'll reflect badly on the Guild." Fryn shook her head, and flit ahead.

She stopped before the covered back-porch and waved him over. "I'm sorry. We were delayed at the gate."

The person she was addressing was a serious-looking butler in a gray suit with a navy blue cravat. "Never mind that now. I hear you come highly recommended. We will need you and your associate to assist in the arrangements in the dining hall, and after that come see me." He directed them inside with his chin, and resumed his post by the door.

Leif scanned the hall from the service entrance, marking the kitchens, the stairs to the cellars and laundry, and the storage rooms, in his memory to match the layout drawn up by Jason. He glanced back out the door and noticed that it had just started to snow. "Well, good thing we got here when we did," he said, jerking a thumb over his shoulder.

"Wouldn't want you getting cut up again," she smirked. "Now, I think the dining hall was this way." She walked through the arch at the end of the hall and turned left.

The ballroom and the dining hall were conjoined, separated by the imaginary line drawn from the hallway that was collinear with the front entrance. While the ballroom had tall windows separated by pillars, always open to the view, the dining hall somewhat mirrored the rectangular space with a thinner rectangle decorated with burgundy curtains that partially covered the skinny windows on the east side. There was already a long table set up on one side of the dining hall, and a trio of servers flitted around it setting plates and cups at each space.

One of them, a girl looking roughly Clair's age, noticed them and stopped her work to walk over. "Oh good, I was a little worried that no one else was coming." She smiled. "I'm Lillen."

They introduced themselves and waited in awkward silence, watching the other staff walk in with chairs for the places they'd just set.

"I imagine that we need to set up more tables, which room are they in?" Leif asked.

111

"Oh, of course," Lillen said, tilting her head. "This way. Fryn, I might need your help on my side."

They wound back down the hall and into a room with table-tops and legs lined up on separate walls, all dark wood without a scratch, polished with care, and with only a little dust. Leif and Fryn managed to carry out one of the long table-tops, with space enough to seat ten, and Lillen brought out one of its three bases.

Another server carried in the other two. They spaced them down the center line of the table and lowered the top onto the pegs. "There's a bit of a trick to securing these," Lillen explained, crouching under the table by the middle base, "there's a locking peg we need to slide into place."

Leif locked the other two without comment, and chuckled as she checked them. She shook her head, but dusted her knees and scratched her chin in thought. "We'll let Byron and Faryll set this one. We can prepare the last one."

They made short work, in two trips since Lillen could only carry two bases at most, and then brought out all the chairs they'd need.

"This can only seat thirty people. Is that enough?" Leif asked.

"There're still the round tables for small groups that we have to set up," she replied, "they're in the next room down the hall." She held up a hand to stop them as they made to go. "But, we won't need those till right before the party. These long tables are for the Guard; and they will be having tea in half an hour."

Leif stopped and put his hands in his pockets. "I guess that makes sense. I wondered why we were setting up the tables so early."

"After their tea, we will need to replace all the dishes and start setting up for the Ball." She looked at the clock over the fireplace on the north side and tapped her cheek with her finger. "Tea at eleven, afternoon tea at three, guests at six, Ball at seven."

"While they're taking tea, how long of a break do we have?" Leif asked.

"We don't get a break till after we've cleaned up from tea. We need to reassemble at 2:30. It won't take much time to arrange." She took a deep breath and scooted a chair into place at the last table. "Just a little more housecleaning, then we can have some tea ourselves while they eat." She opened a well-concealed closet, built behind one of the wooden panels of the wall, and tossed a broom to Leif, and a duster to Fryn, as well as a cloth. "If there is too much dust, we won't want to cast it into the air we are trying to breathe, so get the towel damp and wipe the surface," she directed.

Leif worked from the back to the front of the Dining Hall, careful to keep the dust from flying into the air, and using just a small amount of sparks so that the dust-motes stuck together and stayed manageable. Periodically, as he checked Fryn's progress, he saw her use a thin layer of frost before wiping with the cloth. He shook his head; the regular staff doubtless had no such abilities, for if they had, they would not have joined the profession.

The room was spotless in a minute, and the other staff, Byron and Faryll, if he recalled, were already bringing in trays with tiny sandwiches and carafes of cold soups, among other things. Leif went into the kitchen and found a teapot waiting, so he brought it out and paused, trying to remember where he was supposed to place the teapot, in what kind of setting.

Fryn took it from his hands, and set it one third of the way down from the head of the table. "There should be a second teapot," she said, searching his eyes, "You look tired."

"I'm not used to hard labor," he said, covering his mouth with a yawn.

"Uh huh," she laughed softly, and glanced over at the arrangement of sandwiches. "It's so tempting just to take one isn't it?"

"I can't stop thinking about it." Leif gripped her shoulders lightly, and gave her a small shake. "This job is harder than I thought."

Fryn pursed her lips and smiled. "If we laugh too much, we might arouse suspicion."

"Oooh, suspicion about what?" Lillen asked, materializing beside them, watching them like she was drooling over crème-brulee, or some juicy romance novel.

Leif smirked and pulled Fryn close. "We've been discovered, Fryn."

She sighed dramatically. "Whatever shall we do? Gone are the times in the closet, or the days spent pouring wine."

Lillen chuckled. "There's no policy against romance," she said dreamily, "just don't let it get in the way of your work."

Leif disengaged from Fryn's arms, which had wrapped a bit too tightly around his neck, and straightened his coat. "Actually, we have a favor to ask. When we have our break, would it be possible to take lunch *out*?"

113

"A picnic?" Fryn asked, eyebrow arched unromantically.

"Of course you can, just so long as you are back to help us set up the last tables once afternoon tea is done," she replied. "Now, we'd best move into the solarium so the Guards can enjoy their tea in private."

She led them through the kitchens into a wide solarium with herbs glowing in the sunlight in their planters. There was one of those circular tables she had alluded to earlier set up in the center with a teapot and collection of sandwiches for their enjoyment.

"When did this get here?" Fryn asked, taking a seat.

"Oh, Byron did this. He always does things like this; says he enjoys the little things." Lillen's mouth twitched but she didn't laugh. "It's things like that that make my job here rewarding."

The other two servers stepped in from the kitchen with cups and saucers; Byron, with dark brown hair trimmed close on the sides, and an innocent face, and Faryll with an indifferent expression that clashed with the eager glint in his eyes. He seemed about Lillen's age, so Leif guessed the 'cool' façade was for her benefit.

"I can imagine that you hear a lot of gossip here," Fryn said, accepting her steaming cup from Byron who'd insisted on pouring for everyone.

Faryll nodded, and sipped his tea, looking like he really wanted to say something.

"It seems like every day we hear about something new. Yesterday I heard that Heron went on a date with a clerk from the Commission," Lillen related, leaning over the table.

Faryll blinked. "But he was so shy."

"You would know, Faryll, I don't think you've been on a date for half a year," Byron teased.

"I am not shy. I just have trouble finding someone I like," he said, adding a sniff for good measure.

"Don't worry, Faryll, you're cool, and girls like that. They just don't understand that you're interesting, too," Lillen said, looking like she was trying to be reassuring, but she turned quickly to hide the color on her cheeks. "Just the other day, you told me that rumor about the assassin coming from the Guard—and what girl doesn't like rumors?"

Leif imagined quite a few, but didn't want to disillusion her. He just gave Fryn a look and smiled. She didn't like rumors. She was far too serious for that.

Fryn winked and looked back at Lillen. "I heard that the Pine-Martins might be made nobility."

"No, I don't believe it!" She exclaimed quietly. "I always liked the Pauper Princess, a splash of color and glamour in the weeds. Or at least, that was how my mother described her."

Leif thought it best not to let on about Fryn's relationship with that house. Rumors were best kept vague. "What were you saying about the assassin and the guard?" He asked.

Faryll spoke first. "Well, I heard that one of the tombs had been looted, and that someone in the guard might have helped the thief. See, the tomb belonged to an old criminal, and was buried with some of his loot, or so they say."

While he wondered if the assassin referred to was the one from the Palace, or the one who had killed the one in the Palace, Leif figured it was best not to seem too interested.

They idled over their cooling tea until the bell rang for them to clean up the morning tea, so they waited till the last guards had filed out before removing all the plates and utensils, and taking them to the kitchen. With Lillen's 'okay' Leif packed up a napkin with tea sandwiches and led Fryn out by the hand.

He let go once they were out of sight, and they paused in the storage room that once contained the long tables. "Where did Harissa say we should wait until the party?"

"She didn't. But what did you think about that looted tomb? Should we investigate? If I recall there was a series of catacombs beneath the wine cellar. We should go back out this door, then right at the next hall, and then down the stairs to the basement." She shook her head. "Did you forget?"

"Gossiping drives out information as fast as you learn it." He shrugged.

"Alright, come on." They stepped out, and hovered down the hall, and around the corner, which was just as Fryn had predicted, and landed silently at the foot of the stairs. There were quite a few storage rooms, an armory, a laundry room, and finally the wine cellar.

Without windows they could only guess at its depth. At about fifteen spans wide, it contained four rows of wine racks in the central space, and barrels with mysterious contents along the walls.

"Do they make their own wine?" He asked, flitting over to the closest rack and examining the bottles. He picked up a dusty bottle with green

115

velvet sealing the cork with a wax label imprinted on the top. "This is a '703 Rosenkraun. How can they afford this?"

Fryn stopped beside him and tilted her head. "Remember how Ieffin said they accepted a portion of their taxes in goods? Maybe they also pay a portion of wages to the guard in goods."

Keeping one hand on the wine rack they wandered deeper into the wine cellar, until they reached the back wall. It was roughly twenty spans in length, and they stopped before a hatch door in the floor that was poorly maintained and squeaked when they opened it. "Let's hope no one heard that," Leif said, as Fryn hopped down.

"What are you waiting for?"

"Just forgot something." He picked a bottle at random and followed her. "If we're going to wait in here for hours, we might as well have something to do."

She nodded in the dark, and pulled the door shut. "Well, let's just try to find somewhere to hide. Here, I'll lead. Where's your hand?"

He found her hand, and followed her slow steps through the dark. "We should have brought a candle or something."

She squeezed his hand in response. "I hear this place is haunted by the ghosts of ancient guards."

"Well, I wish one of them would appear, that way we could see by their spook-light." He chuckled.

"Their what?" She laughed. "I don't know how you come up with these things."

"You never know, we might find a lamp or a torch somewhere in here. I find it hard to believe that they'd have catacombs that they'd need to navigate with a lantern." He brushed the wall with his wingtips, hoping to discover a sconce of some kind.

"If we find one, how do you expect to light it?"

He sent a small jolt through her arm, causing her to jump and hover in the air, pulling him up with her.

"Hey, watch where you send those things." She dropped back down. "Do that again and it'll cost you in blood."

He laughed. "I can tell you're smiling."

"No I'm not." She stopped. "There's a passage to the left, let's take it." She fumbled over something on the ground, and crouched to investigate. "It looks like there're some bones here that have been disturbed."

"What, whose bones?"

"How would I know that?" Her arm moved with her headshake, at least as far as he could interpret.

They continued down the new corridor for a while, before Fryn found something in her path. "There's some kind of slab here." She searched the wall with her other hand. "Look, I found a lamp." She placed his hand on a shelf built into the wall, and he felt the telltale glass and metal of a lantern.

"See if you can open it."

"It is open, on the right side." She moved his hand slightly, until he felt the wick move under his fingers.

He created a small arc between his thumb and forefinger, which gave a little blue light and passed it over the wick until it flared to life. Yellow light blinded them for a minute, but before long Leif could see how wide the corridor really was; carved from the mountain, with shelves for storing odd items, and capstones covering the mausoleum's inhabitants' slots in the walls.

"When was the Guard founded?" He asked, staring down the corridor till it faded to black.

"Almost twelve hundred years ago. There are thousands of graves in here." She took the lantern down and set it on the unused slab. The stone looked like it was intended for an empty slot across from where the lamp had been. Above the slot there was a weapon mount, but it was also empty.

"I wonder who was going to be buried here," Leif said, setting the napkin with the sandwiches and the bottle of wine beside the lamp.

The air went cold and the lamp nearly went out and Fryn turned to look at the slab of stone on the ground. "I have an idea. Here, help me turn this over."

He moved the food and light onto the shelf, and helped her flip the stone so that the opposite face shown dully in the light. It had a metal nameplate printed in faded letters.

Fryn took down the lamp to investigate, and shook her head. "This was not a grave, it was a prison."

"Why would the guards ever imprison someone like this, it's a death-sentence." Leif glanced up at the weapon-mount curiously. "And why would they hang up a sword there?"

117

She brushed the dust off the engraving, and caught her breath. "It says here that the prisoner was one Aldyr Havrshyk, imprisoned because he could not be killed on account of his Bloodsword."

"Havrshyk?" She gasped, and took a step back. "Then that must mean the accomplice was a Bloodcrafter."

"So how old is he? I thought Mythrim was the leader." Leif opened the napkin and took a bite from one of the sandwiches, musing silently for a few seconds as he chewed. "I suppose he might follow someone who freed him. When was he put in here?"

"It says that he was defeated and sealed here... seventy years ago. Mythrim must have recruited him, but why?." She sat on the slab, and taking his sandwich, she stole a bite.

"What was that for?" He asked, sitting with his back against the wall. "There're plenty here."

"How much time do we have?"

Leif fished out a pocket-watch, courtesy of Jason, and sighed. "It's twelve-fifteen."

"Well, I know of one way to pass the time." She pulled out her knife and cut off the top of the bottle. The blade sucked in the stray droplets, and the glass edges were smoothed by a thin layer of ice. "It's a shame we couldn't bring any wineglasses, but this should do." She took a long swig and passed it over. "What is this? It's tart."

He examined the dusty label, wiping it with his thumb. "It looks like a something-berry wine. Should I get something else?" He took a drink and grimaced. "It is pretty sour."

"I think we should," she said, taking the lamp in one hand. "Come on, our break is only so long, and I want a short nap before we have to babysit the whole party."

"Ha, ha, I agree." Leif followed her back the way they'd come, and blew out the lamp when they stood beneath the trapdoor. Leif climbed up the ladder and was about to open it, when Fryn hovered beside him and pushed it up just a crack so they could see.

"No one's in there, let's go." She pushed it all the way up and held it till he'd got out, and then gently lowered it shut. "We should get something tannic," she said, scanning the racks.

"How about this?" Leif pulled out one of the Rosenkrauns he'd found before.

"That'd be too obvious." She shook her head. "But this corner over here is filled with untouched bottles, let's take one of these." In the dim light she managed to retrieve a bottle covered in dust and zip down the hole as Leif held it open.

They rushed back, barely keeping the lamp lit, and settled on either side of Havrshyk's headstone. "This time," she said, fingering the edge of her blade, "I have a different idea." She cut her thumb, and allowed a small pool of blood to collect in the palm of her hand, and handed him the bottle. Fryn hummed the tune of the Acorn from the other day as she concentrated on the liquid that she'd gathered, and it started to shift and harden into a sharp spiral.

Leif watched as it went black and turned into ice, and formed a little cross section which she gripped in one hand, as she held out the other towards him.

"I'm ready." She opened her eyes and winked. "I just made history: the very first blood-screw." She twisted it into the cork and pulled it out with ease. Then, the spiral melted and flowed back into the cut she'd made and sealed it shut with a thin layer of ice.

Immediately the thick aroma of the strong wine filled the catacombs, and she held the bottle before her nose gently with a smile. "This is what we should have chosen the first time," she said, took a large sip, and placed one hand over her chest. "What is this?"

"Let me try." Leif took the bottle and tried a sip as she cleaned off the label and gasped.

"Oh my, I think I made a mistake." She looked into the empty slot that Havrshyk had slept in.

"What? This wine is delicious."

"Want to know why that area of the cellar is untouched?" She took the bottle and drank a little. "It's because this bottle is three hundred years old."

"Then I better have some more." He took it back and savored it, while he traded her a tea sandwich. She accepted it but looked suspiciously at the bottle.

"This is going to be fairly divided, Leif, and don't say anything about tolerance levels of fee and fae, this is about the principle, not whether I feel its effects."

119

"You're right, of course, so I should do the gentlemanly thing and drink two thirds of it."

"No you won't." She swiped it from his hand and held it to her chest, and then laughed. "I kind of feel like Grendel, that thief I caught, do you remember him?"

"How could I forget?" Leif sighed dramatically. "He cost you a very nice-sounding bonus."

She glanced down at the bottle, and smiled. "You know, there's something that's been bothering me for a while now."

"What's that?" Leif switched his crossed legs and rested his chin in his hands.

Fryn looked at the headstone between them, with the lamp on one corner, and then at the sandwiches and the tart wine they didn't want to drink. "How did Mythrim know about Havrshyk, if he was imprisoned so long ago, how did he revive him and get him to serve him?"

"You just said the word 'him' quite a lot," Leif said. "Mythrim, from what we know, is none other than Captain Hartlin, right? So there's a chance he got familiar with all his predecessors and their wild stories—one of which had to have been about the rare Bloodcrafter—and when he decided to start murdering royalty he must have found him rather easily."

"You're right about it being rare." She took a sip and passed him the bottle. "I only know of one other Bloodcrafter, well, aside from Havrshyk, and now Harissa I guess."

"Seems almost like its becoming more common," Leif mused. "Didn't it used to be? How did they kill them?"

She shrugged. "It's not like they can't be killed. They age normally, they heal faster, but still have scars, and I know that they can't be separated too far from their item." Fryn's wings shifted nervously. "As for how Havrshyk seems to be our age, I wonder if his imprisonment and separation from his blade froze him, preserved him."

Leif watched her face as she stared at her hands. Her small pointy nose, her thin mouth, and her long eyelashes perfect for keeping out the sand of the desert. She wouldn't do well there all the same, unless it was in the same latitude. Her eyes skipped around all the inanimate objects surrounding them, her gaze skipping past, avoiding his. "How did you?"

Fryn took a bite of her sandwich and frowned. "I only have vague memories, I suspect I tried to forget, but even what I do remember, I don't really want to discuss."

"You look a little cold." He passed her the bottle.

"I don't get cold." She smirked. "No need to say anything like: 'here, we can be warm together, sit here' or anything, you fee-charmer."

"I am not." Leif sniffed. "You're the one more prone to teasing."

"I should hope so."

"So it does matter?"

"Shush." She sighed. "Drink your wine."

They settled to drinking and eating, and telling a few odd jokes; Leif's hints, and Fryn's barbs, till she decided to take a nap, resting her head against the wall. He matched her pose against the opposite wall, checking his clock now and again, but otherwise admiring her peaceful expression as she slept.

Who knew that she'd be fun, or tease, or steal bites of sandwiches? She'd been so serious, reserved, and cold on the surface. Was it just because Mythrim was gone that she had cheered up in general, or was it him? It couldn't be him; he'd never changed someone's attitude before, had he?

He waited, unable to sleep, and shifted at last into a meditation to pass the time. He defocused his gaze, eyes still watching her face, as his breathing slowed. Ten years ago he'd been accepted as an apprentice, his master still had those manacle scars on his wrists and ankles. Ten years from now, what would they be doing? Would they still be partners, even though they'd started working together out of a coincidence? The hour hand of his watch shifted to two and he was mildly aware of the sound of the trapdoor opening and then shutting.

His thoughts refocused. Fryn slept, the lamp burning low beside her, and footsteps 'snick'ed their way softly down the corridors in their direction. Who could it be? Would they get in trouble for their picnic? What if Mythrim had returned?

He roused himself quickly and stood, ears straining to hear the quiet movements of their intruder. The wine in the bottle was almost gone, and only one sandwich remained, but he stole a quick sip and felt it on his lips as he thought. The footsteps were definitely coming down their corridor.

He looked at Fryn and brushed her silvery blunt bangs out of her face. "I'm sorry, Fryn," he said, kneeling carefully over her while trying not to be as intrusive as he was trying to look. Seconds left, he laced his fingers with hers, keeping her hands away from the knife at her belt, and pressed his wine-stained lips to hers.

He felt her shift beneath him, as her lips trembled in response. Her fingers tightened around his, and her eyes slowly flickered in a semiconscious state. Staring romantically, urgently into her glazed eyes, he hoped she'd understand. Her knees moved as her eyes cleared and the footsteps paused outside their view.

It's all for show. Leif thought, smiling with his eyes, pulling one hand up to caress her ear.

It isn't real. He thought, as she lightly bit his lower lip, her eyes cold and bitter.

I hope she knows. But then, if she hadn't, she'd have slit his throat right? She pulled her legs under her and ran her free hand through his hair, and pushed him back against the headstone.

"There's still a little wine left," she whispered, sultry, rubbing the stubble on his chin. "Do you want some?"

"You can have it, all I ever wanted is right here." He placed his hands on her shoulders and held her close, but she pushed him away with a smirk.

"I want that wine." She took a swig and a little dribbled down her neck.

"What a mess, we can't have that." Leif brushed away the stain and pulled her in for a kiss. She wrapped her hands around his head, and they held each other as the intruder's footsteps sounded down the corridor.

She pulled back a little, gripping his sleeves at the shoulder, staring into his gaze, biting her lip nervously; looking more uncertain than he'd ever seen her.

The sound of the door was faint, but they both released their breath and chuckled.

"I'm sorry I couldn't warn you," Leif said, tempted to move her hair behind her ear, his wings alternating between flashes of burgundy and colorless shame.

She stood slowly and flushed, matching the same level of red that he suddenly realized had suffused his face. They stood apart breathing anxiously, until Fryn burst out laughing. "If you hadn't looked so awkward I would have killed you!" She grabbed the last sandwich and polished it off. "Do you think our performance worked?"

You nearly had me convinced, he thought. "I don't know; we might need more practice."

She grinned; wings tinted a reddish color with embarrassment. "I knew you'd say that. Do you know how I knew?"

"How?"

"You're lonely." She pressed a finger into his forehead. "That's why you left home, and decided to fight 'bad guys' right?"

"I thought it'd be time better spent than living in the tavern, or becoming a hermit," he joked. "At least this way, I have a partner right?"

"Partner," she chuckled ruefully, "you're right..." She grew serious for a moment, but smiled again quickly. "For now, neither one of us is alone."

"Did you dream?"

She gave him a knowing look. "You mean before or after you kissed me?"

"Before..."

"Well, I only remember after."

"What was it?"

"That's a secret." She picked up the lamp and stuck the gross wine in Havrshyk's cell. "We should head back upstairs, Lillen might need more help, and we should try to get there while the guards are busy with their tea."

Leif dusted off the dirt that he'd gotten from their display and stuffed his hands in his pockets. "Alright, but you haven't heard the last of it about that dream."

She kicked his foot lightly and took to wing. "Come on now, we should hurry."

They snuck into the cellar as they had before, and like last time, no one was there. Fryn corked the empty bottle and replaced it before zipping out into the hall. "Is there anything on my uniform?" She asked, trying to twist around.

"I can dust it off for you," he offered, but immediately looked away at her glare.

"We aren't that close, Leif." She dusted the back of her skirt and coat purposefully until he told her it looked clean. Even then she gave it a few good pats just to be safe.

They hurried back up to the solarium where Lillen was enjoying a little tea herself with Byron. Where Faryll had gone, no one knew, and they were surprised to see Leif and Fryn back so soon.

"Well, you know, we wanted to help if we could," Leif said, pulling up a seat for Fryn, and then himself.

She and Lillen shared a look, but it was Byron who spoke next.

"It's a shame; you just missed tea-time." He poured them cups of tea and looked hard at Leif. "So where did you go for lunch?"

"Oh we went out, had a little picnic, very quiet, very private." Leif shrugged with his hands.

"Is that so? How nice, I can imagine the parks being private today, what with the surprise snowfall," he replied.

Fryn coughed and shot Leif a look. "We brought umbrellas and were willing to enjoy it despite of the snow."

Lillin reached out and brushed Fryn's mouth, slightly more relaxed than it normally was. "You had wine, and snow… it must have been so romantic."

"It was," Leif interjected, "I think we'll go again sometime, but we've only just started with the guild so, it might be a little while before we can get away like that again."

Fryn sighed. "True."

Just then, the butler entered the room and sat down at the table beside them. Byron passed him a perfectly-poured cup of tea, which he held before his nose and savored before tasting. "Unfortunately there has been a delivery mix-up. I need one of you to pick up the last crate from the Frosthall Winery before the party starts."

They all looked at each other, no one wanting to volunteer. The butler smiled. "I think it would be a simple job, even for a newcomer. Leif, was it? Would you take this receipt to the Floor Manager and pick it up for me?" He passed over a slip of paper, printed in fine movable-type. He leaned over as Leif accepted it and added. "I hear that they sometimes give taste-tests to members of the guild—seeing as we go out of our way to fulfill our service and all."

"Fear not. I will obtain this valuable crate and return it safe through storm and strife." Leif pocketed the receipt and stood, puffing up his thin chest proudly. "For I am a server, and that is what I do."

They all laughed, even the butler, who looked like he was normally stern. "Go on, Leif, we'll manage the preparations till you get back." Byron shook his head. "You're not a Hunter, you're a Butler, no need to stand on a box."

Leif spun on him. "Oh but there is. You see, people do not comprehend the glamour of this work, this calling to which we are called. It is a venerable profession. We get to sip the leftover wine as the party-guests flirt and dance and perform for us, we get to arrange little love-triangles based on where we seat the guests, and we get to learn all about the fun little rumors that fill every ring in this city."

They applauded softly.

"That was well spoken," Fryn said, with a slight headshake. "Now take wing and get out of here before we have a repeat of your magic words' effect from the park."

"You saucy girl," he winked. "I have tarried here long enough, friends, you will see me again: of that I promise you."

"We better, or else you're fired." The butler chuckled. "Now go on."

"Could someone remind me how to get to the Frosthall Winery?" Leif held his arms akimbo and looked off to the left.

"It's clockwise down the Snow Ringroad, then north on the South Cardinal, and clockwise again on the Vineroad. It's where all the major wineries are, and very, very hard to miss," the butler said, "now go on before I have the guards escort you off the premises."

Leif sniffed. "I shall be off." He waved and flew out of a window of the solarium to everyone's evident surprise, and darted in the direction provided.

He was still smiling when he landed with a crunch in the courtyard of the Frosthall Winery. The snow was soft, and wet, and he'd had no trouble avoiding their slow-falling paths, or crushing them with his fists, but he noticed with discomfort that a small amount of cold water had trickled under his shirt and sleeves.

The Winery was far enough north along the Vineroad that the main office of the complex, normal to the street, was almost directly in the western direction. With three stories, numerous windows, and gray stones, it was a magnificent structure. But, Leif's gaze was immediately drawn to the tasting room on the north side of the courtyard, a low building with long windows providing a view of a wide room with a maple-wood bar, armchairs set around little tables, flanking an area in front of a fireplace that sent its smoke in a tiny white cloud up and out of a pebble-brick chimney.

"Oy, you here for a pickup?" A loud, burly voice hailed him from the south.

He turned and scratched his head, blond hair tossed in the cold wind. "I am. Are you the Floor Manager?"

"I am. This is where I'd be. Are you new?" The Floor Manager wore a work apron paired with scuffed boots and a finely-knit scarf that clashed with his work clothes.

"I am new, but pleased to make your acquaintance." Leif bowed perfunctorily, but with a little flair, and smiled. "My name is Leif, and I am here to pick up this crate for the Guardhouse Ball." He presented the receipt and passed it over.

"Hmm… This is all in order. Yes… I will have it packaged for you momentarily." He looked over Leif's shoulder at the tasting room and smiled. "Tell you what, go and taste our new Reserva while you wait. We'll join you when it's ready."

"Really?" Leif stuffed his hands in his pockets awkwardly. "I don't know what to say."

"Say 'thank you' or 'okay' and get in there." He laughed, and walked into the warehouse.

Leif nodded and slipped through the door into the comfortably toasty bar, and took a seat on the stool closest to the door. A few other patrons sipped glasses of wine; a couple nestled in the chairs closest to the fire, whispering with rosy eyes.

The wine steward nodded to him, and glanced out the window, before pulling up an unopened bottle from under the counter and opening it with a flourish. He had grayish-black hair, and perfectly white teeth, which smiled at him as he poured a golden liquid into a glass and swirled its contents in a small circle on the almost radiant finished maple-wood bar. He slid it carefully before Leif, and set the bottle and cork beside it.

"This is our new Reserva. I hope you enjoy it," he said, watching Leif's movements as he picked up the cork and felt its softness.

Leif looked through the glass at an angle over the perfect white of his sleeve to check the even distribution of color, and then he finally took a sniff, breathing in what smelled like rose-petals, and caramelized honey. Then he took a sip and chewed it like he would a steak for several seconds, and swallowed.

The first real sip was normal, and he could taste notes of the rose-petals, caramel, but the finish was dry, cold but not bitter. He drank it thoughtfully, rather quickly, enjoying it with as much attention he could give it considering his timetable.

"That is the nectar of life," he declared. "I will recommend this to the head butler when I return."

"If you are fortunate, there should be enough leftover for him to taste as well." The steward grinned.

The Floor Manager entered with a cedar-bark crate tied with string and set it down beside him. "You liked it? Excellent." He beamed and passed the crate over gently. "These bottles are made of the most durable glass available, but it is still glass, so be careful."

"I am the very face of care." Leif passed the glass back and picked up the crate. "But sadly I must be going."

"This was one of Captain Hartlin's favorites," the steward said idly. "Though, he hasn't been around lately. If you should see him, give him our regards."

Leif gulped and looked at the wood around the cork suspiciously. It wasn't singed like the tablecloth at the party, but he nodded warily and went to the door. "I will tell him."

He walked out to the street and noticed an envelope tied to the crate, addressed... *to the bearer*, sealed with red wax. He tripped momentarily on a loose stone and fumbled to open the letter, vision slightly blurred as he read it.

"Dear Crate-Bearer,

"Sigleifr, is it? It has been some time. I hope this letter finds you well. After all, you thought I was gone, didn't you? I have learned to choose my poisons more carefully, so don't try the same trick twice. I saw you, you know, finally claiming the love of that Bloodcrafting partner of yours; it was amusing, but genuine. She really does like you. She really did enjoy that, but how could I know? How could I not? It is a shame that she's going to die, even more a shame that you won't be there to see it. Take these last few moments to reflect..."

Leif fell to his knees, his sight blurred by the tears of pain as his stomach roiled and burned.

"...reflect on how amateur you are, how I killed you, and how I might kill her. This is very satisfying; surely you see its poetry? I killed you

127

once, shame on me, I kill you twice, well, shame on me. I was surprised, but not again.

Farewell.

-Mythrim"

Leif dropped the letter and wobbled to his feet, and leaned against the wall of the winery. The streets were empty. He had to try, even if Mythrim warned him not to.

He charged his palm with sparks, and plunged it into his gut. The surge went through his bones, through his feet, and into the ground, but the poison still burned, unaffected. He fell, foam at his mouth, and vomited. His vision faded, and snow fell on his back, the old traces of the snake venom burned in his arm, and he wondered if that only made it worse.

Only then did he notice, the crate had fallen too, but then he closed his eyes.

Stagger and Sweat

Frorin:
Rain District
Vineroad

Leif opened his eyes, snow had piled over him, and the cold seeped into his bones. He could feel the hardening of his wings, and taste the metallic tinge of blood in his mouth. Red vomit lay under a thin layer of snow by his face, and his fingers had gone blue. He pushed himself off the ground and sat against the wall of the winery, vision swimming. The crate and its bottles had cracked open where it fell, and its bubbly contents had frozen to the ground in an icy layer.

How had Mythrim known, and more importantly, when had he returned? Leif pulled out the crumpled letter from where he had fallen on it, and reread the contents with a grimace. Why hadn't he assumed that it was *him* that had seen them? He could have stopped him right then in the catacombs but he *had* to stick to the plan. He'd had to let the party go on so he could guard whomever he was hired to protect without alerting them to the potential threat. Sitting there, leaning back and looking at the slowly falling slush, he smiled.

"I should have known, the job was just the thing to put us just where he wanted—unsuspecting, unprepared," he said, glancing over at a figure standing in the gateway to the winery.

Struggling to his feet, he wobbled and fell on his back—the poison still ebbing after he had spat it out. His chest labored as he tried to breath in the fresh, biting air. Leif turned over and tried again. This time managing to stand, he supported himself on the gate. He didn't remember vomiting.

Mythrim had played them for the fools that they were. Even now, the guests, Fryn, the butler, and the staff, were probably all dead... but what if

129

they weren't? Leif had only just survived his mistaken gamble with the poison, and the odds were the party hadn't started yet. Leif's hands trembled for a moment as he remembered the way Fryn had responded to his kiss, before she had played along.

"I need to get back," he said, looking over at the fae standing in the gateway.

With a red scarf around his neck, and a concerned look on his face, the Floor Manager examined him warily. "I don't know what happened to you sir, but the fact you're alive... I don't know who you are, but we had nothing to do with this. The bottle had been left on the counter with a note attached."

"I just need a little food, and I'll be on my way," Leif replied.

"Of course." The Floor Manager waved him over and sat down beside him at the bar in the tasting room. The bartender was a little surprised to see him, skin blue, and blood traces on his mouth.

"You look like you had quite the accident sir," he said, sliding over a cup of spiced wine.

Leif caught it and took a careful draught of its scent before tasting it. "I lost my footing in the ice," he said at last, feeling the polished gloss of the maple-wood bar.

"Do you need a replacement crate?" The bartender asked.

"No, it will be fine as it is. I would like some soup or whatever food you think would go best with this." He lifted his glass and smiled wanly.

"I can think of a few things." The bartender shared a look with the Floor Manager and produced a green ceramic plate from under the bar. "Probably best to give you something hearty, like a stuffed-roll." He placed a dark rye roll on the plate and cut a small pocket in the side, then bringing out a jar of bitter-sweet jam, and a block of smoked cheese, he stuffed it and slid the plate over with a dry smile.

Leif thanked him, ate quickly, finished his wine, and reread the letter Mythrim had left him. Then, parting from the pair with a few assurances that 'he was fine' Leif stole out the front and took to the wing, and flew with a haphazard wobble counter-clockwise toward the South Cardinal.

He paused in a hover before the intersection, a tea-house on the northern corner on his side, and a steel-umbrella store across the way. He wondered why he shouldn't just follow the arc up till he was closer to the Guardhouse and then take the connecting street to the Snow Ringroad.

Mythrim would have expected him to return the same way he came, in a contingency of his survival, so it made sense to return another way.

Leif knew roughly how far north the Guardhouse was, so he continued along the eastern arc of the Vineroad. The sun was setting, so the party would start any minute... but then, Mythrim would just enjoy the party and kill everyone at the end, if he followed the pattern from the last time.

A few minutes passed as he flew up the arc, watching the skies, hoping the snow wouldn't thicken or harden. Then he noticed a figure standing in the road ahead. It looked like a fae in a black cloak, with a sword at his belt.

He slowed and settled onto the icy street, wind in his face, and waited for the only other person on the street to move. The fae measured him with his hooded gaze, and walked forward a few steps, and stopped a few yards away, before reaching up and lowering his hood.

"I told him his little tricks wouldn't work, not even twice," the fae said, revealing his dark hair, shaven face, and steel-gray eyes. "He underestimates you."

"Well, if it isn't Havrshyk the Old," Leif said, hands spread out in a mocking fashion.

"Do I look old to you?" Havrshyk unclasped his cloak and let it fly off in the wind. "So you think you can mock me, for the seventy years spent in isolation, unable to feel my body, unable to move, just think... think... and think, until I lose my mind?" He frowned, lower lip trembling at bitter memories, Leif figured.

"I can put all that to an end," Leif replied, "You never have to go consciously into such a tomb again."

"Ha!" Havrshyk walked around, Leif following, so that they changed positions. "I can't promise you such a nice death, why would you be so generous with me?"

Leif checked his reserves, wishing he had recovered more of his sparks. "Oh, and what kind of death will I suffer?"

"Your imprisonment will be equally maddening, but much longer than mine: when I consume you, you will barely exist—just enough to drive you mad." He drew his sword from its scabbard in a red flash, and examined the polished blade, nearly black from the amount of blood and ice imbued.

"Whose idea was it to hire us and lure us into a trap?" Leif asked, lowering into a stance, wings prepped for a launching blast.

"Mine. Mythrim wanted to leave you be until you really were secure, I just wanted you to *feel* safe. Now, enough of this, I expect you to at least keep me entertained while Mythrim kills the girl." Havrshyk leapt toward him in the same stance that Fryn often used, sword pointing out, with the back hand open for blocking.

Leif skidded back over the ice as he deflected the blade with his fist, and used a wing-burst to propel himself forward with the other hand stretched out to spear his opponent in the gut.

But Havrshyk's feet locked to the ground, and he blocked the punch with his open hand and brought his sword arm's elbow down on Leif's forearm. Leif grunted, and twisted, using a spinning kick to dislodge Havrshyk's hold on the ice, and tumbled over him in a fight for control of the sword.

They rolled over the stones, exchanging jabs, kicks, and slaps until they pushed away and stood staring at each other just out of range. Leif's breath was quick and his heart pounded anxiously, while Havrshyk examined him without any such difficulty.

Havrshyk regained his stance and smiled. "Did you know that Fryn's precious Soft-Point-Fist was invented by an Assassin? He served the king, well, the king of five hundred years ago, and to mask his identity, he created that style."

"And, why are you telling me this?" Leif stretched his neck. "Is this because you wish Fryn had been sent out here?"

"You're cleverer than you look." Havrshyk glanced at his blade fondly. "I am the last student of the true school, the one forgotten in favor of that presumptuous mask that Fryn and her ilk wear."

Leif spread his feet into a wide stance with his fists at his hips, slightly charged with sparks. "I don't think you'd win in a fight against her. You're lucky to be facing me." He slid forward over his front foot and prepared for a lunge, matching Havrshyk's tension with his own.

"I, at least, was smart enough to wear armor. Your fists can't break this," he said, opening his black trench-coat to reveal a light chest-plate and a thin set of scout's greaves engraved with snowflakes on the leather and stenciled onto the steel.

Leif straightened and adjusted his sleeves so that the cuffs were a few inches from his wrists. His vest was free of wrinkles, surprisingly, though a few flecks of blood had dried on the white of his shirt underneath. "I am proud to face you in this attire. It makes you seem uncivilized, and me a proper gentleman."

"That's a sentiment that will get you killed; besides you look more like a butler or a bartender than a gentleman." Havrshyk stepped forward, and they edged toward and away from each other for almost a minute before Leif lunged forward. He dodged the first sword swing and deflected the second, and punched him in the stomach, sending him skidding back over the ice, leaving shavings in a trail from his path.

He jumped up, and flit over to the wall of the building on the eastern side, and rebounded off it, aligned like an arrow with the sword pointed straight at Leif's head. Leif burst forward, under his trajectory and kicked straight overhead as Havrshyk's face appeared, but Havrshyk grabbed his foot and spun him into the air.

Leif floundered to regain control of his spin, and flew away at random just as the sword cut the space he had been falling through, and landed hard on his back on the ground with a flash of pain through his shoulder. Havrshyk was on him in a moment, face pale, sword black, as his weight bore down on him with the edge edging closer to his throat—Leif fighting the hand on the hilt with all his strength.

He charged his sparks through his hands, sent Havrshyk sailing back into the wall, and used the recoil to force his shoulder back into its socket. The scars on his arms burned, and he stared at Havrshyk as he stood up, black and silver with a blood-drained face, and thought of the day he'd fought the Sand-Viper. It had thrown him from one dune to another, impervious to all his attacks, toying with him, trying just to eat him.

Why was it, he had asked, that no one had ever beaten one with sparks? Snow fell thicker now, clouding his view of Havrshyk's seething form, turning blue and hardening his expression till he looked like a corpse, well-preserved. Why? Some said the Vipers also used sparks, so it didn't make sense to fight a magical creature with the same form of magic unless one was more powerful than it.

Leif charged his fists, trailing tendrils of lightning arcing up from the ground, as Havrshyk stepped forward in the thickening storm.

"What do you know of the Bloodcraft?" Havrshyk asked, appearing for a second between snowflakes, his voice tinny and cold as if imitated by some animal. "What do you know of the greatest form of magic in all that is? Why do you think it is a secret, a legend from the ancient days, with tales of gods and beasts, and those who devoured anyone who stood in their way?"

"So far as I know, it is a skill that can only be found in the ice-elementals of Froreholt; but there are tales of other elements using such skills in the past. There were other forms of crafting," Leif smirked. "If I recall, Bloodcraft was viewed with pity, and the people who used it were often despised; people who cheated death, but were left forever scarred."

"Quite so, and so it was in my day." Havrshyk stood before him, his skin covered in a layer of frost, his flesh crystallized into a hard crust, and his sword converted to a deep red bordering on midnight black. "I was called an abomination, even after all my service, even after all I had accomplished, once I learned this skill, once it saved my life, everyone wished that I'd never survived at all."

"That sounds quite sad, have you considered becoming an artist? I think you have the angst to manage it." Leif looked into his now pale-gray eyes, wondering how he could continue to live in such a form.

"I accepted this, and mastered it to a level not seen for thousands of years. This full Lichform is the epitome of the skill, one that few can even hope to control; for the risk of irreparable death is quite significant. So, I hope you will at least respect my skill before I kill you, and perhaps learn to admire me afterwards."

"What are you saying?" Leif asked, but just as he closed his mouth, the tip of the sword flashed toward his throat, and he barely thrust it aside in time and jumped back.

Havrshyk followed quickly, following up with a slash to his shoulder, then his legs, and then a stab at his chest, which Leif barely dodged or parried. His speed, so greatly increased, Leif wondered if it was wiser to save some of his sparks to fight Mythrim.

He flew back and settled on the ground against the far wall. "I know this might offend you, but I had thought of conserving my strength."

"I am not offended, but I do think you should devote the proper amount of force to obtain your object." Havrshyk laughed. "You cannot hope to beat me, much less kill me, if you insist on using less than your full strength."

Leif shook his head, and hoped that Fryn would have things handled. *She would.* She'd been strong in their last encounter facing Fildar, and whatever nameless circumstance had caused her to achieve Bloodcraft in the first place. He drew on his reserves, coursing his sparks through his limbs, charging his nerves with all he had, smiling as his hair stood on end.

Havrshyk grinned, and a slight crack appeared in his cheek as a result. "I wondered why that didn't happen." He charged toward him with unnatural speed and power, which Leif countered with a jab under the flat of the blade and a shocking stab with his braced fingers into Havrshyk's icy armpit, where he felt the tendons snap and harden in place.

Havrshyk switched the blade to the other hand and set his teeth on edge. He used his good hand to strap his loose arm under his chest plate and stepped forward again in an angled guard stance.

"Looks like I can beat you." Leif grinned, running a hand through his blond hair, enjoying the arcs of energy that tingled in his fingers as he slicked his hair back.

A flash of color and a twinge of pain ran through the skin of Havrshyk's face, and he went pale again, as he pulled his arm out of his chest plate. "You do not understand the amount of damage I can shrug off."

"And you are trying to cover the fact that you can only heal while there is blood-flow." Leif pointed at the shifting currents in the surface of his blade. "As long as you cannot send blood somewhere, you cannot heal it."

"What is this, an anatomical lesson?" Havrshyk shook his head and slashed at his face.

Leif spun, lowering down in a crouch, and launched himself up with his fists meeting in a brilliant flash of light on either side of Havrshyk's sword arm, and a pop sounded in his ears as the arm broke and fell to the ground.

Havrshyk kicked off the ground and wheeled overhead and grabbed the sword out of the air, showing his teeth, and bursting downwards with a spinning hacking blow toward his head. Leif matched his spin and skidded sideways, only earning a savage cut along his left arm.

The blood froze, and held the gash closed, but the cold numbed his nerves in his left arm. He burst straight at Havrshyk, using his injured hand to barely deflect the slash but opened the way for his palm to charge in with a bulb of sparkling energy under Havrshyk's chin, and exploded in an arc of light as he gripped him around the neck and brought his head down on his knee.

Dazed, Havrshyk released his grip on the sword, and Leif grabbed it as it fell with his left hand, and cut off his head. Leif collapsed to his knees and laughed, gripping the light armor on Havrshyk's chest.

"I don't know if I killed you, but just in case, I will send you back to that crypt, you Lich. Still, this sword of yours might come in handy, if I am to fight Mythrim." He unbuckled the armor and placed it over his serving

135

clothes and belted the sword around his waist. He stood and placed the frozen head and arm beside the body and fixed his hair. "Since you cannot heal without the blood that is inside this sword, for all intents and purposes, you are dead," he said to the head, grimacing peacefully on the ground.

Leif looked up the street and hoped that Mythrim was still enjoying the party, so that he could have a chance to eat something before smashing in his face. A few sparks sizzled around the edges of the wound on his arm, arcing to the ground, and the sword and armor he had claimed. Leif hoped it wouldn't look too suspicious if he happened on a guard.

***

Fryn:

She watched Leif flit out the window with a mixture of unease and amusement. He was so eager, so warm. She felt her chin, and brushed her mouth with her fingers idly remembering their cover in the catacombs, and shivered.

"Are you cold, Fryn?" Lillen asked; spoons bunched in one hand, and forks in the other.

"No, I'm fine." She picked up the knives from the cart Faryll had brought in, and followed Lillen in a circuit around the tables preparing them for the guests.

"How did your date go?" Lillen glanced over her shoulder at her with a smirk.

Fryn blushed. "It wasn't anything... it was nice."

"Oh? I always thought the fae of Aelaete were dashing, don't you? I wonder how he came here for work." She walked over to the cart and picked up a few crystal flutes and examined one in the pale light of the starlamp in the nearest sconce. "Did you ever read any of Cherise Yarl's *Sandman* series? Oh they're just full of adventure, and romance."

The name sounded familiar, one of her childhood friends used to read those books as they came out. "I haven't yet."

"Oh you must, in some ways your Leif is just like Bradlin from the books, only he isn't a warrior." She went on.

Fryn looked at the glasses fondly, feeling the snowflake-pattern cuts in the crystal. "Yes, I'm sure you're right." If Lillen only knew, she might think he really was Bradlin from the books.

They finished the tables and had to rush into the kitchen to prepare the trays of hors d'oeuvres and wine before the guards started to trickle in. For the first half hour or so, the guard captains sat in a circle by the fireplace with mulled wine; thankfully she didn't see Mythrim among them—even though he was supposed to be gone, she was surprised that he wasn't there.

Lillen appeared beside her with a tray of white wine, watching the small groups of guards with great interest. "I wonder what it would be like to be taken to a party like this," she said, glancing over at the ballroom floor.

Fryn nodded. "I've been to a few parties, but never taken to one."

"Leif hasn't taken you to a ball? I thought he would have taken you to several by now; you look so close." She looked up in shock.

"Well, we met at a party, so in a sense we have attended parties together... but it's not like he invited me per se." Fryn shook her head. "How soon do you think before the guests start to arrive?"

The butler peered at her from around the corner. "I am about to let them in, there is a sizable queue outside the front door. It seems like there are also a number of new faces, so be as welcoming and accommodating as possible."

"Of course!" Lillen gave a quick salute, placing the palm of her right hand over her heart and her left in a fist behind her back, after the manner of the Royal Guard.

"Glad to hear it. Now, go on and begin your circuits." The butler waved them away gently and walked over to the door, which he opened with a generous bow and started taking the letters of invitation and announcing them as they entered.

There were quite a few important names among the list, and Fryn had just finished delivering her second tray of wineglasses to the guests, when the butler announced 'the Lady Pine-Martin and Escort,' and she nearly dropped the tray as she looked over to see Harissa in the same kind of daring black dress she usually wore with the slits down the sides and Jason on her arm.

"It least it wasn't Ieffin." She shook her head and brought a tray over. "My lady, sir, would you care for some wine?"

137

Harissa looked at her with cold elegance, and politely waved her hand in the negative. "I would like sceppe, two glasses, if you please."

"Of course, my lady." Fryn walked away, wanting to laugh, wanting to bring her down a notch, as she filled two tumblers with two-fingers of Kendyn malt sceppe. She delivered them and returned to her rounds, occasionally watching the pair as they chatted with important people from around the Snow District, with Harissa leaning imperiously on her bone cane.

She went into the kitchen and sat on a clean stool with a glass of water and rubbed her temples with her free hand.

Lillen, picking up a tray of toasted cheese on crackers, noticed her and sidled up with a conspiratorial smile. "Did you see the Pine-Martin? I can't believe she's finally been invited to the Guardhouse Ball, we all knew that she deserved it, but everyone was too proud until the Prince himself nominated their house for the nobility."

"Oh indeed." Fryn forced a smile. "It is a wonder she hasn't received these honors before now. I'm glad."

"Well come on, we don't have a break yet, they need more red wine in circulation." Lillen presented her hand, in its white silk glove and helped her to her feet.

"Wait… your bow-tie." Fryn reached under her chin and adjusted Lillen's glacier-blue bow-tie and nodded. "Now, go get them." She watched her go, and shook her head quickly to refocus, and picked up a tray of snacks. She smiled at the chef, a middle-aged fae with thick eyebrows and a gruff voice, and walked out with a tray balanced in one hand and a towel over the other, wishing the serving uniform she'd been required to wear had a slightly longer skirt to more conveniently cover her knife which she'd been forced to cinch up as high up her leg as possible.

Cheerful strains of the quartet alerted her to the beginning of the dances, and she watched the first few couples venture out onto the ballroom floor, eyes only for their partners, even though the sky had faded to a pale dark color and snow fell luxuriously outside the tall windows spaced out along the entire floor.

One of the girls, with auburn hair, and a red and gold dress danced cheerfully with one of the guards, and it took Fryn a second to realize, it was Clair. "I suppose I should have expected her here…" She thought aloud softly, and continued around the room. The music was far more discriminating in its choice than the party at Harissa's inauguration, without even one folk song. Waltzes were in abundance, with mellow melodies that encouraged close dancing and gazing deeply into partner's eyes.

She tilted her head and looked over at the back door through which she expected Leif to return at any minute. He was running late. The group of guard Captains seemed a bit livelier than the last time she'd glanced their way, laughing at a joke that one of them had said. They all wore ceremonial uniforms with white uniforms decorated with blue piping and thin decorative silver armor and matching swords on their waists.

She edged closer, trying to listen in.

The one leading the discussion had his back to her, and the others were too busy watching him to be distracted by her observation. He had a dress cap over his short blond hair and was gesticulating wildly with an unopened bottle of wine in one hand, saying:

"So then, there I was sitting in his study, waiting for him to complain about my absence. But then, he sits down beside me and orders in this kid with a ring of his bell. 'Ceren,' he says, and the kid nods seriously and ducks out, and then he just started laughing. 'Alan,' he says, 'I think this new kid is a fine replacement for that withered butler I used to have.'"

The other Captains nodded and smiled, or otherwise waited for him to continue.

"So I told him that the entertainment value was quite worth the miserable end of his previous servant."

"You didn't!" The Captain to the right said, staring over his mustache.

"I did. So when the ceren was brought in, the Prince poured me a glass and we forgot all about my vacation, and he told me that he was sorry to hear about my mother." The central figure in the group sighed, and the one on the left placed a firm comforting hand on his shoulder.

"That is why we insisted on your coming here tonight," he said.

"Thank you, Gunter, everyone, it is good to get out of the house." The voice was light, entertaining, but oddly familiar, as if Leif had gained a Frorin accent. "Now, does anyone have a corkscrew?"

"Oh, I always carry one," one of them noted proudly.

"That's because you're steeped," Gunter, the one with the mustache, joked.

"I drink moderately, just often," the one with the corkscrew pressed. "I'm not 'steeped.'"

139

"Of course you aren't. If you were, then I think everyone here would have the same problem," the central figure suggested. "Now, this wine is what I just picked up from the Frosthall Winery on my way here."

Perhaps the guards really liked Frosthall, but why had he gone to get wine they'd already be serving? Fryn noticed her tray was empty and Harissa stood beside her watching the group.

"They seem like a fun group to be a member of," she said, sipping a glass of the sparkling wine. "Don't you think?"

"I wouldn't know," she hedged. "What are you doing here?"

"We hoped to watch you and Leif in action, putting your professional butler skills to work. Where is he?" A flicker of worry passed over her face, and she pursed her lips.

"He was sent out to pick up a crate that they failed to deliver…" Fryn bit her lip and looked at Harissa with an awkward smile. "Is it bad that I'm worried? He's late."

Harissa twirled her cane in her hand and took a light breath. "I want to tell you not to, I want to tell you that he'll be here soon… but I'm uneasy myself. That captain, the one with the bottle of wine, doesn't he seem familiar?"

Fryn felt a shiver go up her spine, a sensation she was not used to because of her element, one that only appeared when she was unnerved and suspected something terrible. She walked around one of the tables, picking up used glasses, and moved to a good enough angle to confirm whether or not he was who she thought.

"And so, this Golden Reserve is perfect for such an occasion," he was saying, filling their reused glasses, voice smooth, placating, and charming all at once.

She finally saw his face, and time seemed to pause as she saw the sharp chin, and pointy nose, and piercingly cheerful eyes of Mythrim. His eyes glanced over and she barely managed to return to picking up used glasses until he looked away.

That was close! He's too sharp; he knows when he's being watched… She delivered the used dishes to the kitchen and brought out a tray with the same kind of nuts she and Leif had eaten at Mythrim's Poison Ball.

"I just purchased two crates for my collection," Mythrim explained, smelling his glass with a swirl. The scent wafted over the crowd of Frosthall red and white wines, and Fryn was momentarily distracted by its pleasant sweetness. But still he wouldn't be poisoning his fellow Captains only, so she wondered whether it would be wise to confront him now, or to wait for Leif. *Where are you?* She brushed her bangs behind her ear and bit her lip.

"Oh my, you are worried, aren't you?" Harissa said, appearing beside her again. "Just how close have you gotten since the last time we saw you?"

Fryn wings tinged red for a second, but at least she didn't blush. "Nothing."

"Oh, no, you did something." Harissa leaned in and examined her face. "Why do you keep feeling your lips? Did he kiss you?"

She blushed and looked away, in Mythrim's direction, where to her horror; Mythrim looked back at her with a genuine smile.

She froze and stared.

His mouth moved, but no sound came with it, tracing out the words: 'he's not coming back.'

She tightened her hands into fists and replied: 'what have you done?'

He glanced away, but then stretched and mouthed in response: 'you two were pretty cute.'

Harissa stepped away and moved to the dance floor where Jason had managed to steal a dance with Clair. Fryn approached Mythrim slowly mouthing: 'where is he?'

Mythrim took a deep draught of his wine and set his glass down before his silent answer: 'he's dead.'

Her blood drained from her face as her heart labored in response. "No, but… why?" She mumbled. "No, we only just…" She neared the group, the air growing cold with each step she took, frost forming on her partially drained face, her wings turning purple. Panic drowned her emotions, Mythrim would die, and Leif would still be alive, just as he always was.

They watched her curiously. One of them, Gunter, if she recalled, thanked her and placed his empty glass on her tray. She looked at it, then at him, and let go of the tray. They all watched the tray as it fell in slow motion from her hands, as she lifted the edge of her skirt and her knife appeared in her hand.

Mythrim ducked under her lunge, grabbing the tray out of the air, and looked up at her blinking in surprise, as the Captains pulled back in shock.

"She's got a knife!" he said, bringing up the tray to block her following slash.

She cut through the sterling silver of the tray and burst forward with her free hand pointed like a blade, and was parried by a half tray as Mythrim drew his ceremonial sword.

"Alan, stand back! If she wants you, she'll have to kill us," Gunter said, thrusting himself between them with his silver sword angled before him. All around the room, guests and musicians had stopped what they were doing and stared at the scene, with the black knife, the silver sword, and the broken tray. Lillen trembled in the doorway, and Harissa had vanished in the crowd.

"If I have to fight you, I can at least say that no one else will have to die," she hissed, voice cold, ice forming on the outside of her sleeves and around her vest.

A circle of guards formed around her, silver blades out, some shaking slightly. She burst straight up and rebounded off the roof-supports and landed on one of the tables next to the weakest guards and pummeled one over the head with the hilt of her blade, twisted around a thrust by another and gripped his head with her free hand and knocked him out against the wall.

Two more stood behind her, so she sidestepped the attacks of both and charged between them, and with her knife between her teeth, she grabbed their wrists and clubbed them with the hilts of their swords before diving under the nearest table, and cutting through its base and throwing the table-top, glasses and china and all, roughly in the direction of the Captains.

She twisted as she flew up and perched on the rafters, looking for more easy targets, and dove straight down at a trio of guards near Captain Gunter, who froze when they saw her speed. Fryn landed with a kick in the shoulder of one, and darted under the frightened slash of another and planted a frosted palm strike in the stomach of a third before spinning and delivering a chop behind the neck of the other. All three fell, the ice from her strikes shattering as they hit the ground.

A quick count showed that she had taken out, but not killed, seven guards. Eight remained, and five Captains including Mythrim. The lower-ranked guards were jumbled in a group behind her, as the Captains in front shielded Mythrim from her view. She spun, bringing her back foot forward, and charged, powered by a wing-burst she clove through the first, ducked and kicked away the second, and moved through the group of the guards.

Her old training sounded in her head as she kicked the third one into the long table by the window and continued through their loose formation.

Strike through, cleave, one direction, one path. One hand on the blade, another on the haft. I am the blade that cuts the wind, the wind that cuts the flesh.

She jumped up and spun, as Leif would, with his torque-based style and kicked out two more before landing on the chest of another and punching him out with ice. Ice coated her arms and fists, her legs and chest, forming a layer of cold armor that deflected or took the clumsy slashes of the remaining guards.

Fryn held the last of the eight by the neck and looked at him oddly as he fainted. Dropping him, she looked over at the four Captains guarding her prey. She picked up the fainted guard's sword and advanced with her knife in one hand and the sword in the other. Gunter blocked her first, letting the other three circle around with their blades out, and Mythrim standing behind him protected from her rage. She ignored him, and spun on the Captain behind her, catching his blade with her confiscated sword, freezing them together, she kicked his front foot to the side, dislodging his root, and cocked him on the chin with her knife-hand. She ducked and used the bonded sword to block the double strike from her sides, and froze their blades as well, as she scarcely managed to deflect Gunter's thrust at her heart.

She pulled them in the direction of the knocked-out Captain, and wrested their swords from their hands, palming one in the face with ice, and socking the other in the gut with the hilt of her knife.

Gunter was already on her, with Mythrim closing in behind, slashing with vicious cuts that she couldn't catch with her knife, just barely deflect. She jumped, and encased her legs in ice, and caught his strike with a kick that she followed through with a second, and sent him flying out the window with a flash of light and a clatter of broken glass. The wind rushed in and snuffed out the decorative candles on the remaining tables, and surrounded them in only the pale light of the lamps.

The guests were gone, Lillen knelt in awe or shock in the doorway to the kitchen, and Harissa appeared for just a second to usher her out.

Mythrim paused beside one of the few tables left standing, and picked up a discarded glass of sparkling wine. "That was one impressive fight, Fryn. I almost forgot how beautiful you were." He smiled and looked deeply into the crystal glass he held in his hand.

143

"I don't need your flattery, or your jokes," she said, ice reforming on her legs as she broke the sword away.

"Oh, for sure, but you deserve my compliments. You and your partner have been most troublesome. I have looked forward to cleaning this up." Mythrim raised his glass to her.

She noticed a tray of glasses on the table beside her, oddly undamaged by the fighting. She smiled bitterly and raised a glass in return. "I can also say I have looked forward to killing you."

"She understands." He nodded and drank deeply. "But it is a pity that we *only just* tapped into my bottles," he added once she had drained her glass as well.

Her vision blurred for a second, and she stumbled against the table. "You hired us, didn't you?"

"Of course I did. I thank politics that people expect nobles to hire anonymously and to protect anonymously. Politics is what makes my job easy." He glanced over as she began to drain the rest of her blood. "Oh don't do that, please, I'd hate to have to kill you in that state, it'd be such a mess."

The ice encasing her limbs and body faded and crystallized into a thin layer as she went completely pale and blue.

"Havrshyk really wanted to kill you, said something about the poetry of two immortals fighting… it's a bunch of nonsense. I could kill him, permanently, just as I can kill you." Mythrim set down his glass and adjusted his dress uniform. "Only now, rather than your beautiful body, I will have to leave you in *pieces*."

Her heart stopped, and Mythrim's breath floated away in wisps of fog, as her knife went completely black. "I should have done this from the first," her voice was stale, as if coming from a great distance.

"You were so much prettier before. It's a shame, to destroy you here while Leif is dying in the cold. I kind of wish he could be here just to find what's left." Mythrim's voice was still as light and cheerful as before, but his sword had shifted from the frost-covered silver to a reddish glow, to a brilliant white-hot molten bar. He smiled and winked.

Fryn lunged and caught his flaming blade on the edge of her knife, barely containing the heat streaming into her blood, threatening to melt her knife. She somersaulted over backwards as he cut the air she'd inhabited seconds before, melting away an instantaneous shield she'd thrown up.

She ducked and dodged and tried to parry his attacks, matching his fluid grace with her own toughness and strength. In her flight, she kicked apart a table in his direction, which he cut apart in a flurry of swings, and paused to regard her with a melancholic spread of his arms, presenting the smoldering remnants of the table he'd shattered and burned.

"You cannot defeat me, even in that form, no, perhaps especially in that form. But then, you cannot restore either, because of the poison which sits harmless in your stomach," he said shaking his head. "You should just accept the poison. It is a better death, more fitting to your form, don't you think? It doesn't ruin your face, or permanently scar your corpse. It would be a pretty funeral, with veils and tears; I'd even let your cousin live and attend it."

"Your promises are as meaningless as your compliments." Fryn flew into a dive and roll along the wall, and sprang off it in a lunge with her blade encased in a lance of ice to protect herself and to reach him.

He met her launch with the edge of his blade, cutting through her shield until their blades met, his now faded to a red-hot state, hers still mostly frozen, though somewhat diminished in thickness. She landed in a crouch with his sword pressing down on her blade, and pushed up against him in a burst with palm strike under his chest, sending him skidding back across the floor.

She leapt on him, giving a feint for his shoulder which he moved to block, and then she followed through toward his heart, as the tip of his blade flicked back and sent her knife across the room, the tip sent flying toward the opposite corner from the hilt, and then followed squarely through her heart.

The dull-red blade cooled as it met her heart, melting a hole straight through. Fryn stared up at him as she fell to her knees, and slid off the blade, and collapsed with her eyes gazing out the door in a dull sense of confusion at Leif's face, contorted in anguish where he appeared gripping the doorframe. *So he was safe.* A tear froze halfway from her eye, and her consciousness faded.

Blood and Blade

Leif stared, mouth open as he watched her fall. His fingers dug into the heartwood of the doorframe, sizzling and sparking with the current of emotions that raged through his head at a speed that far outpaced the rate at which she fell. It seemed like ages had passed before she thudded to the ground, before her icy eyes met his, with a look of pitiable confusion, and relief.

Mythrim wiped the gelled blood from his dimly warm blade on his coat and whistled one or two notes from the Acorn. Then, smoothing his hair, he fixed his eyes on Leif.

"I wasn't sure you'd make it in time," he said, feeling the smoothness of his freshly shaven chin. "It wasn't easy to drag this out so long. Bloodknife or no, she was far too inexperienced to be my equal… though, so far as I can tell, there is none." He laughed, softly at first, and then manically as Leif stared back at him.

Leif's arms trembled, threatening to break the door-frame. "I am going to kill you, Mythrim, and she is going to be fine."

"They aren't immortal, Leif," Mythrim replied, pulling out a chair with his foot and taking a seat before the last table standing in the room. He fished out a dented flask from the pocket of his armored coat, and unscrewed the cap. His eyes never left Leif, who watched him without blinking as his mental councilors raged in the senate of his mind. He wanted to skip the distance between them, vanish and reappear, and smash his smug face in. He wanted to run, get him far away, and come back for her, find some way to revive her.

Mythrim took a draught of his flask and wiped his mouth on the back of his glove. "They are resilient, they have tricks, and can steal the life of their victims in order to heal their wounds and prolong their lives."

The speaker of the house decided in his head, the best course of action was to fight, to kill Mythrim before attempting to save Fryn. Leif let go of the door, and walked over the scattered shards of glass from the flutes and windows, and enjoyed their crunch as he knelt beside Fryn. It was appropriate, he thought, that she had fallen in such a state, in such a scene. One Captain had been thrown clear through the window, and the unconscious forms of the others were littered around the ballroom floor and the dining area. He placed his hand on her head and closed her eyes. She was colder than the air outside; red gelatinous blood had formed a ring through her breast where Mythrim had cut her down.

He looked up and fought the muscles in his face, which sought to betray him, let loose a tear or a tremble of a lip, or a twitch of the nose. He sought only Mythrim's contented face, drinking his flask, watching him at ease. "I am going to kill you Mythrim, and feed you to her." He glanced around looking for her knife.

"Are you now? Well good luck finding it, it flew off somewhere, in two pieces I might add. Why don't you just use Havrshyk's blade, it probably has enough blood for ten wiry girls." He chuckled at his own joke, and flicked a piece of glass off the table and out the window into the snow.

Leif drew the blade and settled into the only sword stance he'd ever been taught. Feet shoulder-width apart, the left advanced slightly forward, and the blade held high and angled over his head toward his outstretched palm.

Mythrim straightened his collar, adjusted his cuffs, and stood. He set the flask, open on the table, and dropped its cap with an uncaring laugh. "I doubt you'll live even half as long as she fought."

Leif edged forward, maintaining his stance, scattering glass pebbles as he went.

Mythrim drew his silver blade and brushed its length down between the fingers of his glove, giving it a fresh polish that shown in the dim blue light of the lamps. In the kitchen, the sizzling of a pot boiling over, and the hot scent of burnt wine, told them that the mulled wine had missed its time.

Leif waited, eyes flicking toward the windows, then to him, to the doors, and back, until at last Mythrim saluted him with his blade and

147

bowed slightly with a debonair flourish. He struck, advancing in a quick lunge, sweeping under with a charcoal black arc of his sword, which rang with the parry repost that Mythrim replied with, spinning into his advance and punching him in the ribs.

One of his ribs cracked under his coat, but Leif bit his cheek and continued his turn, grabbing Mythrim at the collar and pulling him down and back and tossing him into the last table in the room. It broke beneath him as he slapped his arm down to absorb the fall, and with one wingburst he somersaulted backwards through the air and landed on his feet. The flask fell and spilled its liqueur on the floor, sending up a bitter herbal smell.

"It has been a while since I've done any grappling," Mythrim said offhandedly. "I never liked such a vulgar form of fighting." He swished his long sword several times and settled into a guard. He launched forward blade straight toward his face, braced with both hands.

Leif caught it just before it would have connected, deflecting it with the back of the arm brace on his free hand, and cut across Mythrim's torso, splitting the silver decorative plate.

Mythrim stepped back just an inch, and cut a fine line across the straps of Leif's chest plate, and smiled as it fell to the ground. "It's almost like a play," he said, catching Leif's sword against his, they struggled force to force, to see who would break.

He was strong, stronger than he should have been, with that thin, artiste figure. Mythrim shoved him back, breaking his root, and brought down his blade in a flash, hacking dents and cuts as Leif backpedaled blocking and redirecting the cuts with his armored knuckles.

He nearly stepped on Fryn, and caught the full brunt of Mythrim's swings, arms shaking from the force, and he jumped, over the blade, over his head, he landed on the other side and stabbed at his face.

His sword went through air, Mythrim spinning, and kicking out at him, and sent him flying back against the wall.

Leif rebounded and dodged his side-slashes and upward cuts, arching and bending in his advance. It was why they'd never been able to defeat the Vipers with their element, they were too similar. He grinned, feeling the sharp cuts and bits of wind sent out by the near misses of the blade, and he twisted with a burst of sparks in his fist, and yelled as he broke through the remainder of his decorative plate, and sent him skidding back with his sword in an angled guard.

"Not bad," Mythrim whistled, "I haven't fought a Viper in many years; not a real one anyway."

"Well, you're my first pompous actor." Leif unclenched his fist and felt the left-over tendrils of sparks dissipate to the ground. They always went to ground. That was why the lightning storms did, but there were times, rare occasions where it leapt up to reach the sky.

"Enter: Lord Graylin, I have been away for just a while, tending to the necessaries of my work, and yet I find I come to return, to a more sorry state than I have ever heard to be either in aged account or history." Mythrim lowered his sword and pressed his hand against his heart and made a melodramatic face, staring up and away toward the kitchen.

"The Ermine?" Leif smiled for a moment, almost forgetting why he had come. "So you were an actor."

"And my 'pomp' is not an act, but a very real fact," he replied in a patronizing musical tone.

"If you were in it, I suppose the reviews must have raved about 'The Vermin" last night." Leif smiled wider at his witticism.

"You are not the first to make that connection, but you are the first foolish enough to demean the arts before my face." Mythrim raised his sword and stepped carefully, his face a mask, watching his eyes.

Leif ran toward him, ducking under his first close-slash, and spinning, aiming for his legs.

Mythrim merely raised his legs, hovering, thanks to his wings, and brought his heel down on his shin with a loud crack. Leif felt the burning, the pulse straining as his bones snapped beneath his heel. He continued his spin, and rolled away on his side, protecting his leg.

The sword forgotten, it remained where he fell, where he tightened and adjusted the greaves belted over his slacks. He tasted blood; he smelled it radiating from Mythrim's friendly eyes. Mythrim was playing, it was all he did, savoring, enjoying the fight as long as he could. Leif groaned as the bones set under his adjustments, and he hovered inches above the ground.

His opponent didn't wait for him to recover; he flew at him, and threw him back against the wall, shattering the window beside him. His sword glowed a dull red as it pierced him in the gut and pinned him to the wall. He smelled his own flesh burning, and fought the instinct to faint.

Mythrim adjusted Leif's bow-tie with his free hand as he drove the blade deeper into the wall. "Did you know, Leif, that your liver is the conduit through which your fancy sparks are channeled? It limits how much is sent through, and how, in your body. Without it, you would simply fry yourself."

"That would only be true, if you were using an iron or steel blade. Silver is not magnetic," Leif said, blood dripping from his mouth, falling on his ruined butler's vest and glacial colored bow-tie.

"Isn't that fortunate?" Mythrim said, nearly shaking with pleasure. "The guards are more miserly than they let on: it's all about the appearance of class, isn't it? That's what those urchins play at in the Pine District, acting like they belong at all to the city. No one has ever wanted them." His hands shivered as he gripped Leif's head and held him up by his hair. "They only plated the outside of the swords with sterling silver." He let Leif's head drop to his chest and twisted the blade a little. "Focus. Don't you think all that soft silver would have sloughed off when I burned her heart? That's the magic weapon, at least according to legend, if you want to kill a Lich."

Leif coughed up blood and glanced over at Fryn's frozen form, covered in bits of broken crystal and frost. His eyelids were so heavy. His heart slowed its beat by one for every beat it gave. "Do you take last words?" He asked between his teeth, his mouth too tired to move more than just a little.

"Oh yes, of course I do," he said, twisting the blade again with a grin. "I also do last rites."

"You're a cheat," Leif said, wearily reaching his hand behind his back to grip the blade that had him pinned against the wall. The connection was already there, but he couldn't focus without the use of his hands. "You said something earlier, about the limit on the amount of sparks I could use?" He drew in all that was left in his reserves, everything at once, small sparks arcing up from the ground around his hand, centering on the blade.

Mythrim's eyes widened and a moment of panic flashed through them before the air popped and a brilliant flash of light arced up from the ground and into the sword. Pain seared itself into Mythrim's hand as the thunderclap sounded right around them, coursing the entire current through him to the sky.

Leif was barely aware that Mythrim was angry, and that time had slowed to a tired crawl, spoons skittered upwards from the ground, Havrshyk's sword swiveled to point in his direction, and all the silverware left about began their slow pilgrimage through the air. Floating softly up and over, seeking out the sword that glowed and radiated its powerful influence over all the iron, and the steel.

The moment ended with a clatter of tiny utensils and a sick 'thunk' as Fryn's broken knife sunk into Mythrim's exposed neck. He let out a panicked yelp but was silenced as his face went pale, his lips went blue, and frost claimed his flesh, as the knife drank its fill.

Mythrim fell back in a clatter of spoons and metal trays, and Leif still hung there on the wall. Fryn's knife turned black, thick and cold, as it sucked in all that was left of the heat. So cold, and so tired, Leif let his eyelids fall, glancing only once at Fryn's face and the frozen twitch of her perfectly shaped eyebrow. He was dimly aware that the hole in her heart had closed, filled in with a sliver of dark red ice. His hands went limp, and he slumped over the blade that kept him standing against the wall, his blood dripping, from his mouth, and from his hand, and from the hilt he'd twisted in his gut.

***

She thought she'd heard someone shout, but it had been so quiet, so far away. She opened her eyes slowly, staring out, not understanding what it was she saw. Leif had been there at the door. She moved her mouth. It was cold, and tasted like ice. She drew on the blood she'd hidden in her blade and curled up closer to her knees, and saw the frozen cap of ice over her heart. It smelled like snow, and a chill wind trailed through the windows and the door.

Fryn hugged her knees and turned to look around the room. Wood and glass were splintered everywhere, but the silverware had all moved toward some space behind her, a spoon pressed against her shoulder, trying to get through. She shifted to her knees, and held herself balanced with her hands, and turned to find out why. The spoon danced up and through the air and sailed to the wall and fastened itself with a clear ring against the bloodied sword of Mythrim where it held Leif pale and cold against the wall.

But he was safe; he was just there by the door! She reeled and managed somehow to stand up to her feet. Her wings drooped lifelessly, colorless and dry. "No, no, nonononono." She walked over and tripped over Mythrim's corpse, and found her knife fixed in his neck. She ripped it out, the tip still reforming, and put it in her sheath. Her skirt was cut and torn, but she'd worn shorts underneath, so she didn't care; she didn't think about much at all.

151

He hung there like a painting on the wall, grotesque, yet beautiful. His blond hair platinum in the little blue light, the purplish hue that his bloodstained tie took on, and the peaceful expression that was tinged with just a little regret. She walked up to him softly, wondering if she should disturb it, when someone's footsteps sounded on the floor.

Glass crunched like fresh snow at the approach. "Oh Fryn," Harissa's voice said, the light tapping of her cane measuring her time. "Oh Fryn," she repeated.

Fryn touched the tip of the hilt and brushed off some of Leif's dried blood. The sword was still hot. The spoon clung to it, resisting her faded strength to remove it. "What a fancy trick," she said, smiling at him as she hugged her arms around her chest. "Don't you know any others?"

He didn't answer, but she supposed he still clung to life with the same tenacity as the little spoon. His flesh was seared around the blade, cauterized perhaps. He hadn't lost it all yet.

Harissa placed a gentle hand on her shoulder, and she let it stay. "We should cut him down." She said, almost a whisper.

"I can't." Fryn looked at her and tilted her head. "What do we do?"

"Yes you can, Fryn. You can still save him." Harissa pointed to the knife on her leg. "You can cut him down if the sword is brittle."

"Steel undergoes a ductile to brittle transformation at low temperatures," she quoted, her master's voice sounding off from somewhere in her head. "Bae, what do I do?" She asked aloud, her old friend dancing somewhere in the past. She shivered and closed her eyes. She wouldn't know, not anymore.

Fryn opened her eyes with a deep breath ignoring the pain it caused her to disturb the hole in her chest. Harissa was right, she could still save him. She placed her hand on the portion of the blade that fused him to the wall, where a bloody handprint showed where *he* had held it. She drew out all the heat in that portion of the blade and raised her knife over her head, and brought it down with a sharp crack that split the sword and returned him to the hands of gravity.

Harissa rushed forward and caught him, and lowered him to the ground. "He doesn't have much time… there must be a doctor nearby… maybe one of the guests." She gripped Fryn's shoulder tightly in her hand and flew back out the door.

One of the guards groaned and shifted behind them, and the sounds of people slowly returned to the scene as they came to see the aftermath of the fight. Lillen knelt beside one of the guards and stared at the body and then at them.

"Why?" She asked numbly.

Fryn ignored her and placed her hands against Leif's wound, freezing it before easing the sword back out. "No doctor can save him, even if they were already here," she mumbled, searching the ground with her other hand, till it found purchase on her blade. "There's only one way that I can think to bring you back." She pressed her lips together and froze the water gathering in her eyes. "I need to see clearly," she said, voice wavering softly.

As the people gathered around them, and the guards woke up in shock, she bent over him and pressed her mouth on his. "That's for stealing one before." She wiped away the tiny crystals forming in her eyes and slid her knife into his wound. She poured in what blood she could, and felt his heart fill and twitch in response. "You need to at least try," she whispered, one hand white-knuckled on the blade, the other on his face. "Just one spark, that's all you need; just one." She pushed on his chest, and felt the blood move. She pressed again, pumping his veins with her blood, felt his heart twitch again, and pushed and pushed, as Harissa returned with a pale doctor in an evening dress.

"Just one," she repeated, "just one." She kissed him again. "You can't just come in here and leave me after all that." She patted his face in a mock slap. "Some gentleman... you're supposed to walk it off, play the dashing Sandman."

The doctor knelt beside her and noticed the blade. "We should remove the knife and stitch his wounds immediately," she said in a shaky voice.

"I can't," Fryn said without looking at her. "I'm just holding it together," she could feel what was left of his blood, it was so much warmer than what she had transfused, it shied away from hers, afraid to touch the cold, with little dancing sparks remaining by the wound. "I will herd them then." She nodded, biting her lip until it bled. She pushed his blood back to his heart, and hoped, as the tiny sparks caused it to twitch.

It beat.

She leaned back and hugged her arms. "Is that it?" She asked, bending back and pressing her ear against his chest. It beat again, accepting what she'd given it, even if it was a little cold. He breathed in, and then out, and then back in.

"You did it!" She exclaimed, lifting him up in a close embrace. "I knew you wouldn't die like that," she said, even if she hadn't.

The Captain she'd thrown out the window appeared inside the door and coughed, suddenly standing close but far enough that she couldn't attack him. His mustache moved, as she stared him down protectively, holding Leif closer. "Do you mind explaining what happened here?" He demanded softly.

Fryn nearly shot him a word of warning or a defiant look, but Harissa stood and went over to him.

"That fae was Mythrim, the one responsible for the Poison Ball. These Hunters were among the only survivors of that event, and have been hunting and been hunted by Mythrim ever since," she explained, gesturing delicately with her cane and wings. "They were hired to protect someone at this Ball… but I suspect it might have been Mythrim who hired them so that he could finish them off and finally be free of suspicion."

"That 'fae' as you so indelicately put it, was my friend. His name was Alan," Gunter pressed, hands shaking at his sides. "You mean to tell me that the fae I've known for fifteen years was some kind of sociopath?"

"He was!" Fryn shouted. "He was… so bright… so cruel," she added, trailing off into silence, looking down at the top of Leif's head.

Captain Gunter shook his head and scratched his mustache vigorously. "I don't believe it… I just can't…"

"Then how do you explain what he did to us?" Fryn demanded, pushing Leif back and showing the wound through her heart and the knife in Leif's stomach. "Would you do that? Would you toy with us and torment us, let us die slowly just so you could watch?"

Leif breathed softly in her arms, looking like he was on the verge of waking, but then slept deeper than he had before, completely limp, like a boiled egg. She smiled at the comparison and shook her head. She knelt there for a few minutes, no one disturbing her, talking in low voices gossiping, yet somehow mindful of her mood.

Finally, Lillen came over and crouched before her. "I was wrong to be frightened," she said with a small frown, "thank you for being here."

Fryn nodded and combed Leif's hair with her cold fingers, idly watching her face. "You're a sweet girl, Lillen," she said at last.

She *was* a sweet girl. All the guests stood back, almost huddled against the wall, wary of getting close, but Lillen had come with a smile, an apology.

"Don't you think you should take Mythrim over to the Bounty Office? I hear there's a royal commendation as well as the bounty," she suggested.

Fryn laughed. "From that ne'er-do-well Prince?"

She got a few laughs. The Prince had a reputation for being willful and impulsive, which was usually forgiven him because of his welcoming charm. Just then though, a kid in a butler's vest burst in through the broken door and stood as straight as a staff and announced the arrival of the Prince.

Ieffin stepped in after with a blue scarf around his neck, looking distastefully at the glass strewn about the floor, and the blood spattered here and there. "When they said there was a fight at the Guardhouse Ball I thought they meant there had been an altercation over someone's mistress." He sniffed and snapped his fingers. "Could someone bring in a chair that hasn't been smashed to bits?"

Lillen ran off to the store rooms and returned moments later with a polished and dark wood chair carved with decorative flowers and placed it in the light of the lamp closest to Fryn.

The Prince sat down loftily and took off his gloves with deliberately slow movements, his piercing eyes never leaving Fryn's face. "I can't believe I missed the fight."

"There wasn't much to see." Fryn glanced up at him, still guarding Leif, hoping that no one would decide to arrest them.

"My lord," Gunter interrupted, "they say that Captain Hartlin was the assassin responsible for the Poison Ball, and that they were pursuing a bounty on his head. Is this true?"

"It had come to my attention that there might be a dangerous character in my guard and I think that this destruction proves that there is something cogent in what they say about him, don't you?" Ieffin held out his hand expectantly, and the kid butler produced a snifter of ceren from somewhere. "Now, I expect there will be some pompous gathering at which I will have to say some fancy words, so I'll speak my mind now: that was a fine operation, if I say so myself."

"What do you mean?" Fryn asked.

"I might have been less than honest when I told you that Mythrim had left the city… might you forgive me? I didn't expect you to win… I had hoped that my personal guard would arrive in time to save you though when I was to catch word of your fight." He took a small sip and smiled.

"I'm sure my sister will want to talk to you. She's quite invested in her fascination with the Commission and its adventurers."

"So they are free to go?" Gunter asked incredulously, arms wide like his eyes.

"Not to leave the city. I expect them to turn in the Captain's body, and stay long enough to hear my speech… that I now have to write. Thank you for that," he added the last part with a slightly annoyed look at Fryn.

Jason moved over to the body and struggled to get it over his shoulder. "He's heavier than he looks," he said, fluttering his wings to lighten the load as he dragged him to the door.

"You're… who is he?" Ieffin narrowed his eyes as if he needed glasses. "Whoever he is, he's right. Go drop off the body and get some rest. I will want you two to be properly standing when I bore you with my speech."

Harissa chuckled, twirling her cane. "You've never bored a single person with your speeches yet. In fact, in case you haven't noticed, your appearances always bring in the largest crowds. You might think that people tire of boring officials, but they love you sire."

"Perhaps not as much as their Pauper Princess," he countered, swirling the contents of his glass with a sneaky smile. "I see why though, you are very witty, and have the most remarkable face."

"Oh my," she said, covering her cheeks with a false blush, breaking out into a laugh. "The people would never accept it if we spent too much time at the same venues."

His smile vanished. "Yes, you're right of course. We serve a similar purpose for very different people. Still, you had best go before Fryn can no longer stand on her feet." He waved them away and turned to his kid butler with a snap of his fingers. "Have a seat, Graham, I need you to test the food left over before I eat it."

"Of course sire," he replied with a childish squeak in his voice.

Harissa stooped over and supported Leif's body as Fryn wobbled to her feet. Leif's wound was mostly sealed over with ice, and she could feel his heart pulsing as if it were her own, as she carefully took her knife and placed it back in its sheath. They hobbled to the door after Jason with the body, and Fryn could only just hear Ieffin compliment and then order Lillen to serve the kid as they stepped out.

It had stopped snowing, and the stars blazed out of the sky with a defiant look in their sparkling. The street was covered in a deep blanket of snow, forcing them to support Leif's considerable lean mass and trudge in a bank that rose just above their knees. Harissa was talking about something, laughing at her own joke, trying to be supportive.

How was it that after ten years they talked as if they'd never been apart? Fryn's entrance at the Soft-Point-Fist left her little time to visit family, and she'd felt pressured to avoid the 'seedy' elements of her past. How was it that they forgave her for being ashamed?

They wandered down the Snowring Road, aware that no one else was out and about. Fryn supposed the people were busy making merry at the pubs, or dining out romantically with their loves, or sitting quietly by the fire reading a book. She wished that she could enjoy that kind of warmth. It was an idea she'd never fully understood, not after she had started her training, and forgotten the graceful touch of the sun. Now it just seemed bright, and sometimes stifling. She'd given up her taste for warmth the day she claimed the ice.

It seemed like forever before they finally stood, hunched over and exhausted before the doors of the Bounty Office. Its marble walls had pillars carved into the archway around the thick, iron-bound oak double-doors. She half expected to see the drunk, Hamish, passed out on the bench in the lobby, as they entered, shouldering aside the heavy doors. The glass-fronted booths were empty but one, where the clerk Caelyn sat biting her nails reading what looked like a cheap romance novel.

She hadn't heard the door, so they placed Leif on the bench the drunk had once occupied and Fryn knocked with an angry wrap against the glass—which mirrored back a reflection of her blood-drained, blood-stained face.

Caelyn gave a yelp of fright at the sound and the sight of Fryn's face. Fryn was struggling to maintain both Leif's pulse and her own, saving just enough blood to work on her injuries, leaving the rest almost completely frozen.

"I thought you were a ghost!" Caelyn hid the book in a drawer with a deep red flush of color through her cheeks and up her wings. "What is this about?"

Jason followed them in and dropped Mythrim's body on the floor with an unceremonious: "I have a special delivery for the Commission. I need a signature."

"Whaaat?" Caelyn pushed herself off the desk and rushed around the counter and knelt beside the body. "Who is this?" She looked back at them and noticed Leif. "What happened to him?"

"That is Mythrim. We are here for our reward." Fryn gave a smile that she didn't feel and hoped that Caelyn would buy the bravado.

"It must have been quite a fight." She made an 'o' with her mouth and rushed back to the counter, and rifled around her drawers until she found the papers she needed. "I know you must be tired, but I need you to sign these and fill in the necessary information right away. Proper record-keeping is not just so that you can be assured of your payment, but also so that your reputation has a solid foundation—which I imagine will be stellar after this." She shoved a few sheets in Fryn's hands and gently set a matching set next to Leif's head, where he still slept in an almost suspended state. "When do you think he will wake up?"

"Not for a long time I should think," Harissa said, looking at herself in the glass partition. "He was technically dead for who knows how long."

"Oh Leif, what happened out there?" Fryn asked. "Where's Mythrim's accomplice? We need to secure our bounty on him too."

Caelyn glanced up sharply. "He had an accomplice?"

"Yeah, it turns out the chef at the party was in on the whole thing. Leif must have fought him off… or killed him… but he can't tell us now." Fryn sat down by Leif's head and sighed. She scooted over and rested his head on her knees and relaxed. The papers asked about the tracking, the actions leading up to the fight, but she didn't want to risk her position by describing Ieffin's involvement in their past week and a half, so she simply wrote that they used disguises and moved around a lot till they thought Mythrim had left the city and taken on their new job.

Harissa chatted with Caelyn about the book she was reading, apparently a Stone-Market fan-fiction based on the Sandman books, and much more affecting in its romance. It sounded pretty base… but she supposed that some girls liked reading books that fired their imagination sometimes.

Jason said he'd met the author, and that the girls would not like him at all, a very low-class person with no sense of taste. They debated that fact, but Fryn imagined that the author of the cheap knock-off books was just as crooked and vulgar as the thief she'd caught on her first day.

The door opened and Captain Gunter stepped in, his ceremonial dress coat scuffed and the silver plating dented and bent completely out of shape from their encounter. He took a seat opposite her and shook his head at the task he'd just been asked to complete. "The Prince sent me here to facilitate the authentication of the corpse and to authorize the transfer of funds into your accounts."

He looked bitter and despondent, but kept a straight back and proper posture all around, as he sat down opposite Fryn.

She felt the need to apologize herself. "Captain, I…"

"Do you need something?" He asked, raising his eyes from his loosely bunched fists on his knees.

"I wanted to apologize for kicking you in the stomach, stepping on your feet, and throwing you out a window… and… that we killed your friend." She bowed her head, hoping that he'd at least take it silently.

"I'm angry, of course," he said, fists tightening, "I'm livid, that I was entertained and deceived and toyed with, by someone I thought was my closest and oldest friend and confidant. I am enraged at this betrayal." He took a deep breath and sighed. "I just can't believe it."

Fryn nodded, signing the end of the last page with a proud F and a delicate Martin written with little swirls. She nodded and caught herself as she nearly fell forward over Leif.

"Oh, did you finish?" Caelyn took the papers and stuffed them in a green envelope and took it in the back. On her return, she brushed the front of her uniform and grinned. "Fryn's account is on file, unfortunately before we can dispense any reward, we will need Leif to write down his side of things. Captain, you came here to confirm the identity of the corpse. What can you add to this?"

He stood and walked over to the body, hands shaking, and he kicked it in the side, and immediately yelped and held his bruised toes through his boot. "I didn't know he was frozen solid."

"What is the identity of the body?" Caelyn held her pen in her mouth, and a small drop of black ink fell from the nib to the floor.

"This is the body of the former Captain Alan Hartlin of the Guard; posthumously disavowed entirely, to be left unburied in the northern wastes. This is the body of the murderer, responsible for the deaths of three members of the royal house, of Mythrim," he said stiffly, and sat back down, nursing his sore foot.

Fryn leaned over Leif's head and rested her chin on her hands. She was so tired, and their talk was lulling her to sleep. Harissa gave her a light shake and broke her reverie.

159

"Caelyn said that everything is in order for now, and that you should head over to the Hunter Lodge," she said.

"What? Oh, alright." She shifted Leif to the side and propped him up on one shoulder, with Harissa on the other. Jason offered to help, but they told him to stay with the body and help the clerk if she needed to move it.

As they neared the Lodge, Fryn suddenly had a thought. "Harissa, what happened to Clair?"

"I guided her out, with great protest, as soon as I spotted Mythrim. She didn't see any fighting," Harissa replied, leaning on her cane, bending forward to see around Leif's head.

"Oh, that's good. I forgot all about her once I saw him," Fryn said, covering a yawn. "I think I need some food."

"I think you need some rest." Harissa guided her through the door to the lodge and the secretary at the desk immediately ran over to them.

"Please, have a seat by the fire, you look exhausted," he said, his eyes dodging to and away from Fryn's short and ruined skirt and the athletic shorts she wore underneath.

She followed him to the couch and they released their burden thankfully. Leif sprawled out in his mismatched bits of armor and butler's garb, and Fryn chuckled then at just how silly he looked: the massive patch of ice, the bloodstained bow-tie, and the demolished greaves. She frowned. There was something wrong with his leg, why hadn't she noticed?

"Fryn, what is it?" Harissa asked, halfway to the counter.

Fryn held up a hand and examined his leg; it was tightly bound and fixed to its armor. She felt the way through his veins, with the blood she had infused, to the swollen mess around his broken bones, and she gasped. "This is a terrible fracture." She placed her hands on either side and encased the leg with a thin layer of ice to reduce the swelling, and hoped that her regenerative skills would extend to the healing of his wounds as well, that it wasn't just a styptic.

Beneath the plate of ice in her chest, she could already feel the blood at work rebuilding her broken form. The poison that had been in her drink had also somehow vanished, was that because she'd been revived by Mythrim's immune blood? She slumped onto the couch beside him and sighed.

Harissa brought over a couple blankets and a tray of tea. "It's no Gin-Martin, but it will help you recover your strength," she said as Fryn wrapped herself in a blanket and draped one over Leif's spread-eagled form.

"I hope he doesn't get sick from the cold... but it is necessary," she said with a yawn.

"I'm sure you'll nurse him back to health." Harissa found her own blanket and sat across from them in one of the red velvet armchairs closest to the fire.

"Mhm." Fryn nodded and slipped off her boots, and curled her legs up on the couch.

In the morning she found she'd used Leif's softly rising and falling chest as a pillow, and that his heart was beating strong and proud with the blood that she'd provided. He opened his eyes and looked at her tiredly. "Oh, it was just a dream," he said, placing a hand on her head. "Come on, we'd best head up and help Lillen set the tables before the party starts."

"We have plenty of time," she said, pressing her chin down on his chest.

"That tickles," he groaned.

"Just take it easy, you need to rest." She smiled and sat straight up in the couch, and leaned against the opposite arm to hide her embarrassment. She hadn't meant to fall asleep or to wake up like that... but it was a comfortably warm morning to wake up to, comfortably warm. She'd forgotten how it felt, but now she could hear it in his pulsing heart.

Call and Capital

Frorin:
Rain District
Hunter Lodge

Whatever she had done to save him, Leif was both amazed at the speed of his recovery, and the constant chill caused by the ice suffusing his wound. It clawed its way constantly, eating away at his memories of the warm desert sun. His leg wasn't healing as quickly, because it was only incased in ice, he supposed. Leif examined his teeth in the mirror and leaned on the white oak cane he'd taken from the forgotten-things box behind the lobby reception desk. Its handle was smoothed by years of use, and he wondered if it had been left behind after its owner died.

He enjoyed the simple golden light of the stained starlamps in the restroom, glinting off the marble of the sink, and softening the darkness of the wood paneling.

The door opened a crack as Fryn addressed him, facing away. "We should go now, Leif, if you want to eat something before Ieffin's speech."

"Right you are." He twirled the cane, or tried to, in the same way as Harissa, but quickly lost his balance and caught himself on the sink with a loud thud.

Fryn pushed the door to and stopped with a worried smile. "For a second I thought you fell."

"Well, for a second there, so did I." He pulled himself upright and slowly made his way out the door. "At least we can fly the rest of the way… only, landing might be a problem."

"Then I'll just have to catch you," she winked, "you'll be fine; with that cast you could survive a collapsed building."

They sat down in the chairs by the fireplace in the lobby, and Leif couldn't help thinking of the moment he woke up. He covered his face with a light cough, and noticed the tray of teacups on the coffee table. A thin trail of steam rose from the spout of the teapot, a cheerful piece of white china with blue snowflakes and sets of scales painted in a delicate hand.

Fryn followed his gaze and poured him a cup. "After we finish our tea, bitter as it is from steeping so long, we should meet up with Captain Gunter at the Guardhouse."

"Look, it's Hunter-themed." He pointed at the scales on his cup and repressed a laugh at the twinge of pain that shot through his stomach. "I thought you said something about breakfast."

"Did you think we were going to a café in your condition?" She unfolded a throw blanket over her evergreen skirt and smoothed its wrinkles before picking up her cup and examining the design. "Yes, it's very cute."

"That's not what I meant." He somehow felt that anytime someone said 'cute' they were being patronizing… and he was certain of his conviction that she was laughing at him right then. "So, where are we eating?"

"I'm sure you wondered why we had to get up so early," she pointed to the wall clock as the dull sound of the Rain District clock tower rang seven bells, "but we are going to join the Captain for breakfast."

"Oh." He drank more deeply from his tea, glad that it no longer scalded, and savored the rich pine-needle and mint aroma.

They finished quickly and stacked their cups on their saucers in a neat pentagonal arrangement on the tray with the teapot in the center. The other cups were unused, but Fryn hadn't complained when the secretary sent them tea. She folded the blanket and draped it over the back of her chair before helping him to his feet.

He groaned at the weight on his leg, and quickly rose to a shaky hover. A glance outside told him that it wasn't snowing, and that a brilliant sunrise would light them on their way. Fryn walked to the door and held it open, returning a polite wave from the secretary, as Leif flew out.

His layered suit was a closer fit than he was used to, but not uncomfortable, since he guessed that the last few days in recovery with little food had resulted in a pleasant degree of emaciation. Fryn looked equally worn down but she looked really well all the same. She'd been partially drained ever since he'd woken, but it just accented her perfectly white skin and silver-blond hair, with glacial blue eyes and matching lips.

163

I guess I know now why so many of my friends were obsessed with Frorholtian girls, he thought, watching her as she flit over beside him.

"You're a bit wobbly in the air. Do you need support?" She asked, eyebrows coming together kindly.

Just say yes. "What this? No, I can manage just fine." He straightened the knot of his black, red-striped tie.

She smiled. "Whatever you say, now come on." She led the way down the southern arc of the Rain Ringroad till they met the heavy traffic running up and down the South Cardinal.

"Why don't we ever take one of the other Cardinals?" Leif asked, sliding his cane through his belt like a child's sword.

Fryn gave him a look as if to say, 'what, you want to talk about this now?' and bit her lip. "Do you really want an explanation?"

They waited for a slight opening in the crowd of carts, flying and walking foot-traffic and darted in along the thick lines to the north.

"I just mean it's awfully crowded," he said, and grunted when a burly trader shoved past with a fancy briefcase in his thick-fingered hands.

Fryn caught him by the shoulder and supported him till he'd recovered from the unexpected attack. "Well, it's just the time of day. All these people are rushing to open their shops or make it to their firms before their manager so they can open at seven-thirty. Also, the South Cardinal usually sees more traffic to the south than the north because space is limited in the inner rings, so a number of people living in the Snow District are forced to open up shop in the Rain District, and people from here sometimes extend their business to the Hill District and so on." She pushed away a careless messenger, who almost collided with them, and continued.

"That's why it is easier to go north because sixty percent of these people are going south." She was silenced as a person burst through the cluster before them, and ran straight into her, sending her barreling toward the street.

Leif watched mouth open, as the youth responsible hefted her purple velvet coin-pouch and stuffed it in his coat. Fryn recovered quickly and flew up, straight as an arrow, and Leif barely reacted in time, catching the kid at the ankle with his cane.

The kid looked back at the cane gripping his foot, and Fryn's drained face, and went pale. He threw her the coin pouch and tried to get away, but Leif pulled him closer. "Sorry kid, but you've made quite a mistake if you think you can try to pickpocket a Hunter and not get turned in for a reward," he said, giving him a pat on the head.

"Hunters?" The kid asked, shifting his brown eyes to Leif's cast on his leg, and Fryn's concealed bandage around her chest. "You aren't *those* hunters, are you?"

"I'm not sure I know what you mean, but I could use the support, so keep using those wings, we're going to the Guardhouse." Leif shared a look with Fryn and they returned to their course.

The kid looked roughly fifteen, and hung his head sadly; helping Leif fly straight like it was some kind of cruel penance, humiliation before his sentencing. They arrived at the front door of the Guardhouse a few minutes later than they had expected thanks to the interruption, and found that the windows had all been replaced, and the door repaired in only the past few days.

They were met by the butler, who thanked them for 'earlier' and invited them in to the dining area they'd only just recently trashed. It was also pristine, and they noticed one of the few extra circular tables that had happened to be left over in the storage, set up in the center of the room. Gunter was already sitting there facing the door, with the newspaper held in front of him, unaware of the corner floating in his tea.

"Good morning, Captain," Leif said, noticing the butler close his mouth with a slight frown. "I'm sorry; you were going to say something."

"No need to apologize, Master Aellin. Ahem. Captain, your guests have arrived." He finished with a proud smile as he waved them to their chairs.

"Yes, thank you for showing them in," Gunter said as they settled in, "but who is this third person?"

The butler examined him carefully. "He looks like a street fellow. I imagine they captured him on their way here… in their current state no less." He tapped the kid's forehead idly and then placed a firm hand on his shoulder. "Come with me lad, I could use the help, my old back you know."

"Come where, sir?" The kid asked, looking suspiciously at the hallway.

"I just have a little community service for you to attend to is all. Better to learn a useful thing or two about service, than to be taken to the Office." The butler led him off with a firm hand and waved to the Captain. "We will return shortly."

165

Captain Gunter folded his newspaper and set it aside before taking a sip of his tea. He sputtered as the piece of paper floating in his cup stuck to his mustache, but wiped it away with his napkin as if nothing had happened. "I hope you have had some time to recover, at least well enough to attend to your Royal Commendation."

"Commendation?" Leif said, nearly losing his balance. "I thought this was a simple 'thank you' party or something."

"I trust you have met the Prince. As much as he talks about how tiresome his business is; most have come to understand that he actually enjoys it. Among the many things he enjoys, a party where he is not the center of attention is the most significant," he explained.

"He did sound annoyed that he would have to practice a speech," Fryn recalled, "but I just thought he would forget to rehearse and make it up as he went."

The Captain nodded, soundlessly tapping his finger on his cup. "He gives that impression, but the truth is he loves his duties, and practices his pomp before any occasion."

The butler and his new recruit brought out their plates with finch eggs on hare and toast topped with a mild hollandaise sauce. Another pot of tea, this one bittersweet and hot from the dried orange and cinnamon mixed with the leaves, was set in the center, and they returned to the kitchen. Lillen stood in the door surreptitiously watching them with a tasteful, ribbon-covered, white and pink apron, and red and green oven mitts over her hands.

"I think she wants to ask us something," Leif whispered to Fryn, regretting hunching his posture as it shifted the slightly thinned block of ice that held his insides together.

"It looks like she made the food, we had best enjoy it," she advised.

The Captain glanced at the door and smiled warmly before cutting a bit and testing it with his teeth. "This is even better than usual," he said loudly, "I must push through her promotion to the kitchen staff."

Leif agreed that it was delicious, but suspected that the guards would miss being served their tea by the excitable, quick-to-blush Lillen. They ate their food without talking for a while, each absorbed in the smooth textures and warm flavors, until Leif saw fit to interrupt them.

"What time do we need to arrive?" He asked twirling his unused spoon.

Fryn and the Captain exchanged looks, but she quickly replied. "We should arrive around 9 o'clock; I thought I had told you."

"You did, but I forgot," he said, scratching his head and glancing away.

"Well," Gunter interjected, "we will be ushered into the audience hall and those who were invited will already be in attendance. I will then escort you to the front in the presence of the prince whose charge it is to give a short speech before your reward and the following celebration."

"Ief... The Prince is hosting the party for us?" Leif smiled.

"On the surface that is the case, however its main purpose is to include the nobility and assure them that these trying crises have come to an end. This has had the whole city feeling uneasy and he hopes to dispel the emotion with a lavish toast," Gunter replied.

"I hesitate at your use of the word 'party,'" Fryn glanced to the door as Lillen walked by, "with the Prince it is more likely to be a serious social gathering where you must observe all the niceties and remember names."

"I am not so bad at that..." Leif said, finishing his tea.

She frowned slightly and set her cup on its saucer with a soft 'clink.' "I don't think you are bad at recalling names, but it is your manners that I find somewhat lacking."

"Really I must protest," he said importantly, "I received the same training you did. From your cousin, if you recall."

"That was to prepare you for service; manner at court is entirely different." Fryn closed her eyes and took a sip of her tea. "Say as little as possible, and accept compliments and insults with the same degree of courtesy and respond in kind. You must remember social hierarchies and give more or less discretion depending on who you are speaking with. Treat nobles and the royalty as above yourself, and everyone else as your equal if you want to be liked." She took a breath and then another bite of her breakfast.

"Sound advice, though I doubt it will be as difficult as you imply," Gunter said, noticing the street-kid, and waving him over.

He stood before them with an apron tied on loosely over his patched jacket, with the ties dangling needlessly down to his boots, looking awfully repentant.

"I think I have seen you before," Gunter continued, "not two months ago you were brought in having the misfortune of attempting to rob Yarrow the Silver-blade."

The lad winced and nodded.

"I am surprised that you have once more made the same mistake in trying to rob a Hunter." The Captain smiled. "Perhaps you hoped to make a name for yourself—some sort of challenge, am I wrong?"

His eyes widened and he stared at the Captain, and then glanced to the door.

"Trying to audition for a certain job?" He pressed.

"No sir…" The thief's hands were clasped behind his back, fingers white from the tension.

"But you wanted to prove you were just as capable," Gunter inferred. "Sadly, you are not. It would be wise to forsake an occupation for which you are not suited."

His face turned red, and his wings twitched with a flash of purple, but he relaxed and unclenched his hands. "Perhaps you are right…" He looked up just as Lillen walked by with a steaming tray of biscuits.

"Hope I am not interrupting anything important, I just thought this would go with your tea." She said, all smiles, as she set it down in the middle of the table.

The thief stared at her, forgetting his words. When she'd returned to the kitchens, giving orders to the butler to find more milk, the Captain examined his face.

"You were saying?" he suggested, finishing his tea.

"Are there any positions for a messenger or in any department?" The thief continued to stare in the direction of the kitchen.

Gunter shook his head. "First things first, you must complete your community service: aiding the staff under the guidance of Mister Hesson, our butler, for a period of three weeks. At the end of that time, we can discuss the possibility of hiring you."

Leif took a bite of his biscuit with a bit of butter stuffed inside. "Why would you hire a criminal?"

"Why would you hire a killer?" The Captain looked at him. "Just because your talents are appreciated, and his are not, does not mean that they are useless. If a thief can put his skills to more productive uses, then I cannot say that developing them had been a waste of time."

The kid straightened at this praise and nodded. "We…"

Gunter held up a hand to silence him. "Now, go ask Mister Hesson what to do next."

"Right." He bowed his head slightly, and walked off.

"Now, we had better get moving." Gunter stood and retrieved his coat from the concealed closet by the door. He pulled at the space between two of the square wooden tiles of the wall, and one side slid back into the wall revealing a dark space with a dozen or so coats hanging inside. His had the two-swords of a Captain pinned at the lapel and a different gold embroidered pattern at the end of his sleeves. A gold line, then a series of parallel slashes or dashes, Leif couldn't decide which.

When they were ready, Leif followed them into the sun. It was a little warm; since it was still the summer, and he wondered just how cold it would be in the winter, and then where he would be in the winter and what he'd be doing. Would Fryn still be with him then?

"Leif," she interrupted, "are you coming?"

"Right, of course," he said, collecting his thoughts. He lifted to a slight hover and trailed after her and the Captain. When they reached the gate to the Crown District the Castle Tower tolled the half hour, and they were shown into a small atrium across from the attorney's study they had investigated the week or so before.

Leif wobbled on his cane to one of the leather armchairs by the hearth in the corner and frowned when its warmth didn't reach him, and examined the room. It looked like a waiting area. There was a light brown coffee table behind the chairs facing the fire, with a trio of smaller chairs facing it, and to his left a bay window looked out at the courtyard but the thin day-curtains were drawn so he couldn't see much out of it.

Gunter took a seat beside him, and covered a yawn. "I should explain the procedure here."

"It would help to pass the time," Leif said, noticing a wall-clock that somehow made little to no noise at all. "I admit this makes me a little nervous."

Fryn nodded. "I'd be more worried if you weren't." She settled into the chair closest to theirs by the coffee table and turned it to face them. "Dealing with the city's most important people should be taken seriously."

There was a light rap on the door, and Gunter went over to check who it was, and promptly let in a servant with a tray bearing several steaming cups of tea, four cups.

"I wonder who that's for," he whispered to Fryn.

"The Prince?" She guessed.

169

It wasn't. When the servant had gone, the door opened again without warning and Princess Savis walked in with a pleasant smile. Fryn and Gunter stood out of deference, and Leif managed to grab his cane when she motioned them to sit and pulled a chair over to join them.

She'd had her hair pulled back into simple yet elegant bun with two small braids from the sides that wrapped around the back and were tied with a light blue bow. This matched her white dress, covered with a blue-crown pattern. She must have gotten up awfully early to dress as she had. With her gray-green eyes, and the colors of her dress and bow, she looked like a character from one of those Ydfell paintings. Fryn would probably like his work; he'd have to point it out if they came across one.

"I had hoped we might have a word before the ceremonies begin," the Princess said, her full mouth barely moving.

"Nothing would please us more, my lady," Fryn said, beaming.

Leif stared, he'd never seen her make *that* expression, so open and friendly. "I am sure that anything you could say would be welcome." He shot a glance in Fryn's direction, hoping for some kind of approval of his courtly manners.

The corner of her mouth twisted up for a moment at his look, and her eyes met his in what looked like irony. Fryn picked up her teacup from the tray and held it and its saucer over her lap.

The Princess gave a light smile and held her cup in the same way before continuing. "If you recall, I am the Ambassador to Gaersheim, the home of the Commission, and I have come just now with a message that concerns you both."

Leif leaned forward in his seat, and held his cane loosely in his fingers in suspense. Fryn took a sip.

"First, a few veterans of your Commission will be attending this ceremony, and I would advise you to meet them. It would be good to make some connections with some of the more well-known members of the organization. Those who came with me are interested in meeting you as well, seeing how you took down one of the most notorious assassins in the world," she explained.

"Famous hunters?" Leif grinned. "Who?"

At this Savis laughed and covered her mouth with her white-gloved hand. "A few names you might recognize. I came home in the company of Yarrow, a veteran of some thirty years."

Fryn's wings twitched with interest, and Gunter nodded in approval.

"Then we were joined by Trel the Blackbow the next day. They said they were merely going north on their own errands, but I confess I think they came because I was going." She chuckled again. "Always so protective, I can't imagine what they could be worried about; since the roads have been safe for over a hundred years."

"They may have been uneasy because of the tragedy involving your cousins," Fryn said looking down at her tea.

Leif waited as everyone solemnly allowed a moment to pass. "Mythrim was still alive when you came up here, were Yarrow and Trel also pursuing him at the time?"

Savis nodded with a smile. "They didn't listen when my brother assured them that he'd fled the city and spent the whole week searching. He must have been quite the assassin to have avoided them."

Leif frowned. That meant that the only reason they'd found him first was because Mythrim had wanted them to. But then, he'd already understood that it was a trap. "I'll be sure to tell them that our tracking was just as fruitless."

The Princess narrowed her eyes. "Oh they found something, but perhaps they'll tell you about it. But there was something else I meant to tell you." She closed her mouth and let a moment's silence pass before continuing with a pleasant blink of her eyes. "I also wanted to invite you to attend the Harvest Festival in Gaersheim, it is a little over two-weeks away, and there is still time to travel."

"I've heard that they have the grandest parties." Leif leaned forward over his cup.

Fryn placed a hand on his shoulder and shook her head, whispering. "Need I remind you who we are speaking with?"

He covered his mouth by taking a gulp of tea and composed himself. "I had forgotten it was still summer because of the snow; I have little desire to remain in the city when winter comes."

"Indeed!" Savis chuckled. "You are quite right, though it does get cold in certain areas of the desert does it not?"

"It does, but it is a simple matter to pull up stakes and move south for the winter." He explained. "We have only been late once and only then because of the untimely birth of my sister... that was a cold winter."

"You have a sister? What is your family like?" Savis asked refilling her cup.

"Now is hardly the time to talk about such a mundane topic, your grace, but if you wouldn't mind telling us more about the Harvest Festival," he humbly interjected.

Her nose wrinkled in a cute but somehow regal way as she gave a light 'snort' and conceded. "You are quite right; there will be plenty of time to talk on the road."

"So it is decided then?" Fryn asked with one eyebrow raised.

"It is quite decided." Savis confirmed. "Now I will tell you about it." She set down her cup and saucer and smoothed the wrinkles on her knees. "The Harvest Festival is celebrated on the first day of Autumn each year throughout the whole kingdom of Gaersheim. The King and his entourage enjoy a private party in the north where the fading of the grass is quicker and more noticeable, and most of the grain is already quite gold."

Leif could almost see it, green walls of the Forest of Grass, and the golden stalks of grain towering even over the grass, their bunches almost invisible, but the scent filling the whole land.

"The wineries set aside a selection of their freshest batch of wine from that year and young wine is shared among all the guests. There is dancing, and toasts, and music, and those who have served the kingdom, or as an acknowledgment of their merit or service, are invited to join the festivities," the Princess continued, "that is why I am sure you are qualified to attend, and if anyone should complain, they will be silent when they hear of your deeds."

The Captain coughed lightly to interrupt. "If you are in the company of Yarrow I doubt you will have any trouble from the King's Guard, or the other guests."

"Oh Gunter, you have no idea; the people of Gaersheim are hopeless gossips and love nothing more than to determine the difference in social standing on a first acquaintance," she corrected.

"As opposed to the nobles here…?" Leif asked in a subdued tone.

She flushed. "Well perhaps it is a universal failing of the aristocracy."

"But aside from us, are there going to be many Hunters in attendance?" Fryn asked.

"Of course! The President of the Commission and his lieutenants will be there, as well as a few veterans or retired Hunters, and those who have made a name for themselves in the past year, like you." She replied. "Aside from them, all of the nobles will be there with their heirs, and foreign delegates like me will be there, too."

"It sounds like a large party," Leif smiled.

"But first you need to see to your duties," Savis said, standing easily. "There are only a few minutes before you will be called for, so I must be going."

They bowed their heads as she slipped out and considered their discussion. "She seems quite intent on our going with her," Fryn said at last.

"Perhaps she thinks that we will not be safe here?" Leif said, but quickly laughed. "That can't be it. She shouldn't concern herself for us, and what threat could there be?"

Fryn shook her head and walked to the window, pulled aside the drapes and peeked out saying. "She may have just cause. I wonder who hired Mythrim to kill her cousins, and I wonder what they will do to those who killed him."

There was a light knock on the door, so Captain Gunter walked over and opened it a crack, and conversed with whoever was on the other side for a few moments before closing it and turning to them. "They are ready for you."

Leif shared a look with Fryn and waited for her by the door. "We may learn more about that, but for now I think it would be suspicious if we disappeared too soon."

She adjusted her jacket and her wings twitched nervously, but they stepped out the door and looked down the hall to the Grand Assembly. They could hear the subdued din of people whispering, as stray words echoed about the domed room, but the doors to the chamber were still closed with one of the palace guards waiting on either side with silver halberds in their hands.

Leif stepped forward, but Fryn hesitated.

"What are we doing?" She asked.

He took her hand and drew her forward. "We're just doing our job," he said, giving her a reassuring smile.

She chuckled but pulled her hand away and the doors parted to meet them. It was hard to believe that this was the room they'd found Fildar in, every seat filled.

Prince and Praise

Frorin:
Crown District
Grand Assembly

The Assembly opened up before them, with sunlight streaming through the far windows, casting beams from the circular windows in the dome that shunted down on the desks filled to capacity with the well-dressed nobles of the city. The walkway had two ramps that ran off from the door to the top of the seats, as the main path descended to the center comprised of a small circular space with a square dais occupied by the attorneys' chairs, and the figure of Prince Ieffin, standing where the empty culprit's booth would have been.

Fryn caught her breath at the sight, and the gentle, yet hearty applause that greeted them, and walked forward purposefully to the center. The cream-colored banners hanging beneath the windows trailed down unmoving to the floor, with the icy-blue crown emblazoned in the center, matching the long thin frame of the Prince as he watched them approach. The bell tolled nine, echoing throughout the Assembly.

Captain Gunter followed a few steps behind them and moved to the side of the room when they arrived before the Prince, and held up a hand to quiet the people surrounding them.

Ieffin wore his white suit with a blue cravat under a short-waistcoat with gold thread, glittering from the medals pinned, unearned Leif supposed, to his chest; though it did make him look more official. Leif and Fryn stood a few paces from the dais, watching him and being watched in turn for about thirty seconds before Ieffin turned his head away, glanced at them out of the corner of his eyes, and gave a shrug, as the last ringing of the bell faded.

Fryn's wings twitched irritably, and a shade of purple flashed through them.

"You forgot to write a speech?" Leif asked in a low enough tone that only the Prince could hear.

He coughed and straightened up magnanimously. "While there are many disadvantages to the continued support of the Hunter's Commission, there are rare occasions where their service becomes not only irreplaceable, but invaluable to the health of our society," he began with a wave of his hand, and while most of the murmurs in the crowd seemed impressed, Leif thought he heard a snicker or two.

"Indeed, in spite of the constant busy-bodying and leisure of the organization, it still has the potential to protect us from the threats we haven't the wit to see; almost as if they have foreknowledge and are able to chase down their targets at their convenience—which is what I would like to say." Ieffin bowed his head politely toward one of the corners of the crowd. "Many have known of my distaste for the organization aforementioned, for the reasons I have also given, but even I must concede that their dedication, diligence, and professionalism have once again been of inestimable service to our country. Their presence is every year legitimized, much to my personal displeasure, for they are never satisfied to retain their position only on the merit of their previous accomplishments; they prove themselves again and again."

There was a general applause, which he allowed for a few seconds before raising his hand and continuing. "But," he said in a low voice, "no one has impressed me so much as these Hunters who stand before me today. Novices in the Commission, their heart, and persistence, and their very good sense and taste, have avenged even my family on the assassin Mythrim, the very Venomsword who has plagued the Three Kingdoms for fifteen years."

This time he let them clap till they tapered off of their own accord, and then waited for several silent moments before nodding to himself. "Sigleifr Aellin, Fryn Martin, it is my hope that you obtain a fitting reward and recognition from within the Commission, but I cannot deny the debt of gratitude my family owes you. You have ended the unrest, avenged my family, and unmasked the corruption that had infiltrated my Guard."

They bowed their heads as Gunter had suggested before entering, and waited for him to go on.

"You are already being paid a suitable bonus in mint," he went on almost as if he could hear the sound of the coins clinking, "but there are a few tokens I would like to bestow upon you." The Prince held out a hand, and a servant appeared with an object about arm's length wrapped in white cloth. "Sigleifr, for your service in the defeat and recapture of the dangerous criminal Aldyr Havrshyk," he drew off the cloth and cast it in the air, revealing the black and silver scabbard and hilt of Havrshyk's sword, "I grant you his blade."

Fryn's eyes widened and she bit her lip, looking more than a little puzzled. "But how can he...?"

"At present he cannot." Ieffin drew the sword and looked deep into the dark-red blade, and the currents that shifted in its depths. "He cannot until he can claim it, and there is only one way to do that."

Fryn subconsciously took a step back, and Leif looked at her with a start.

"What do you mean?" He asked her, but she didn't reply, Ieffin smiled and lunged toward him with all the grace of a dancer, and ran him through with the blade in his heart.

Leif's vision went black and he felt the rush of fresh blood through his veins, and a faint whisper from the one who used to own it. He didn't realize it at the time, but he fainted, and awoke in a strange open space.

There was what he could call a sky, but it was dark, without even stars, and seemed a shade of red. He stood on a small platform of cracked sandstone in the middle of a desert without wind, and sand-dunes going off like mountains into the far distance, where the bones of an ancient Sand-Viper lay coiled, an expression of its long lost death throes.

He looked at the podium, standing in the center of the stone, it was shaped like a pillar of glass, and there was the sword in its center, beside a chipped fang. He felt cold, but it wasn't nearly as unpleasant as before and as he reached out his hand to touch the podium, his hand passed through the glass and he grasped the hilt of the sword.

He came to in the Grand Assembly with his hands closed around Ieffin's holding the hilt where it pierced his heart. The Prince was smiling, and Fryn had gone white as if ready to fight him: she even held her knife in her hand but made no move against him.

The Prince let go and belted the sheath around Leif's waist, and returned to the podium. Fryn stared, and when Leif finally realized what he was doing, he had drawn the sword from his chest, and sheathed it at his side, as a thick layer of black frost closed the wound in his heart.

"I guess that makes me like you," he said, wobbling on his feet, cane forgotten.

She shook her head. "Not exactly, you can now use that sword, and what it contains, but I doubt you can become a Lich." Fryn pursed her lips and turned to the Prince.

"And for your gift," Ieffin said, looking at her carefully, "I cannot grant you what you already have, but I can give you something new." He stuffed his hand in his pocket and pulled out a silver-chain necklace with a blue stone pendant. The air around it grew cold, and a slight amount of fog coalesced as he stepped forward and fastened it around her neck. "If you are going to travel, I thought that something like this might be useful for bearing the heat."

Fryn touched the stone, the length of the chain settled the pendant just below her collar bone, and she looked relieved as the frost that formed on it spread to the rest of her exposed skin and stiffened the cloth of her blouse. "Thank you, sire," she said, giving Leif a telling look.

"Thank you," Leif added, adjusting the weight of the sword at his waist.

Ieffin nodded distractedly, spinning his hands, directing them to turn around.

They did. Fryn meeting his eyes for a second about halfway through the turn, and then they saw everyone in the audience stand and applauded when they stopped. Leif's sword hung awkwardly by his knee, and Fryn's pendant looked frozen to her skin, but they were equally happy, even if Leif was a little nervous.

He leaned toward her ear. "Do I have to maintain it?" He whispered.

"Later." She faced the crowd and waited for him to do the same.

The Prince stepped off the dais between them and placed a hand on their shoulders. "This city is once more safe and secure, after all the things that have happened, and it is largely thanks to these two standing here. I know of only one way to forget what happened, and that is in celebration. So if everyone would meet in the Ballroom of the Palace, we will continue there." He waved and watched the people file out, one or two young ones racing through the exit on their wings, and smiled. "That used to be me and Savis, always in a hurry to have fun…" He said softly, looking through the door when it was empty.

"This may sound a little crass," Leif said, immediately regretting his choice of words, "but I half imagine that the reason everyone came here was for the party alone."

Ieffin patted his shoulder. "I thought I told you that… still, even if no one appreciates your talents or wit, I will."

"That's very kind of you." Leif grinned. "You know I feel like I can walk more easily now, I don't know if I need this anymore." He pulled the cane up and caught it halfway from the top.

"Well, don't get rid of it, the cane suits you," Ieffin said covering a smile.

Fryn shook her head. "Our Prince has a reputation of being meddlesome and mischievous. I'd take his fashion advice with reservation."

They watched her straight face for a few seconds before the Prince reacted. "I wouldn't dream of giving *you* fashion advice, because there'd be nothing to advise about."

Fryn's wings twitched with a slight flash of red, but she kept it from her face. "Well, you also have a reputation for your compliments."

"Still, we should join the others. There's nothing like a glass of Frosthall in the morning," he said at last. "But, I meant what I said when I warned you of the Commission: they are a pseudo-national entity, without borders or laws, just a lot of power and influence."

They started up the ramp in silence. Leif scratching his chin thoughtfully. "But what threat could they pose? They have no army."

The Prince just waved his comment away and turned to face them when they reached the door. "No, I'm afraid I shouldn't burden you with my paranoia, for a ruler or a potential ruler, seeing threats—or supposed threats—is a daily occurrence."

When they had passed out into the courtyard, it was empty except for the string of coaches parked by the aviary behind the Assembly, that and a few guards sipping tea in the booth set up by the gate.

"Ief… Sir," Leif stumbled over his thoughts.

"Heroes of the city may be allowed to call me by my name." The Prince rolled his eyes with a smile.

"Ieffin, why are the guards so relaxed?" He pointed to the pair of guards with their swords hanging from a rack in the nearby guard post, sitting at their portable table under the pale-blue awning.

The Prince nodded seriously and started in their direction. "You know, you're right, I ought to frighten them."

"That's not what I meant." Leif trailed after him, Fryn keeping pace beside him with exaggerated steps. He switched his complaints to her. "That's not how I'm walking."

They caught up with the Prince in a matter of seconds, where the guards were stumbling over their chairs to rise and salute, with their left hands pinned to their sides, their wings straight out, and their right hands stiffly placed with the palm over their hearts. "Your majesty!" One of them blurted, and then bit his lip.

"Our guest here," Leif wished he hadn't mentioned it, "says you ought to be more careful in your duties."

"Of course sire." They bowed their heads in true repentance.

"And so I will tell you how to do your jobs properly," Ieffin continued, pointing at the cups sitting on the bare wood. "You need to use the saucer, and, I recommend dipping your cookies in the tea to soften them a bit. It's very nice."

"Excuse me?" One of the guards said, lifting his head. "Do you mean we are not in trouble?"

"I mean nothing of the sort!" He almost yelled, cowing them with his withering gaze. "You might have left circles on the table."

"My apologies, sire." The one on the right nodded, picked up his cup and moved it to the saucer. Then, sitting down, to the amazement of his companion, took a thin bran wafer cookie from the plate in the center of the table, and dipped it in his tea. He took a bit, and then a sip of tea, and smiled. "Is this better?"

Ieffin nodded. "You may return to your duties," he said, looking to the one standing at attention.

Leif and Fryn watched in confusion as the second guard gulped, and sat down across from the other and copied his movements, chewing his cookie as if his food had turned to ash.

"Yes, that is better. Now, we will be inside the palace enjoying ourselves, and since we are suspending our work for the day, it is only right that you do too. If anyone comes to the gate, it is your duty to talk with them, and if they are nicely dressed, to give them tea, and if they are of nobility, you should escort them up to the Ballroom," Ieffin said, turned on his heel, and waved for them to follow.

Leif's footing was still a little uncertain, and as they followed after him, he tripped on one of the loose stones and fell straight toward the ground. Ieffin stared, and in one split moment, he was caught and pulled back by Fryn, who supported him on her arm.

She was slightly pale, but her color returned fully as she smiled. "We can't have you ruining your suit in the dirty snow."

"Thank you, Fryn." If he had fallen, the handle of his loosely-held cane would have likely pierced, or at least seriously bruised his stomach. "That would have been painful."

She resisted his attempts to be free of her support as they ascended the stairs. "I can't have you tripping here where the snow is compacted and icy, it's even more dangerous."

He allowed her to lead him through the door, and they found the Prince had gone ahead, and his new favorite servant was waiting for them, all disheveled in his butler's suit.

The kid had an empty silver tray, a wrinkled towel over his arm, and his hair was mussed on one side. "The Ballroom is this way, if you'll follow me," he said, suddenly heading down the hall.

Leif didn't even have time to admire the entryway of the Palace, as they rushed down the hallway under the double staircase, but he noticed all the walls were made with beech paneling and decorated with gold leaf and extravagantly framed paintings of the members of the royal house doing various things. He saw a group of four girls playing cards, he saw a young fae with blond hair staring down a towering white beast in a snow-filled scene, and a few other frames flashed by with blue and white robes and swords of gold, and a blue-faced king in brass spectacles.

Fryn ignored the paintings; she'd probably seen them all before. Leif wished she'd explained them, but before he could complain, she had dragged him into the Ballroom, and they stood in the archway breathing heavily, staring at the wide space and the tall ceiling.

There were even more people in the Ballroom than had filled the Grand Assembly, lords and ladies stood or sat together patiently by the refreshments area, and the younger ones stared eagerly at the dance floor.

"Fryn, I may have said I had an easier time walking since Ieffin did whatever he did to me, but I don't think I can dance today," Leif said, looking at the blue in her eyes.

She didn't meet his gaze, but the corner of her mouth curled up slightly. "Then we should focus on making friends like Savis suggested."

"I thought we were already friends," Leif said, looking for the Princess. He couldn't see her through the crowd.

Fryn squeezed his arm. "You've got a long way to go before I can agree to that."

"That's cold." He started toward the refreshments, but she held him back.

"You forget who I am," she teased, and pointed to the left. "I think I see her over there." She led him off into the group, greeting those who deigned to notice them with a distracted smile, until they broke through a thick circle and came face to face with Yarrow.

Leif had heard of him, everyone had, that he had hair blacker than ink, that his silver eyes were sharper than his sword, which was rumored to be very sharp, and that he was once engaged to the Princess of Gaersheim, and that it had ended in tragedy.

Fryn held her breath, lips pressed closed as they met him, and she held on to Leif's arm nervously.

Yarrow, veteran Hunter, watched them with an amused smile, which was slightly twisted because of a pale scar than ran across his lips. He wore a traditional suit, a black short-coat with tails, a white shirt, and a silver cravat, and a thin saber belted around his thin waist. He was a famous duelist and fencer, having won the Grass-Blade tourneys twelve times in his thirty-year career.

He opened his mouth to greet them, but was interrupted as a dark-haired fee in a green dress slid through an opening in the crowd beside him with a wide smile on her face. "Well, I'll be, look who it is. Yarrow!"

He looked at her with a serious glance and then returned his gaze to their apparel. "Welcome back, Trel, how goes the day-drinking?"

"Splendidly," she grinned. "So these are the kids who took out the Venomsword? That's an awfully large bounty for one so young." She bit her lip excitedly and examined their faces. "Yes, yes, a pair of close-range brawlers if I'm not mistaken. Reminds me of when we started."

"And how does it?" Yarrow lifted his eyebrow sardonically and shook his head. "How can you compare us to them?"

"You're complaining about the difference in range, of course, but if you discount that, we're very similar, aren't we, Leif?" She frowned. "Perhaps I'm being too familiar."

Leif smiled and held out his hand. "No please, call me Leif. I never thought I would speak so casually with you, in fact I wondered if I'd even meet you."

181

She blushed graciously. "It is the curse of being well-known wherever you go, everyone's too nervous to speak with you."

"Or too eager," Yarrow interjected wryly, "but I suppose we are somewhat alike, don't you agree, Miss Martin?"

She nodded with understanding, tightening her grip on Leif's arm unconsciously. "You came in the company of Princess Savis, did you not?"

"Yes. When we heard of the danger in the city, we could not allow her to travel alone," He replied, looking off in thought.

At this, Trel laughed. "I wanted to catch this Mythrim for myself." She snuck an arm through the opening at Yarrow's waist and linked arms. "Now, let's find Miss Savis."

As they moved through the distracted crowd, Leif caught sight of Clair sitting at one of the tables talking with the Prince. "We should see how she's doing," he said, pointing her out.

"Oh, that is one of the Yardall's," Yarrow said, eyes narrowing when he saw the Prince. "One of their family works for the Commission."

As they approached, Ieffin covered a look of displeasure with a smile, and greeted them with an outstretched hand. "It is good of you to come. Thank you for looking after my sister, as always."

"Thank you for looking after our novices," Trel said taking his hand and giving it a firm shake. "I don't know what would have happened if you hadn't taken them in."

Ieffin scratched his head and sighed. "Well it seems my efforts to protect them were unnecessary in the end. They were able to manage him."

"Frankly, it is a wonder that we did. You were right to keep us out of things that week," Leif said, looking over at Yarrow. "You heard that they were coming, didn't you?"

"I did, and I thought it best to take you off the case, especially when the assassin died in prison," the Prince said, turning to Clair. "But I am very glad to see *you* again. You were friends with my Elena, and I daresay you are my friend, too."

"You've always been gracious, Ieffin," she said, bowing her head a little. "Leif, Fryn, I heard you were injured, but I didn't think it was this bad," she added, turning to them with sympathy brimming in her eyes.

"Quite bad, I'm afraid." Leif sniffed. "But we are bearing with it."

Clair slid her tumbler across the table, and he caught it as it went over the edge. The sceppe sloshed a little, but only got on his hand. He drank a sip and was about to pass it back, when Fryn stole it and finished the glass.

"Now, I'm sorry, Clair, but you're going to need a fresh glass," she said. "We were looking for the Princess, so we must be going."

Ieffin nodded. "Then I will be the first to dance." He held out a hand toward Clair. "Will you help me start this Ball?"

She stood at once. "I would like nothing more."

They left them at the dance floor, and found the Princess chatting with Harissa by the window. Harissa wore a suit, almost matching Yarrow's, except that she had a red cravat and a more pronounced hour-glass waist, and wore a black vest that dulled the curve of her bust. She held her cane in her hand, and wore a gold ring with a red stone that caught the light and held it in.

"My lady," Yarrow said, standing an appropriate distance away from them so they could finish their conversation privately.

"Ah, Master Yarrow, you have the best timing," Savis said, pulling away from Harissa with a smile. "I would like to introduce you to Harissa, the Pine-Martin."

Yarrow nodded, "My pleasure."

Harissa smiled and let the tip of her cane slide to the ground with a light tap. "I didn't imagine I would meet you so soon."

Savis was about to speak, but Trel shoved her hand forward, and grasped Harissa's hand that held the cane. "I am very glad to hear of your ascension, welcome to the Snow District."

"Actually, I will remain in the Pine District," Harissa said, placing her other hand on top of Trel's, "and I am very glad to meet you."

"And the Pauper's Princess, I just love the stories about you, are they all true?" Trel asked, looking at Fryn.

Fryn shrugged.

Harissa coughed politely and pulled back her hands. "I have had many adventures, but I am still very young."

"You are twenty now, correct?" Trel confirmed.

"Y…yes. You?"

"Of course I am twenty, and I'll never be anything else." She chuckled. "Leif, you couldn't be much older than her, what are you?"

"I'm a man," he said awkwardly. "What do you want my age for?"

"Now, now, be polite, and humor an old fee." She pressed.

"I'm twenty-five."

"Oh, now that's disappointing. I thought you were much younger... how could you maintain your youth, what's your secret?" She winked and then looked at Fryn.

"Twenty-four," Fryn said without prompt.

"Then it's almost perfect." She nodded, tapping her chin.

Fryn glanced down at where she still held Leif's arm and released it with a flush of color. "You mistake me."

"I am old enough that I enjoy nothing more than matching people." Trel smoothed the front of her dress. "In fact I matched myself." She stole a glass at Yarrow. "But things don't always go according to plan."

"Some relationships work better than others for certain people," Yarrow explained, "partnerships can become complicated otherwise."

Leif adjusted his sleeves and watched them. Certainly they looked close, but Yarrow had a lot of reserve, as if he wouldn't let anything go any further, and Trel looked convinced that she could change that.

Savis finally had the opportunity to interrupt. "Now. I wish to discuss the Harvest Festival."

Leif nodded. The Princess seemed very relieved to be speaking again, and her earnest face was a refreshing change from the energetic eagerness of Trel, who, for a legend, was a bit exhausting.

"If you are going to attend, then we should travel together. I was just inviting the Pine-Martin. Have you decided?" She went on, placing a hand on Harissa's arm.

"Yes I have. Unfortunately, I am still rebuilding my house after Mythrim's attack. I cannot leave at present, but if I receive an invitation in the following year, I would be happy to attend," Harissa said, and looked out the window. It had started snowing again: those thick, full flakes that only fall when it is just above freezing. There wasn't even a breeze, and they fell slowly, straight down.

Outside, there was a view of the garden where they had gathered to feed the fish in the pond. It seemed like a long time ago, though it had only been about a week. The snow had already left a thin layer over the greenhouse, and Leif thought that at least from the inside, snow was very nice as long as he wasn't cold.

"Leif, Fryn, have you thought about my invitation?" Savis asked, startling him from his thoughts.

He noticed Fryn's agitated hands and posture. "Well, we haven't had much time to talk about it. If you wouldn't mind…" He pointed to one of the doors leading out onto the Ballroom balcony overlooking the garden it accessed via a few stone steps.

"I understand, you have been very busy." The Princess smiled shyly, and led her friends toward the refreshments.

They were left standing there by the window together, with Trel shooting glances in their direction. "I suppose we should step outside if we are going to have any privacy," Fryn said, moving to the door.

Leif followed without response, and they soon stood on one of the ledges leaning over the uncovered section of the garden, protected by a jutting overhang from the roof. It was a semi-circular space with a stone bench built into the railing, and a large brazier stood in the middle of it giving both warmth and light. Fryn stood on the far side looking at the pond through the glass, but Leif hung back a moment to warm his hands by the fire.

"We've had quite the adventure, haven't we?" She said, glancing up at the clouds.

Leif followed her gaze and walked up beside her, her wings shifting wistfully. "When I first met you, I thought you were very serious," he said, resting his hands on the rails.

"And I thought you were frivolous." She looked in his face and turned her head slightly. "But it seems we were only half right."

"That's better than saying we were half wrong," he allowed, and took a breath and looked north, toward the rising mountains that separated Frorin from the Ice Wastes. "I never thought I'd learn so much about this place, it always seemed so far away, but now, the thought of leaving comes as a surprise."

She leaned against the railing on one side and watched him curiously. "You've learned an awful lot about me, or rather my family, but I still feel like I don't really know you," she said, turning and resting her chin on her hand. "You don't talk much about your home."

"I told you a lot, I was sent out as a right of passage. I killed a Sand-Viper, and I have a large family." He frowned.

"I still feel like you're hiding something." She smiled.

"What could I possibly hide from you?" He asked.

"Oh, nothing." She blinked.

Leif crossed his arms. "Well that's not good."

"Sure it is." She sighed. "Leif, do you… would you still like to… you know."

"Work together? You bet your right knee I do." Leif looked away and hid a blush.

Apparently she hadn't noticed, because as he turned back, he saw that she had looked away as well—likely trying to make sense of his comment.

"My right knee?" She looked down at her leg. "Why, is there something wrong with it? Are my knees different from each other?"

"Of course not, I just said the first thing that came to mind." He shrugged.

Fryn continued looking at her leg. "But, why would you be thinking of my knee?"

"No particular reason, it just has a sort of general appeal." He bit his tongue; that came out wrong.

She smiled. "I guess I'll take that as a compliment. So, Gaersheim?"

"We're only just getting started, Fryn. They can't stop us, not as long as we're together," he said, straightening up proudly.

She laughed. It had been quite a while since he'd heard her laugh, honestly laugh, not since they'd been playing cards and trading jokes with Mythrim, and it almost made Leif regret killing him. Leif grinned, and as she laughed, he joined her, but they were interrupted by Trel shoving her head out of the door with a napkin wrapped around her face, as she stared.

Fryn shook her head. "I don't know what you expect to see."

Trel's eyes winked, and she pointed at Leif.

Leif turned to Fryn and took her hands and settled into a stiff dancing position. "Is this what you want? I'm afraid dancing is a bit painful at the moment."

The door opened more fully, and Yarrow sidestepped Trel and walked up beside them. "Well, are you going to attend?"

"Of course we are." Leif straightened.

"Right." Fryn smiled and pulled Leif close, and stepped out so only their arms were linked again. Her wing brushed his, and quickly snapped back to a safe distance.

"Well then, come on back in and have your wine, it's a tonic, or at least that's what the old physicians always said." Trel removed her disguise and waved them in.

When they were alone again, Fryn held him back a moment. "Friends should stick together, right? I've never had many friends, I'm glad we're going."

"I've always had lots of 'friends' but I can also say you're my first," he replied. "I'm glad, too. Plus, this way you don't have to spend much time with His Foppishness the Prince. He'd definitely dote on you."

"Oh really, why is that?" She asked, sidling closer as they reached the door.

"Because: you're the prettiest, strongest, smartest, and cheekiest fee in Froreholt." He nodded several times and they sat down at the large round table where the two veterans, Clair, and Ieffin and his sister were relaxing.

Fryn beamed as they were brought tumblers of Agalia Liqueur, tempered with ice to calm the heat. She took her glass and swirled the liquid around its block of ice, and waited for Leif to receive his. "I admit, I always thought I would I hate it, but now I can say I'm genuinely excited to taste it."

"As well you should be," Leif added, and just as he was about to take a sip, Ieffin held up a hand and said "sky!" in a loud voice, and thrust his hand over the center of the table. Everyone was obliged, by his voice, or force of habit, to join in, and there was a loud clash of tinkling glasses as they met, and then tasted the fiery cold liqueur.

Fryn frowned. "I thought it'd be easier." Her face was red, and her wings flushed. "But it's still really good." She wavered on her feet and found a seat beside Leif.

"I wonder if you're weaker to alcohol that is aligned with the opposite element." Leif said, looking at her cheeks.

"Don't be a fool Leif," she said, pitching forward and resting her chin in her hands, pressing the cold glass to her face. "Alcohol has 'heat' so, the more 'heat' it has the more alcohol. I suppose this is just a really strong liqueur."

"You're from Aelaete, Leif, how much do you usually drink?" Clair asked, just as flushed, if not more so than Fryn. "This is much stronger than any sceppe we've made."

"I'll have you know, I can drink two of these glasses." He grinned, though he wasn't about to say he'd wake up with a hangover.

Ieffin raised a hand, his hair now as disheveled as that of the servant who appeared beside him. "Another round," he said, "today we day-drink, and may we remember the death of that assassin every year on this day, during the day."

"Are you sure that is wise, my lord?" The kid asked. "It smells awfully strong."

The Prince lifted his head and raised his mischievous eyes to his servant's. "If it is something I have decided then it becomes 'wisdom', understand?"

"Of course, my lord, today is now Day-drinking Day." The young servant rushed off to find more of the liqueur.

"That's not a very good name for a holiday," Leif observed.

Ieffin narrowed his eyes. "Leif, didn't you hear what I just said?"

"I did, *sire,* but you must admit it is a very plain name," he went on. "Why not call it 'Happy Day' or even 'Party Day'?"

"I see your point... and I happen to like the sound of 'Party Day'." The Prince yawned. "I got up so early today, being a Prince is hard."

Clair chuckled, but everyone else was a little nervous. "I'm sorry you're having a hard day," she said.

"I know, I'll call this 'Halcyon Day'," he suddenly declared, "so then people will finally understand what it means."

Fryn rolled her eyes. "I don't think that's what that means."

"See! No one knows." Ieffin sighed and rested his head in his hands. "Where is that boy?"

"I didn't know you were a sad drunk," Leif said, shooting a glance to Trel who immediately joined in.

"No, see, he's one of those talkative drunks."

"No, that's you two." Ieffin looked up. "I'm a sad drunk."

The new butler returned, his hair combed for seemingly the first time in his life, since he appeared with a wide smile and looked admiringly at

Clair. He poured them fresh glasses, and this time it was Trel who gave the toast.

"To our new Hunters. May we all be invited to the wedding!" She thrust her hand in, and Leif and Fryn did as well, and had already taken a sip when they realized what she'd said.

Fryn blushed, and Leif choked on his drink, and everyone laughed at their expense. Even Savis seemed excited by the prospect, and that was all it was, a prospect, nothing more. Leif shared an embarrassed look with Fryn, who avoided meeting his eyes.

No, he thought, he wasn't a talkative, or a sad drunk, he got flirtatious.

That evening, after they had tried and failed to dance because of their injuries, which weren't very painful because of the alcohol, they sat around the table playing Serendipity. It wasn't a drinking game, but Ieffin had a bottle of ceren brought in and they all kept sipping while trying to carefully get rid of the cards in their hands.

Leif forgot that he could play multiples of the same number, and Fryn didn't realize that five of a kind cleared the pile, but they all made mistakes, and only Yarrow won in the end, and that was because he alternated drinking water and white wine.

At the end of the night, Ieffin had passed out, leaning over the table, his cards stuffed in his unbuttoned vest pocket to keep them safe, and Clair had been escorted to one of the guest rooms, and Princess Savis had long gone off to her own. Yarrow and Trel stood out on the balcony by the window, whispering, and moving slowly to half remembered music.

Leif and Fryn watched them, less intoxicated than the others simply because they now had a greater pool of blood to filter through and absorb the alcohol, but Leif could feel it weighing on his mind. It was a pleasant evening, Fryn sitting beside him, her arm subconsciously linked with his, and they were watching the veterans in their moment.

The imagined music stopped, and Yarrow paused, Trel in his arms, and he bent forward stiffly, and kissed her.

Fryn's mouth hung open, and Leif smiled as they looked at each other. "I guess they hide it pretty well," he said under his breath.

Fryn shook her head. "I thought he was against her advances."

"Maybe that's what they want people to think." He yawned and leaned back against his chair. There was a little ceren left in his and Ieffin's glasses, so Leif passed her his forgotten glass, and they shared a silent toast. "To requited love then."

Her smile was idle and sweet, as she lightly tapped her glass to his. "Shh… I don't think that's a word."

They drank down their glasses, and leaned back, thoroughly exhausted. He could feel sleep closing his eyelids, and heard the muted clock toll one. He rested his free hand on hers, and felt her head on his shoulder. Whether it was the wine, or the busyness of the day, or whatever else, that night he slept very well, and only woke when Ieffin started awake at the table and rang his silver bell for breakfast. Fryn didn't open her eyes, so he waited for breakfast before pretending to wake, resting his head against hers.

Epilogue

Of course, he thought, the journey south had been quite enjoyable. Princess Savis knew a lot of stories, and was always happy to play cards. Yarrow and Trel had been slightly more open about their romance, though they probably imagined they were being discreet. Why they should hide it, Leif had no idea, but it just made him think about Fryn.

She had passed off that evening as simply having gotten too tired with wine, and wouldn't even speak about their 'lover's tryst' as Trel called it when they had found out about Havrshyk's origins. She'd been more reserved lately, and if he even thought about flirting with her, she suddenly became distracted and busy. She was avoiding him, he decided, and he didn't like it. What with their antics and constant teasing, spending time with the others was tiresome; and spending time with Fryn was refreshing, if a little frustrating at times if they remembered some of their more embarrassing lines.

Luckily, they'd left Savis and the others at the edge of the Forest of Grass, and spending the past two days in the Iron Wind on the outskirts of Fassen had brought back some of Fryn's spirit, so that she'd even been a little playful. He suspected that Trel's nosiness had made her more sensitive.

The wind shifted to the south, ruining the arrangement of his scarf, casting both tails forward, from where they had been thrown behind his back. It was a really long scarf. He'd bought it while they'd been exploring the town, and he thought it really suited him, though Fryn hadn't commented on it yet, even though its tan set off the blond in his hair.

Fryn walked furtively ahead, following the idle windings of the dirt path as it worked around the clusters of the grass. She wore a fashionable travel uniform that Harissa had given her, a durable white blouse unbuttoned at the collar to display the cold pendant Ieffin had given her, with a thick canvas weatherproof blazer, that was only beat in utility by that of her boots. He was still impressed with her boots; they looked like those adventurer boots that were often shown in paintings, with the folded-over top at the knee, and the extra-thick lacing up the back, and even given a slight heel. Her pants matched the jacket, but that would be obvious.

Leif hadn't just bought a scarf; he'd outfitted himself with a set of custom scout's armor, and a fashionable long tan coat with red embroidery and lining. He'd begged Harissa for the name of Fryn's cobbler, and only just been able to procure a custom set of boots before they left Frorin.

"Leif, we're going to miss the beginning!" Fryn called from around the next bend.

The wind picked up and tossed the tops of the grass shifting the flexible forest overhead, and blocking the sunlight. "Are you sure they want to host the party today? The weather seems to disagree," he asked.

She came back and watched him try to fix his scarf. "Well, we don't let the weather decide when we gather."

"*We* do, and it might be wise if there is a storm coming." He sighed and jogged up. "How much further to the clearing?"

She shaded her eyes and stared down the path. "About… who knows?" She chuckled and walked faster, forcing him to rush to keep up.

The sword's awkward weight made him swagger uncomfortably after her, and he wondered, not for the first time, if it was messing up his gait on purpose. He felt more and more, that the sword didn't like him, and that one of these days it was going to really trip him.

Gaersheim was the largest of the three kingdoms. The surrounding lands had their own peoples, and in some of them the Commission had a presence, but Stanaedre, Froreholt, and Gaersheim had a long history. The kingdom of the Forest of Grass was famous for its food, its wine, and its culture, and was constantly associated with ideas of games, and trifles, and sunshine. Leif was a little disappointed. So far it had been quaint. The air smelled slightly damp, and sweet, and the tall golden stalks of the grass-pods towered more than twice the height of the regular blades of grass.

The town smelled like roasted wheat, and honey, but the trail south wasn't quite as nice. Leif shook his head and rose to a hover. Flying with a sword wasn't convenient, but its imbalance was localized, so he could still manage easily.

He caught up with Fryn in moments, and the grass walls parted before them, revealing a wide clearing filled with tables, and chairs, and people talking in little groups. Leif flew straight into the rope barring the way and grunted as the air was forced from his lungs.

A guard in a grass-colored tunic surveyed him from the side, smirking at his inelegant position, hanging over the rope. "Your invitation is required to permit your entry, sir," he said, tracing his thin trimmed mustache with the back of his fountain pen. He held a small portfolio in his other hand, and scanned Fryn's face and clothes, twirling his pen in his fingers.

Fryn grabbed Leif by his scarf and pulled him up. "You should have let me carry the invitations," she said, absently adjusting his collar.

Leif stifled a yawn. "I didn't know it was a two hour trek to get here."

"How does that connect with what I just said? No, don't answer that." She covered a smile and glanced at the sword at his waist, and checked his jacket pocket.

"What are you doing?" Leif asked, stepping back against the rope as she worked.

She found the invitation in his jacket, signed and sealed by the Princess, and handed it to the guard. The guard read it, and frowned when he saw that both their names were listed on one card, and unlatched his end of the rope from its post and crossed to the other side, unbarring their way.

They entered the clearing, covered with lines of hanging lanterns crisscrossing the area with green, and gold, and red. To the right they saw the tents filled with crates and kitchen smoke and behind them the finches' corral, where a soft trilling occasionally traveled on the wind.

All the tables had been set up on three terraces, the lowest had eight long tables stretching in their direction, the middle had four slightly shorter ones above, and behind, and perpendicular to the first group; the third and highest was just one long table, parallel to the second tier, with regal chairs flanking a woven-grass throne.

Fryn pointed to the gazebo and dance partition, straight ahead, between the tables and the tents. "Do you think they have refreshments there?" she asked.

"I couldn't say," he said, looking over the heads of the people crowding the open space in the center of the area. There were a number of covered booths, and everywhere, well-to-do people walked in twos and threes down the aisles looking at trinkets and buying souvenirs. "We could try one of those."

She tugged on the end of his scarf, and led him through the first line of party-goers to the closest booth. The proprietor was an old fae with drooping wings, wearing round glasses and an apron. He was weaving grass caps with surprising speed, then dipping them in a basin with various dyes and patterns, and selling the dry ones that hung from the pegs and hooks covering every open surface of the booth.

Leif fished a couple Commission-stamped mint from his pocket and scanned the caps. There were green ones with blue stars, and yellow ones with green blades of grass, and he was getting slightly bored when he saw something perfect. In the upper right corner, he saw the right one, and pointed it out to the shopkeeper as soon as he had hung up the cap he'd just dyed.

Fryn was busy looking at the other wall, and the old fae didn't talk much, so Leif paid five-mint for the cap and spun it on his finger. It was gold, and had a profusion of brown and red maple leaves tossed about an idle wind. While Fryn was still searching, Leif stepped over, and lightly placed the cap on her head, and spun her around to see.

She raised her hands to her head, about to take it off, but he stopped her and stood back with his hands on his hips, and a satisfied breath. "Yes, that will do perfectly." Her silver-blond hair, mixed with the gold and brown was very pretty, and accented her pale blue eyes.

The old fae noticed them with a smile, and found a mirror under his work-table and held it up so Fryn could see. She posed, and turned, and cocked it to the side a bit as she tilted her head with a teasing smile. "You have a good eye, Leif," she said, wings twitching as she looked at herself. "Now, you close your eyes and I'll find one for you."

He turned around, and waited, watching the people at the other booths. Fryn muttered and murmured as she combed the wares, and through a break in the crowd he saw Trel and Yarrow sitting contentedly together on a bench, eating pieces of chocolate shaped like grass-stalks.

Suddenly, the shade of the brim of a hat fell over his eyes, and Fryn appeared before him with a grin. "No, that won't do." She took it off and dashed off with a quick "don't look" and returned moments later and placed a fresh hat on his head. This one was shaped a bit more like a fedora, and woven of a thinner grade of grass, and as he turned to look in the mirror, he saw that its golden-yellow base was accented by orange and brown birds, flying off into the distance.

"I like this one," he said, tipping his hat to the dyer who nodded gratefully and then started working on his next hat.

They moved on to the next booth, laughed at its rock candy and honeyed trifles, and walked arm in arm to the end of the row. Aside from the hats, they didn't find much that they'd consider buying, though Fryn did pause and stare at some of the jewelry in a glass case at the third booth from the end.

He kept that in mind for later and confirmed that the booths would be open all evening, that is, they would open again after they had all eaten. Trel had said that the Harvest Festival was one of the biggest celebrations in Gaersheim, but he had only expected food, not trinkets and games. The next row had a few games, where people could pay a mint to roll a few dice and a number would decide their reward: a special cravat or pair of fine gloves were among the hardest to acquire with rolls of twos and twelves. The most common items were badges and pins shaped like bunches of grain, or grapes, and the like.

Someone had set up a miniature pond, with a few large fish swimming around, and Fryn immediately bought a bit of food and started tossing the pellets into the water.

"Do you think they fight over it?" she asked, turning to him with a piece of the food held up before her eye.

He stole one from her little satchel and examined the water. "I'd imagine that there's enough for everyone." Leif flicked it into the air, and a dark green monster of a fish jumped from the water and ate it as it fell. "Did you see that?" he asked, pointing at the pond. As he did, a small white fish leapt up, and fixed itself to his fingertip. "Ow!" He brushed off the fish and stepped back, rubbing his finger.

Fryn laughed, and held out a piece of the food. "Won't you try again?"

"No, thank you, I think I'll keep my distance," he said, eyeing the little white fish. "He's probably friends with that big one."

"I think that one's a girl." Fryn crouched by the pond and dropped another piece of food. It floated on the surface of the water briefly, but was sucked under within a few moments. "She just wanted a kiss."

"Well, kindly tell her I'm taken." He frowned, and crossed his arms, regretting his choice of words.

Fryn threw in the last piece and walked over to another booth, and found a table hosted by a new winery, providing free tastings. She ran back and dragged him over by his sleeve and crossed her arms to match his posture. "See," she said in a knowing tone, "there's something you can't refuse."

"I drink other things than wine…" he complained, but followed her up to the table. The staff behind the table were extremely busy. It seemed like everyone at the festival wanted a taste while they had a chance. The employee who stood before them wore a simple suit with a brown vest and tortoiseshell glasses, and held a guest-list. When he saw them, he held out his hand expectantly, so Leif clasped it and gave a firm shake.

The fae looked down at the hand, and then up at him, and pulled his hand back with a blank twitch in his eye. "Your invitation?"

Fryn still had it, and held out the card with her lips pressed together like she was hiding a smile. He took it from her, and compared its contents with that of his guest-list and placed a check by their names, before passing back the card. "You each can taste four wines. We have six to choose from. To your right you will see our Pyrincel, and moving left the White Silvi, the Estlin, and then the reds; from the center we have the Wellsey, the Norenan, and the Rosenkraun blend."

"Blend?" Fryn asked.

"Roughly 65% Rosenkarun, 15% Eirenau, 12% Soranil, and 8% local Fassen: the flavor profile is light on the tannins, but full bodied and slightly fruity on the palate." He poured two small glasses and passed them over, gesturing them to smell. "The nose contains notes of hay, cherry, and blackberries, and a warm touch of cinnamon. This is our most popular red at present, and is selling for 10-mint a bottle, or 50 for a crate of six."

Leif and Fryn tasted the wine, and nodded approvingly together. "It is a shame we are traveling, purchasing a crate would be inconvenient," Leif said, "though it is an excellent wine."

The wine steward—or at least Leif supposed that's what he was—read their names on the list again and nodded. "I take it you are here on business then?"

Fryn nodded. "You could say that coming here was our business."

The steward nodded in return and smiled. He had extremely prominent dimples, not cute or charming like Fryn's, and Leif thought it was very distracting. "Hunters, if I am not mistaken, and if you are not currently on a case, I suspect this is a reprieve. In that case, you might be able to take a case of wine back to your hotel?"

He knows our names, that we are by all accounts wealthy after Mythrim, and can afford his wine. Leif thought, searching his face.

Fryn nodded. "But first we need to taste the others."

Why did she nod? Leif sighed as they finished their glasses and moved on to the Pyrincel, which was alright, and then the White Silvi, which Fryn liked and he didn't, and finally the Estlin which they both enjoyed.

Softened by the wine-tasting, and the lack of food, Fryn pitched her hat back on her head, borrowed the steward's pen to fill out an order for a mixed crate, and left the deposit on top.

They'd spent too long wandering the booths, because in a moment, the band in the gazebo started playing a fitting entry for the first tier guests, and everyone went quiet. At the end of the clearing, a trail of richly dressed figures exited one of the larger tents, walked up the terraced steps to the first row, and seated themselves at the table.

The king of Gaersheim was in the middle. He had dark brown hair that was wavy and threatened to fall over his eyes if not for the gold-dipped woven-grass crown that was illuminated by the various paper lanterns overhead. To his right was a fee in a white dress covered in a pattern of golden wheat sprigs, with elbow-length gloves and her chestnut hair pinned high on her head.

Fryn stared at them and hushed him when he was about to comment. Princess Savis sat in that row, several chairs to the left of the King, in a blue dress with white crowns, and a woven hat similar to Fryn's but matching the pattern of her dress.

Yarrow and Trel moved to the edge of the crowd and watched the King, who stood with his hands wide apart and a grin on his face. He looked young, probably 35 at the latest, and the Queen, if that's who the fee in white was, looked a few years younger. Leif thought she seemed a little silly, with her wide eyes and her blank smile, admiring the view and the lights.

Then he looked at Fryn, who seemed just as enthralled with the spectacle, eyes shining, wings glittering under the panoply of lanterns. Leif shook his head, he was just as silly: staring at her like she stared at them.

The King spoke in a light tenor, with his feminine hands swishing through the air to still the music. "Now, everyone, it is once again my greatest pleasure to welcome you back to this clearing!" He waited, and everyone applauded. "A King is many things: Governor, Administrator, and most importantly, a Host." He lowered one hand and held that of the fee in white, who stared at his face sweetly as he continued.

"The Harvest Festival is the most important, the oldest, and richest, and the best aspect of our heritage. It celebrates the bounty of the previous year, and symbolizes our commitment to establish the prosperity of the next. It is a picture of our gratitude, and recognition of our labor, and it is a promise to our children that just as we have enjoyed these fruits, we will plant the seeds of their fortune, of their future, today!" He finished this with a flourish of his free hand and a slight bow to great cheers and whistling.

The Queen, Leif supposed she could be nothing else, spoke next. She had a sweet alto voice that sounded like she was talking to a child, full of wonder and excitement. "I would like to thank our people, for sponsoring this celebration with your dedicated efforts, providing food, and drink, and music." She nodded to the gazebo, and many in the crowd agreed. "But I would also like to thank our foreign delegates for joining us in our most treasured tradition, the Princess Savis, Lord Wellsey, Master Trivell, Prince Jorrin, and Sir Ebby; you grace us with your presence."

The crowd applauded them gratuitously, but Leif got the sense that they didn't really care. Fryn pointed to one of the figures near the end of the table. "Look! I think that's President Hans. I thought he'd sit closer to the King."

Leif leaned over to whisper. "But if the King favored the Commission more than national delegates that could cause problems. It's just like in a family reunion, the heads of the branches sit closest to the Master, even if the cousin or uncle is more useful and reliable."

Fryn looked at him, her face so close, and blinked. "You still haven't told me much about your family, and that sounds like a really odd situation."

He smiled. On the first terrace the Queen was still talking, but they were focused on each other. "I wouldn't know where to begin, I have a large family, and a large clan, and I'm not very important in it. They say only parents see the value of their children, and I am inclined to agree."

She glanced to the side, as if realizing how close they were. "I had no idea there was such a saying. But I'm sure they'll notice you now."

He swallowed and looked back at the Queen, and took a deep breath. Fryn could see him, even if he was just one child out of seven, in a family of a clan of a hundred.

Fryn was focused on the Queen, so he tilted his hat down to shade his eyes, they were wet, but nothing so bad as to need to be wiped on his sleeve.

The Queen finished speaking, whatever she had said had pleased the guests, and people started moving to their seats. Fryn checked their card, and found that they were second-tier guests, and would be seated by Yarrow and Trel and a few other Hunters of note.

Yarrow sat at the end closest to the middle aisle, with Trel beside him, then Fryn, and then him. Across from them were a trio of brothers, and a bookish fee with a shy smile. The middle brother, that is the one sitting in the middle, nodded to Yarrow with recognition, and then held out his hand to Fryn across the table.

"I don't believe I have seen you before, I am Grifton, and these are my brothers Gerard, and Germaine. My mother had a thing for 'g's and we've never really known why," he said in a deep, but kind voice.

Fryn started at his suddenness, and shot Leif a look, as if for confirmation. He shrugged, so she took his hand. "I am Fryn, and this is my partner Sigliefr, out of Frorin."

Leif nodded. "But you may call me Leif. Are you the Francis brothers? The ones responsible for the capture of that smuggling ring a few months back?" he asked.

Grifton, presumably the eldest smiled. "It is good to be known for one's work." Then he turned to the fee sitting at the end. "I am sorry miss; we do not mean to exclude you, what is your name?"

The girl looked frightened, and glanced up sharply. "Oh, no, I'm no one of consequence, sir."

At this Trel leaned forward and scanned the girl's face cheerfully. "What nonsense are you talking about? I know you; you are the one who invented that windfall enchantment: that is not inconsequential."

The girl blushed furiously and stared at her knees. "I never imagined I would be complimented by the Blackbow."

Leif rested his chin on his hand and whispered to Fryn. "Speaking of which, why is she called that?"

She arched an eyebrow. "You know, I don't really know."

Yarrow reached across the table and gently took the girl's hand. "And tell me, what is your name?"

She looked away but let him hold her hand for a moment. "My name is… Melanie, Sir."

"I thought it was." He smiled and settled back in his seat, releasing her hand.

Just then however, several servants and waiters passed through the aisles, checking that everyone was sitting according to the arrangements, and placing ice-buckets and carafes of sparkling and young wine.

Fryn turned to Trel. "What do we do? Do we wait for a toast, or…?"

Trel placed a finger over her mouth and pressed it shut. "Yes, we must wait. Once everyone is seated, and their glasses have been filled with new wine, the King will make a toast, and then the first course will be served."

Yarrow interrupted in a soft tone, "There is of course, a slight break between courses, whereupon the band will resume playing and the concourse will be filled with dancing."

The three brothers searched the other guests, looking for pretty girls and bright dresses. Melanie was forgotten, and Leif felt bad for her, but didn't really want to dance with anyone besides Fryn, but then felt guilty, and bit his lip in thought. Yarrow had the reputation of being the 'perfect gentleman' and he knew that when he saw her sitting alone, he would ask her to dance, thereby making the rest of the fellows at the table look like inconsiderate snobs. Fryn watched him for a moment and then smiled when a waitress filled her glass with a light pink wine.

The waitress counted the glasses on her thin fingers, and pulled an extra glass from the pocket in her green apron, and wiped it clean with a velvet cloth before placing it before the girl and filling it more than the others with a look of pity in her brilliant green eyes. Her brown hair fell in a thick braid over her shoulder, well past her collar bone, and she wore a primly ironed brown blouse with a red vest, and a similar set of trousers that were rolled up above her ankle-high leather boots.

It was an unusual uniform for a waitress, but Leif decided that Gaersheim had good taste and pointed it out to Fryn.

Fryn smiled playfully as she lifted both eyebrows. "See something you like?" She shook her head as he worked his mouth and said nothing. "Well, I suppose it is a little odd, but we are new here," she said at last. "Oh, shh, I think the King just stood up."

He had. The King was almost directly behind them, and Leif suddenly realized just what excellent seats Savis had arranged for them. "Box seats" she'd said during their travel, and he chuckled at how right she was to call it that. This close, he could see the playful banter and whispers of the King and Queen, still young and fancy.

The King broke away from the Queen regretfully, and faced the people at the tables. The servers stood at the ends of their tables with their own glasses in hand, and everyone else took their cups and held them in the air.

"It is my pleasure to initiate the feast. This cup, of the freshest wine, is rich, and plain, but it is very, very good. This cup, we raise in thanks for this year, and we drink for the next, and for the following years; for we will taste this wine next year, to see how it's come, and the year after that, until five years hence when by rights there should be none left," he began, earning a few laughs. "The second toast will be last year's wine, and the third, the year before. Between each course the wine will grow stronger, and so shall the food be made to match. Please, join me in the first cup." The King's high voice rang out clear across the tables, and everyone raised their glasses, and took a drink.

Leif swished it in his mouth and swallowed. It was very young, still mostly juice, he supposed, but it was also light, and sweet, and as he considered it, their waitress returned with small plates of salad, a vinegary mélange with toasted nuts, mixed greens, and diced grapes.

He took a bite of the salad, and washed it down with the wine, and savored the combination. The meal was light, and so was the wine. It made sense that as the food got heavier to match it with bolder wine, but as he thought about how they did it, with the wine going through several years, tasted each time, he laughed.

"What is it?" Fryn asked, covering her mouth as she finished chewing a piece of lettuce.

"I just like the way they bring out the same wine each year to compare it." He swirled his glass and took a sip. "It's light and fresh now, but in a few years, what will it become? I hope we can come here next year to find out."

She smiled. "Of course we will." She returned to her food, and blushed at something Trel said in her ear. "Stop it…"

The salad wasn't very large, but when they had finished it and the wine, they felt satisfied, and they noticed the band members moving back from their table to the gazebo. Leif turned to Fryn, and seeing that Melanie was still eating, felt a little relieved. "Fryn, would you like to dance?"

"It's been a while since I've been able to dance," Fryn said, placing her hand on her chest in thought.

"I admit I am glad things have closed up at last." He patted his stomach with a knowing look. "Now let's see how we've healed." Leif stood and helped her to her feet. They walked arm in arm down the few flagstone steps and watched the first few couples stand ready on the concourse marked by fitted stones and roped off around its border with hanging lanterns.

They matched the posture of the neighboring couples, standing with their feet together, but with the left foot pointing out at an angle, and their opposite hands clasped, and their free hands at their sides. Fryn curtseyed playfully, and Leif bowed, as a lively, but somehow stately waltz began. They weren't really dressed for dancing, more than once, Leif's scabbard brushed a neighbor's leg, and Fryn's outfit made her look like a girlish boy. But they didn't mind it, their dyed hats tipped coquettishly, Leif's free hand on the pommel of his sword, and Fryn's on top of it.

They moved in slow circles, parting, and turning, and switching through partners till they returned, and settled into a close stance, pressed against each other with their hands together. The music stopped, and they waited in that position for the next song to start.

But it had been a rather long dance, and the musicians filed off to their table again. Leif and Fryn returned to their table, and saw that Yarrow had indeed danced with Melanie who had finished her meal slowly. Luckily, since Yarrow had danced with her, the three brothers were in competition to be the next partner so he didn't have to worry about her anymore.

The second course, served with the previous year's wine, was a pumpkin soup. It was slightly sweet, but hearty, and served with a small slice of bread for dipping. Fryn looked deep into the dark pink wine in her glass and tipped her hat back to a proper position. "This does look richer," she said, flicking her eyes in Leif's direction.

"It still looks sweet and mild, not unlike a Pyrincel, I'd guess," he replied, smelling it. It had notes of clove, orange, and unsurprisingly, grapes. This time it was the Queen who gave the toast, praising the virtue of their labor, and exhorting them that it is all worth it in the end, and that it only gets better with age.

The pairing was very astute, and they decided that the chef must have been allowed to taste the wine before anyone else, and that he or she must be one of the most intelligent chefs to date. Trel agreed. Yarrow made no comment except to sigh occasionally after a sip of one and then the other, and the brothers were content to devour their food. Melanie didn't like the soup. Her bangs shaded her eyes, and her nose wrinkled if she smelled it. So she focused on drinking her wine, which was fortunately inoffensive to her taste.

The second dance was a bright folk dance known only as 'the harvest' and there were several waiters and waitresses standing by in pairs to instruct newcomers in the dance. Their waitress, the one with the boots and the thick braid, paired up with the tortoiseshell glasses steward from the winery, and waved them over.

The music began, and Leif and Fryn followed as best they could, joining hands with their neighbors, and forming into lines, they alternated running between the joined opponents, and making the arches for them, before skipping away to their partners, and standing side by side so that the gents had their hands out to the side, and the ladies all had their hands in the center of a series of circles that formed instinctively, before they turned, switching position, and moving in the opposite direction, so that the gents had their hands in the center and the ladies shot out their hands.

They spun away from their circles into pairs, skipping, and jumping, and tossing their partners in the air, where they would spin, and then land, and throw their partner up instead.

At the end, everyone was covered in sweat, but no one more so than the musicians, who had worked the music to a frenzy, and finally collapsed over their instruments panting. The waiters passed out hand towels; fresh with steam, and everyone wiped their faces and returned for the third toast.

Princess Savis stood as they poured the wine from two years ago, her face white, her hands fidgeting, but everyone stared at her clear, guileless face and admired her reserve. The sound of pouring wine filled the clearing, and everyone was beginning to feel the effects, just slightly, with the light food, the wine tasting even before the toasts, and the dancing.

"Greetings everyone, as the Delegate of Froreholt, it is my honor to be invited here once more, and my great privilege to pronounce the third toast. Two years ago was my first Harvest Festival, and so I am glad to be able to raise a toast with that same wine I had at first." The people clapped, nodding their heads, and whispering.

Savis went on, gaining courage. "Two years may not seem like such a long time, but a lot can happen in a day, in hundreds of days, and I would like to remind you that time is not short, that it is long. That every day is filled with the opportunity that you cannot see, and that every trial is overcome with each moment of shared joy." The crowd grew solemn, and the Princess wavered, her eyes glistening. "I lost three of my cousins this year, my dearest cousins, we traveled the capitol together many times, visiting the Rosenkraun Estate, or the Chateau of Lord Wellsey, who sits here beside me, and though I am sorrowful, I am also grateful for the fruits of this year, for the harvest we have reaped."

The people cheered, and Leif clapped furiously, and saw tears in Fryn's eyes, and in many others.

"I raise this cup to share my joy, because I have a joy that no one can take, but can only be given, and today I give it to you." She smiled, and tears streamed down her face, and she looked at Leif and Fryn, just when she said 'you' and everyone cheered as they clinked their glasses and drank from the rose-red wine.

It was much darker than the previous two, full, and strong, but without even a hint of bitterness. Trel wiped her eyes and took a large gulp of the wine and set her glass on the table, and turning to Yarrow she said, "It is the love of friends that redeems our sorrow."

He reached over and held her hand, and smiled sadly.

Leif didn't know why, but it made him sad, he looked away, and fingered the edge of his glass, resisting the urge to cry. What was it Fryn said, about his past, that he'd been engaged to a princess, and that she'd been killed…? Leif took another sip, and placed a hand on Fryn's shoulder. "I wonder what they will pair with this wine."

She looked at him, her eyes red and wet, but no tears had fallen, she'd frozen the surface of her eyes, he wished he could do that. "Maybe some kind of cheese and meats with crackers," she guessed, tilting her head so that her cap fell forward over her eyes.

They looked at the Princess, who, holding her glass of wine in one hand, dabbed her eyes with her napkin in the other. Leif thought of Ieffin, of his forced jokes, the amount of ceren he'd drunk, during the day, saying brash things and pacing wildly when he wasn't hunched over a table or sitting uncomfortably in a chair. The death of his cousins must have hit him hard too. "So that explains the Prince's grief," Leif said aloud, watching Savis as she finally managed to taste her wine.

Fryn looked over at him, and then at her, and nodded with understanding. "I suppose you're right, he was always bright, and cheerful, and everyone loved him; but since they died, he's been wild, willful, and unpredictable."

They didn't have the heart to join the next dance, and it was a very short waltz anyway. Fryn had been right about the meats and cheeses, and for the fourth toast, it was President Hans of the Commission who stood, the one Ieffin had complained about.

The President was over sixty years old, but most still thought he looked just over forty. He had clean gray hair combed in serious fashion in an asymmetrical part, and had a clean-shaven face with a prominent, but thin nose. His voice too was prominent, it was baritone, with a resonance that went to the end of the clearing without his raising his voice, and he had a stellar record as a Hunter, and as a manager. Twenty years serving as a Hunter, ten more as a manager, and then he'd been voted the President of the Commission five years before; (according to Trel, who gossiped as Hans coughed and readied his glass).

The wine was dark red, rich as a Wellsey, and smelled like a Norenan, but they had to wait. Their waitress still hadn't appeared with the food, but when she walked up the steps with the loaded trays on her arms, and the steam rising from the food, no one complained. It was pheasant steak, and mashed veggies, robust with pepper, and salt, and even a little ginger, if smell was any indicator.

Hans cleared his throat and smiled. "My lords and friends, my employees, and my employers, life is not all business." Leif liked the beginning.

"My organization has a history running back three hundred years, and every single one of those years, I have something to be proud and thankful for. This year, I am thankful to be here, in such fine company, and for being a part of such a company, where even the initiate can be recognized." He paused and looked at their table. Leif and Fryn shared a look and sunk into their chairs. Trel didn't seem to notice, but Yarrow smiled.

The President continued. "I have heard from a reliable source that a few members of my company have already been thanked for their work in Froreholt, in relation to the string of venomous murders that occurred there…"

Leif sunk lower, and Fryn gripped the edge of his sleeve.

"Your brother, Princess Savis, is well-known for his celebrations, but he does not have the best reputation when it comes to speeches or of giving notice where it is due. But he is a Prince, so it is better that he does so, whereas I am free to be free with my thanks." Hans smiled at them, and raised his glass. "I am grateful to these newcomers and all our protectors, who keep us safe so we can prepare for the next year, and raise our children in peace. And I would especially like to thank, not just the guard, or the soldier, but a few specific people who have impacted us today: Fryn Martin, Sigliefr Aellin, my thanks and congratulations. This glass is from me, and it comes with the expectation for your continued efforts."

The people applauded generously, not nearly as moved as by the Princess's speech, but they were eager to see the new celebrities, and laughed at their awkwardness.

The steak was delicious, and the dancing was fierce and close, with slow movements, and spins and trades, and they ended in an embrace, but it was the fifth toast the Leif enjoyed most.

This was the last, the wine from four years before, paired with a chocolate cheesecake, when everyone was tired, and tipsy, and willing to clap for anything. Melanie smiled at the brother who now sat beside her, since they had begun switching places between dances, and Yarrow seemed distracted by the color of Trel's eyes. Fryn stared into her glass, and mumbled something about that brooch she should've gotten, and Leif, just stared at her.

The final toast was to be given by the King again, and he set his crown before his cheesecake on the table. The wine was deep red, and rich, but it was fortified only by age, and it smelled like pure tannins. The King stood, and raised his glass. "My friends, the feast will soon end, but the festival will not. Please enjoy this taste of our efforts from four years ago, and remember where you were then, what you did, and what you were trying to accomplish. Did you do it? What then? What will you remember in four years when you taste the first wine again? Think, and look forward, because in a few years, you will remember what you still had to do this time. It is a simple thought, but good to remember, so join me now in celebration of where we have come from, and in anticipation of where we will yet go!" The King raised his glass in the air, and everyone joined in, alternating gasps of pleasure from the wine, to expressions of awe and disbelief because of the cheesecake.

It was only when they had half finished their cake and wine, when the King gave a horrified, startled cry, and stood pointing at the table.

Everyone watched in silence, asking a question with their eyes.

"The Harvest Crown is gone!" The King sputtered in a pitiful voice.

Leif's eyes scanned the crowd, and saw a far-off figure running into the Forest of Grass, as the last light of the lanterns reflected off the gold in its hand.

Fryn grinned, and the three brothers raced each other to stand. Leif took her hand, and they flew off in the direction of the thief, flying over the lanterns and the crowd.

"It's a race then!" Fryn said, squeezing his hand.

"To whoever catches the crown," Leif replied, and they flew into the grass.

The End

About the Author

As a devoted reader that loves a well told story and artfully turned sentences, Stephen Hagelin pursues his tale with imaginative scenes accented with hints of humor, vivid fights and a comfortable command of the language. He is a native of Seattle and resides in various places in the region.

Upcoming

Stephen Hagelin is working on the next book in the Commission Series: *The Viper's Chase*. Follow his progress: www.facebook.com/stephenhagelinbooks, @HagelinStephen

Varida Publishing & Resources is a small company run by authors from a variety of genres and styles collaborating to produce high quality work. Each one contributes extensive time editing, advising, and proofing one another's work, upholding high standards of grammar, storytelling, and consistency.

www.varida.com

CPSIA information can be obtained
at www.ICGtesting.com
Printed in the USA
FSOW03n1750290417
33603FS